JUMP ZONE
CLEO FALLS

WYLIE SNOW

Jump Zone: Cleo Falls
Copyright © 2013 by Wylie Snow. All rights reserved.
First Print Edition: 2013

Published by PG Watkinson
Jump Zone: Cleo Falls © 2013 by PG Watkinson

ISBN-13: 978-0-9919395-2-7

Editor: Megan Records http://www.meganrecords.com/
Proofreader: Susan Helene Gottfried
http://westofmars.com/susans-editing-services/
Cover and Formatting: Streetlight Graphics

This is a work of fiction. Names, characters, places, and incidents either are the product of the author's imagination or are used fictitiously, and any resemblance to locales, events, business establishments, or actual persons—living or dead—is entirely coincidental.

DEDICATION

To Simon, James, and Spencer, who encourage, nurture, and tolerate my creative ups and downs with unfailing support. And to my mom, for giving me Everything.

Dear Readers:

As a special thank you, my creative team has designed a Jump Zone game for your iPod, iPhone or iPad. Please visit my website www. wyliesnow.com for instructions on how to download this complimentary app.

Available from September 9, 2013 for a limited time.

PROLOGUE

Taiga Forest

I'd always presumed the moments before death would be fuzzy and warm.

They're not. Death is painful. And cold.

Death is terrifying.

For me, there are no sepia vignettes of my childhood, no sign of my mother's smiling face to usher me into a blissful afterlife, open armed. There's nothing to distract me from the fright that slams me every time my mouth fills, every time my head slips under.

No matter how hard I kick or thrash, the current is merciless, dragging me downriver, closer to the edge, closer to the—

I can't even think *the word.*

I claw for the surface, flailing desperately for something to grab onto. But there's nothing.

Not a rock, not a log, not even a stray root. Even if by some miracle I don't drown, there is nothing to save me from the fall.

Seventy feet, straight down.

And the rocks at the bottom... I'll be smashed.

My chest burns so bad, I want to scream from it. Can't, don't dare. I bite down on the inside of my lips to seal them from another mouthful of icy water and taste the copper of my blood. I will my legs to get me to the surface for another breath, but I'm tumbling through the blackness, not sure which way is up.

The rapids twist and toss me, pull me fast and hard as if they're doing me a favor in getting me to the edge quickly. It'll be over soon. Yet every agonizing second feels never-ending.

The more my muscles ache from cold, the heavier my limbs become, the slower time goes. Death is a cruel bitch.

My lungs are on fire. And no matter that my eyeballs feel like they've been dunked in acid, panic won't let me close them.

There's a legend amongst my people of a Ghost Warrior, a survivalist from Old Canada who lost his life in the Polar Wars. They say he guides folks home in their time of need, gives them a second chance. Where is this phantom rescuer for me? Am I not worthy?

I already know the answer...

The pressure in my chest begins to crack me open. I acknowledge my fate, look it in the eye, welcome it. The thought frees me. The simple act of mental acquiescence releases my fear, replaces it with regret. And anger. I'll never get a chance to make amends to my tribe, to Jaegar or my father, never feel the love I've tried so hard, so damned *hard, to earn.*

Anger fuels my strength, gives me a final burst of energy. My anaesthetized legs push off of something solid. My head breaches the surface.

I scream in Death's face.

Then water fills me, douses my fire. I am numb, unable to feel my extremities, unable to feel anything. Like a piece of flotsam, the current tosses me over the precipice toward the jagged rocks below. My world goes dark.

ONE

"Easy now, darlin'. Get it all out. Breathe for me now."

His voice came at her through a long black tunnel. Cleo ignored it at first, but it grew louder and more persistent. She couldn't connect where she was, or who kept insisting she breathe. Before she could get a grasp on her senses, her stomach muscles twisted, convulsed as river water filled her throat and exploded out her mouth. She could vaguely taste the tang of her last meal; a strip of jerky and a couple of handfuls of trail mix, eaten in haste.

Images flooded her mind—the flash in the sky, the kayak, the rocks. Her head spun like the vortex she'd been trapped in. She needed to breathe, needed to—

Gripped by another spasm, she opened her

mouth to scream from the agony ripping up her insides but all that came out was another mouthful of river.

There was a spot of warmth on her back, the hand of whoever was keeping her propped on her side so she wouldn't drown in her own sickness.

So, not dead.

Or alone.

The Ghost Warrior must have come. She'd always been skeptical of the legend, but who else could have possibly brought her back from the journey into dark?

"That's it. Let it all go."

Retching, loud and vulgar in her throbbing head, masked the words of the rumbling, reassuring voice behind her. There couldn't possibly be anything left in her, yet her body still heaved, still gagged until every ounce of strength was spent. Exhaustion made it impossible to keep her cheek off the ground.

Blackness beckoned her to come back to the place where she wouldn't have to fight, wouldn't feel the pain or cold, but Cleo refused to succumb. She clung to this discomfort, to life, and struggled to shake off the disorientation. She prised open her burning eyes and through milky vision saw a shimmer of light reflected in the shiny pool of her own vomit.

Lovely, she thought as her eyes drifted

closed again, *I survived, but my dignity didn't.* She groaned and tried to roll away from the mess, but the movement triggered more retching.

"You're going to be fine. I got you. Just concentrate on breathing," the voice reassured calmly while she ejected more from her stomach. "Quite a bath you took there, darlin'."

As her wits returned, she began to tremble, gasping for precious air, afraid to let her lungs go empty.

He draped something over her, something heavy and warm, but her wet leather clothing held the chill and she couldn't stop violently shaking.

"You're going into shock," he said, bundling her tighter. "Try to slow your breathing down. Don't want you to hyperventilate on me. In and out, nice and slow, on my count."

Cleo closed her eyes and focused on the Ghost Warrior's voice, concentrating on his instructions. She tried to inhale deep and slow, tried to savor the feeling of each inhalation, but she gulped greedily and let it out with fearful reserve.

Tingles, sharp and searing, spread through her limbs as her core warmed. The discomfort shoved away the fog and confusion from her mind. The details of the accident buzzed behind her eyes, but Cleo swept them away like an annoying horsefly. She couldn't go there. Not now. It was more important to focus on surviving.

Ghost Warrior talked her through the worst, all the while rubbing her back. He counted slowly as she breathed, in and out, in and out, until her panicked gasps calmed.

It was working, whatever he was doing. She was glad the legend was true. The Ghost Warrior, born of the Taiga, the northern wilds, protected his people.

He smoothed the clinging tendrils of her hair from her neck and cheek with a gentle touch, his silk-smooth fingertips gliding across against her forehead. Softly...so softly.

Too soft.

People of the Taiga did not have soft hands. So who was stroking her hair? Not a triber. Definitely not a warrior, even a ghostly one.

Don't trust outsiders.

Instinct kicked in. Cleo rolled away from the gentle touch as fast as her protesting limbs would allow. She grasped for the knife at her thigh, only to find an empty sheath, then felt for the weapons harness that normally crisscrossed her torso. Gone.

Her muscles protested as she jumped to her feet in a graceless, jerky motion and assumed a stiff version of attack stance. Hot pokers stabbed through her right leg as she fought to keep her footing. Her body swayed as her brain struggled to maintain equilibrium. The last thing she needed was to faint.

"Whoa, whoa." The stranger got up slowly, palms outstretched like he was talking to a spooked horse.

Soft hands. Not one of us. Even the tribe medics and scholars chop their own wood. The youngest children develop calluses from working fields and learning to handle a bow.

Never trust outsiders.

He was backlit by a potassium nanowire lantern that threw his face into shadow and blinded her with its glare. Cleo tried to peer into the darkness behind him, around him, and as far as her peripheral would allow without letting him out of her sight, trying to ascertain if this outsider was alone.

From his silhouette, she could see he was a much larger man than she wanted to face while unarmed and half stunned.

He moved toward her. Cleo stepped back, ignoring the pain shooting through her lower leg, worse now that the ice in her blood had thawed. Her shin was on fire, but she couldn't take her eyes off the outsider.

"Take it easy, darlin', before you hurt yourself," he said, his voice even. He inched toward her, hands open, fingers spread.

He was taller than her father, but not as broad. She might be able to take him...if only the damn world would stop swaying.

"G-get back," she warned, but her throat burned and her croaky voice sounded more squeaky than fierce. She was in position, ready to execute a roundhouse kick to his side, but her leg wouldn't bend, wouldn't move. And then there were two of him, rushing at her. She shook her head to clear the spinning black discs that danced through her vision, but the movement made them grow bigger until they swallowed her.

For the second time that night, Cleo's world went black.

TWO

LOATH TO LEAVE THE HAVEN of sleep, Cleo squeezed her lids tight against the penetrating light. But consciousness took hold, bringing with it a mother of a headache and an underlying sense of urgency that made her blood surge.

Jaegar! It was crucial she get to him before the recruiters washed the Taiga ways out of him. She drove him away and now had to bring him home, restore him to his rightful place.

Memories of the previous night tumbled forward with the velocity of the waterfall—the cold, the pain, the helplessness...the retching.

Then the voice, the big guy with the gentle touch. The Ghost Warrior.

No such thing as the Ghost Warrior.

Instinct again took over and snapped her into high alert. Her muscles contracted, ready for action, ready to defend, to fight, to survive. But she couldn't move her arms. Something tight constricted her wrists.

She'd been bound, tied up like an animal.

She flexed her ankles, relieved to find them untied. She fought the urge to jump up, run away from whatever was making her heart pound so hard. No, that wouldn't be wise, and she was *supposed* to be wise—the elder council deemed it so. Freaking out would not help. She would remain calm, determine her surroundings, and then decide on a course of action. She squeezed her lids closed and focused her acutely trained senses.

The muffled sound of water hammering rock told her that she'd been moved away from the falls, but not too far. She could tell without opening her eyes that the sun had barely breached the horizon. The sounds of dawn in the forest were unmistakable: birds singing their morning songs, animals scurrying through the underbrush looking for a breakfast of insects, the rustle of leaves as the dew evaporated.

She smelled the pungent scent of a fire made with green, damp wood.

Novice.

She smelled him—woodsy, masculine, and not entirely unpleasant. No sour stink of fear. And he was so close, she could hear shallow breathing. A sign her companion maintained a calm state or, better, still slept.

Whatever she lay upon enveloped her like a warm bath. She couldn't feel the morning breeze on her body, so she assumed she was covered. Using as slight movement as possible, she wiggled her finger and felt a practically weightless cover, so unlike the heavy pelts and woollen blankets she snuggled beneath at home.

So her captor had bound her but seemed concerned with her comfort.

Don't trust outsiders.

Cleo cautiously tensed and released each muscle, but it took everything in her not to wince. She ached everywhere. It even hurt to breathe. The bottom half of her right leg throbbed in a rhythm out of sync with the pounding in her head. She didn't think it broken, but the bone along the front of her shin felt hot and tight—swollen, for sure. Hopefully not infected.

Every inhalation, even the shallowest, made her abdominal muscles hurt, likely the result of throwing up half a glacier. And her right butt cheek stung as if she sat on a pine needle. Damn, there was likely one stuck in her pants. Then something struck her like a low-hanging branch. She wasn't *wearing* pants. Her calves and thighs rubbed together, skin on skin, and her arms were crossed and tied over a bare midriff.

For the love of ducks, she'd been stripped naked! He must have taken her clothes off after she passed out.

Bastard. Sick, perverted dirty outsider.

The rational half of her brain yelled, "*Hold up, he needed to get you warm,*" but the indignant she-warrior in her busted with anger and humiliation. It took a great deal of forbearance to keep her facial expressions in check.

She was sore and knew it would be a bitch of a morning if she had to fight, *naked,* but at least there was no serious damage to her body. Her forehead felt tight and her cheekbone hurt just above her scar, but she didn't need her face to take her captor down. Clothes would be nice. It would be embarrassing to fight naked, but she would if she had to.

The bound wrists were a problem.

"Hey," he whispered, his voice thick with morning rasp. "You awake?"

Cleo mustered the most menacing look possible before turning in his direction and opening her eyes. He sat on a log not three feet away, eyeing her intently. The dark shadowy figure from the previous night was completely opposite by the light of day, a fact that scrambled her throbbing, angry head even further. The soft dawn light fell across hair the color of golden wheat, thick and entirely uncontrollable.

His eyes—it must have been a trick of the forest, because she'd never seen anyone with eyes like that—pale silvery blue, rimmed with sapphire. More wolf than human.

Don't trust outsiders.

"Why am I *naked*?" She tried to sound fierce, like a kick-ass warrior should, but she had her own case of morning voice that cracked on the one word she was trying to emphasize, making her sound vulnerable and, well, *naked.* She cleared her throat. "Where. Are. My. Clothes?"

"And a good morning to you, sunshine."

She squinted, unamused, to show she meant business.

"And the lady has some spark!" He grinned, showing off a row of straight white teeth, another sign he didn't belong in the Taiga.

He scrutinized her, his eyes unnerving as they traveled over her face, but she couldn't look away. He caught her stare head on and held it until the heat in her cheeks made her look away.

"Glad to see you got your color back. That shade of dead-blue didn't suit you, darlin'."

Despite her attempts to look threatening, he remained in good humor.

Don't trust outsiders! Outsiders bring evil and death and destroy families.

Feeling a surge of alarm, Cleo tugged and twisted her wrists, but the cord wouldn't give. As the panic built, tears formed in the corners of her eyes. Cleo grit her teeth and swallowed. She couldn't, wouldn't let him see her cry. Warriors, even third-class ones, did not crumble into emotional heaps.

"Why am I tied up?" It came out *WhyamItiedup.*

"Hey, relax." He stood and circled the fire pit. Only then did she notice her clothes, spread on the ground close to the dying embers.

Cleo felt violated at the thought of him peeling her wet leathers off. Of course it was to keep her from going into hypothermia—she'd have done the same were the roles reversed—but her natural fear of outsiders kept nudging her across the border of rational thought right into terrorville.

"How about a little gratitude?" he huffed as he leaned over to snatch up her leathers. In falsetto voice, he mocked, "Oh, Mr. Knight in Shining Armor, thanks for risking your life by jumping into that freezing river to save my skinny little ass."

Manners. Right. They seemed to be tied up, just like her hands. But for the sake of her grandmother, her moral compass, she struggled to push the words *thank you* from her lips. They wouldn't come. Certainly not while his hands skimmed over her clothes, down her pant legs, squeezing, patting. It was too distracting, too personal.

Should she be grateful? Should she push her fears aside? What if she misjudged him? He didn't look mean. He had a great smile.

But just because he's attractive doesn't mean he won't—

He would have done it already if he meant to harm her.

Maybe he already did, while I was unconscious. Maybe he'd keep me, bring me to others, then kill me...

Something deep inside of Cleo started to unravel. If his intentions were benign, why did he truss her up? She was naked, wounded, alone. So very alone. There was no reason a man would tie up a woman unless—

"Untie me!" She strained her neck as she lifted her head off the ground. The covering, silver and light as air, slid from her shoulders down to the rise of her breasts. Horrified, she slammed back down. "Untie me now!" Her demand sounded like pleading.

Her quickened breathing made her pendant roll off her chest. The raging river that took everything else of value that she owned had spared her prize possession. Just knowing her mother's crystal remained close to her heightened her resolve to survive.

Instead of answering, her captor threw her leathers across the clearing. Cleo flinched, but they landed in a stiff heap on the ground next to her. He speared her with a curious look, the light in his eyes gone, along with his quirky smile.

He continued mocking her, ignoring her outburst, "And that mouth-to-mouth resuscitation, those chest compressions," he said with a dry, humourless tone. "Where ever did you learn those handy little tricks?"

She averted her eyes. He had saved her *skinny little ass.*

She tried to swallow the lump at the base of her throat but it wouldn't budge. Their eyes met as he pulled on a tattered grey shirt. Not that her judging-people skills were honed, but he didn't look dangerous or mean. Just wary. She didn't see anything in his pale eyes except a measure of disgust, which made her feel worse.

"Thanks," she croaked through a constricted pipe. She cleared her throat and tried again. "Thanks for pulling me out of the river, for giving me CPR, for holding my hair while I puked." There. That wasn't so bad. "Now untie me."

One of his eyebrows shot up.

"Please." Grandma would be so proud.

"Are you gonna do something stupid?" His approach was guarded, which struck Cleo as rather ridiculous considering her current state.

"Define stupid."

"Bite me, scratch me?"

"What do you think I am, an alphakitten?"

"I don't know what to make of you, darlin'. You were ready for a fight last night."

"And I'd have kicked your skinny little ass if I hadn't hit the ground again."

His widened eyes preceded a deep throaty chuckle. "Of that, I have no doubt."

Cleo braced as he approached. Maybe she wasn't being fair? He hadn't threatened her. Yet. But her head throbbed and she couldn't think straight, couldn't get an accurate read on him.

"I'm sorry," she said. "Really." Common sense said she had every right to fear him. But his cautious approach made her wonder if he was more afraid of her. "Here's the deal, Mr. Knight. I won't attack you if you don't attack me."

"I realize you're disoriented after what you went through, but I did jump in after you. Do you have any idea how hard it is to drag a water-logged corpse from the bottom of that river? I hardly went to all that trouble if I meant harm, don't you think?"

Unless you intend to use me first, like they used my mother.

Before another bout of panic could render her stupid, she buried those thoughts under a ton of here and now. He carried no weapon, his expression remained guarded but focused, and she watched his eyes for any tell-tale flickers. The eyes almost always gave away an intended attack.

"It'd be easier if you could slip your hands out the side of the blanket," he said, dropping to his knees next to her.

"Just give me a knife and I can do it myself."

He shook his head. "Not this time."

A girl had to try. She rolled sideways and slipped her arms from under the covering.

"It was dark. Real dark," he said without looking at her. "You needed to get warm."

Cleo looked him up and down while he worked the knot. How should she play this when he, clearly, had the advantage? Instead of cooperating, the only thing her reanimated brain could focus on was *him*. This outsider. His broad shoulders and flat abdomen, the way the muscles down his arms flexed as he deftly worked the thick clump of polycord. The faint pulse throbbing on the side of his neck.

Clearly, she still suffered from some kind of hypothermic delusions. He was an outsider, not to be admired, not to be trusted. He was big, with ripped muscles, and she was completely and helplessly alone, naked, and, for the moment anyway, completely at his mercy.

Cleo prided herself on her ability to keep a cool, logical head in challenging conditions, but her current situation had her thoughts as scattered as autumn leaves. Maybe he didn't intend to hurt her. Maybe he was just being kind. But what was he doing in the Taiga? Recruiters wouldn't dare venture this far north, and sightseers tended to stay close to the Trading Post for safety.

Though he travelled alone, he definitely wasn't a Banger, that much was obvious—those poor wretched creatures were more beast then man—and Drifters usually travelled in packs and hung around the walled towns in Lower Amerada, living off the scraps of civilization. Her self-proclaimed knight was too well fed and well behaved to fit in either category.

"I didn't mean for them to be so tight," he said, his gaze flicking to hers for a split second before the black polycord fell from her wrists.

Cleo's fingers tingled as the blood rushed through. He took her hands and rubbed the circulation back into them. Her instinct was to pull away from him or deck him, but...it felt nice.

He could be a soldier with a build like that, but the Lower Ameradan Army knew better than to cross the Cut into the protected lands. She could count on one hand the times they'd tried to do that in her lifetime, and it never ended well.

Where the devil had he come from? She could ask him outright but sometimes, pretending to be a stupid female was the best defense.

"You were thrashing around in the night," he said, interrupting her thoughts. "I didn't want you to hurt yourself." He tried to smile but only one side of his mouth went up, and damn it if it didn't give him a charming appeal. "Or me."

The skin on his hands was soft, almost slippery, as if the top layer had been sanded smooth, or worn completely off, but his grip was strong, his touch warm.

She made a decision. He wanted to be a knight, so she'd act the naïve, vulnerable female-in-dire-straights. He would underestimate her and she'd find a way out of her current predicament and get on with her mission.

"I'm sorry I caused you so much trouble," she said, adding a good dose of humble. It helped that her voice was scratchy. Made her sound pitiable.

"That you did, darlin'." He let go of her hands and pushed her clothes toward her. "Do you need some help getting into these?"

"No. Thank you."

Crouched on his haunches, his hands casually resting on his knees, he studied her with a look of bemusement. His eyebrows knit together over an intent gaze, like he was trying to solve a mental math problem. An angular jaw lay under a day or two of stubble, his lips pressed into a thin line. "You got quite a bruise on your cheek," he said matter-of-factly. "Right above that birthmark—"

"Scar," she blurted. "It's a scar."

He canted his head, staring openly at the garish slash mark. Most people had the courtesy not to gawk. "Some animal claw at you?"

She flashed him a look that instantly killed his curiosity.

He rose abruptly and walked away. "Go ahead, get dressed. I won't look."

A little late for that.

As soon as he started rummaging through his backpack, she pulled the leather halter over her head and tightened the laces that criss-crossed her back, bringing the ends around to the front to tie. Her fingers were still stiff and tingly, making the process a bit of a challenge.

"So what happened?" she asked, pretending the situation wasn't weirdly uncomfortable. "How did you happen to be at the falls the moment I needed you?"

"Just one of those crazy things, you know?" he laughed.

"If the story's that funny, I definitely want to know the details." Death generally wasn't a laughing matter.

He didn't reply. Cleo wondered if he'd even heard her. He seemed distracted by something in his backpack. She was about to repeat the questions when he spoke.

"I'm not sure you do."

"Oh, I do. Right down to the last giggle."

"Fine. Just remember, you asked."

Silence thickened as she waited for him to begin. A beam of sun cut through the trees and caught his hair, turning it to gold as he raked it with his fingers. "I'd just finished making camp and went to the river to clean up before dinner." He paused, cleared his throat. "I uh...I was taking a leak in the river when I thought I heard a scream. I looked up and saw a dark shape fall over the falls. It took me a second to realize it was a body. It was fair dark, so if you hadn't screamed when you did, I would have completely missed the show."

That didn't explain his nervous laughter. "Tell me again about the funny part."

"I uh... I jumped in as-is," he said. "Without...you know...doing up my armor."

"I'm not seeing the humor."

"Yeah, well," he mumbled, "I reckon it's guy humor. I have a few friends back home who're going to love it."

Cleo rolled her eyes and wrestled the unyielding hide over her sore legs. It would take a few hours of wear and movement to soften and stretch back to a comfortable shape.

There was an unmendable tear from the knee down on the right side that matched the bandage on her leg, but closer inspection of her injuries would have to wait—she wanted to dress as quickly as possible in case he got bored sorting through his things. She tugged the laces that ran up the outside length of each leg, loosening them as quickly as her fingers could fly. She lay back on the air cushion—a lightweight bag of nothing—shifted her weight onto her good leg, and hauled her trousers up over her hips.

"Ow!" A quick sharp poke had her wondering if a bee hadn't got into her pants.

"You okay?"

"Yeah...I think so," she said, rubbing the sore spot on her right butt cheek. She craned her neck to see over her shoulder but could see nothing; no bee, no burr, and from what she could feel with her fingers, no scab, no cut, nothing to indicate the origin of the pain. "I think maybe I bruised my backside coming over the falls. Or some nasty bug bit me in my sleep."

She lay back, exhausted from the effort, leaving the side laces on her pants loose for the moment. She'd worry about tightening them up once she regained her stamina. "Then what happened?"

"Excuse me?"

"After you jumped in. What happened next?"

"I had to dive down a couple of times before I found you—you were pretty limp by then. I dragged you out and started CPR."

Cleo turned her head to the side and watched him zip up the various pockets on his pack.

"And at what point did you put everything back in place?"

"Oh, that?" he laughed. "I don't recall. I reckon during one of the dives, otherwise my pants would've fallen off."

"Good to know," she said, not bothering to hide the smile in her voice. She closed her eyes, a wave of exhaustion making her feel drowsy and light-headed.

The Taiga, vast and great, was ninety percent unpopulated, so the chances that anyone would be within a hundred miles of her at any point in time, especially when she needed help, must have been divine intervention. In hindsight, his story was rather amusing. Such a boy-thing, peeing in a river, probably seeing how far he could splash—

Don't trust outsiders.

She fought against her heavy lids and caught him watching her with a calculated expression. He replaced it with friendly openness before she could fully blink away the haze.

"You can go back to sleep if you want. I won't leave you, if that's what you're worried about."

"I'm perfectly fine," she replied, sitting up, the leather straining against her hips and abdomen. "I don't understand how I survived the fall. How did I *not* get smashed to bits? The pool at the bottom has more rocks than water. Explain how my bones are still intact."

"Don't ask me, darlin'," he said with a shake of his head. "I thought I'd be pulling up a bloody corpse. Even questioned my own sanity for bothering to try, especially in the dark. I couldn't see shit. When I got you ashore, you looked pretty intact, so I decided to see what you tasted like."

"Tasted me! What's that supposed to mean?" She may have sounded indignant, but for the love of all things fishy, she was shocked at the images his choice of wording invoked. She could feel a blush rush up her chest.

"Whoa now. I only meant that I gave you mouth-to-mouth, banged on your chest and tried out those life-saving techniques I learned in Ranger Boys." Wolfish eyes raked her body. "But if you want me to be literal, I don't reckon dead girls have much of a taste."

Cleo turned her flushed cheeks away and tried to focus on her lower leg. "Thanks. Thanks for doing that."

Out of the corner of her eye, she caught his smirk.

She should assess her wound, figure out what kind of first aid she'd need, but as her hands worked to undo the sloppy, blood-encrusted bandage, the only thought in her head was, *he has nice hair.*

She heard his feet scrape the ground as he came over. The smirk was gone as he crouched beside her. "I did what I could, but I was too wet and cold to do much more than make sure you didn't bleed to death."

Cleo unwound the strip of material, exposing a six-inch gash. It wasn't critically deep, but she would have benefited from a few stitches. The tender, swollen skin had jagged, torn edges. *Lovely.* Another attractive scar to add to her collection.

Had to have been caused by hitting a rock. Dark purple flesh surrounded the wound, a bruise so sensitive, her own prodding caused her to hiss with pain. A thin trickle of blood oozed through the encrusted lesion. Feeling a tad wobbly, she straightened her spine and placed her palms on the comforting firmness of the ground.

Blood loss. Had to be. Because a little scratch like this wasn't enough to make her queasy.

He bent down next to her, invading her space, so close, she could smell him. "You okay?"

"Sure." She waved her hand dismissively. "I've had worse."

He leaned over her shin, scrutinizing the gash while she studied the profile of his squared jaw. "Two inches toward the front and whatever you hit would have snapped your shin like a twig."

Just like that, the world began to spin at the same rate as her stomach.

"Zhang hell, not again." She felt his arm go around her shoulder. Warm, strong, supporting. "Hang on, Cleo. Deep breaths."

Lacking the strength to pull away, she sagged against him. "I... I..." Her mouth suddenly filled with saliva. She swallowed and willed herself not to retch. "I'm fine."

"No, you're not."

No, I'm not. "I will be. Just give me a sec."

"You want a drink?" He lowered her gently back down into a prone position. "I'll be right back."

Cleo closed her eyes until her head steadied, embarrassed by her weakness.

Think! Clear the mind, regulate the heart rate, and think.

She had to get away. Had to continue her mission. *Yes—concentrate on the goal.* She couldn't go very far on that leg without risking infection. She had to stay put for a day or two.

But Jaegar might not have a couple more days! *Think, think, think...*

It was so hard to focus with a head that refused to stay attached. It floated like a spectral above her, floating, refusing to stay in the moment.

Calm, focus on breathing, remember the training. I am a warrior, trained to fight, to defend, trained to lead, trained to...

It came to her.

Tobacco.

THREE

C LEO RUSH WAS *NOT* WHAT he expected.

Libra was told she was a savage, like all the people who inhabited the remote northern wilds of Old Canada. Technically, they were Upper Ameradans, but everyone in Lower A knew they were a few DNA strands short of civilized and didn't like the association.

Her dossier described her as a motherless girl who would fight to survive and to kill if she were threatened. He half-expected pointed teeth, a spear, and excess body hair.

They were wrong.

He was told she'd be carrying weapons and to expect resistance. He was told to get her while she was alone, drug her, bag her, and transport her back to Gomeda. He was told she was dangerous.

They were wrong.

He didn't know it was Cleo Rush when he pulled her limp body from the water, but armed with the physical description that would ensure her identity—the distinguishable birthmark on her cheek—it wasn't hard to figure out. The thrashing and shouting in her sleep confirmed it, especially when she called her brother, repeatedly, by name.

They gave him a cover story, which he'd memorized in case of capture and questioning, but they were skeptical about his ability to make it sound convincing. Though that was before the last-minute change in his target.

Either way, they needn't have worried.

If he was anything, he was a great liar. Always had been. His life depended on it. He would have lied, bluffed, and fibbed his way into her world if that's what it took. But this—her literally falling out of the sky at his feet—this was so much better. Luck or fate, one of them was on his side. How else could it be explained?

Instead of the wild animal he'd anticipated, Cleo was an injured, frightened, and unarmed woman, with heart-stopping, double-take beauty. He couldn't stop himself from staring. When she was cold, puking, and blue in the face, not so much... But by the light of day, *wow*.

Bringing her back to life was no picnic, but four billion cashpoints and a get-out-ofjail-free card was pretty good incentive. He'd done dirtier jobs for far less.

"Spade-shaped hairy leaves around a spiky formation with yellow flowers," he murmured, reciting the items she'd requested as he headed out of the small clearing where he'd made a camp.

Armed with a mesh pouch for collecting her grocery list, he also surreptitiously tucked his DEL-48, special edition direct energy pulse laser, into the waistband of his pants at the small of his back, in case he met a real wild animal. If there was one memorable fact that stuck out in his training, it was that the Taiga had a problem with misplaced polar grizzlies with a taste for human flesh. While the DEL wouldn't kill anything much over two hundred pounds, it would stun the zhang-hell out of whatever he hit long enough to make a clean escape.

"And chamomile," she called after him, interrupting his thoughts. "Don't forget the chamomile."

She might as well have been asking for moondust. He was so out of his league in this place. *Spade-shaped hairy leaves and chamomile, feathery green, low to the ground, spade shaped feathery leaves—zhang!* "Let me find the hairy spades before you clutter my head with more green things," he said with a quick glance back. She was sitting up in those barely-fastened pants, sipping a cup of water.

Aside from the pink puckered scar that marred her cheek, her skin was a delicious shade of bronzed honey. Didn't see much of anything past ghostly pale complexions in Gomeda.

She looked tired, a little worn out from her ordeal, but that was a good sign as far as he was concerned. He fervently hoped it wasn't an act, that the wound was as serious as it looked and she wasn't sending him on a wild goose chase so she could flee. Then he'd have to rely on the tracker, and turning on his satcom was a risky move in the Taiga.

He'd been careful to do nothing to make her distrust him. In fact, he'd purposely been reckless, leaving his blade behind when he went for water earlier in the day—she hadn't touched it—and just now, he left behind his pack, unguarded, hanging on a tree in plain sight. He counted on her rustling through it while he was gone. The important stuff was well hidden a good distance away. She wouldn't find anything but some basic hiking equipment—rain shield, food packets, satcom.

Zhang hell! That was a careless mistake. Though without his biorhythm, she couldn't turn it on.

One thing he learned from his stint at the penal colony was the fine art of poker.

More specifically, simple observation, since it helped to figure out if someone was bluffing. Cleo's tell was the chunk of black rock that hung around her neck. When she became unsettled, she played with it. If she *did* go through his stuff, Libra expected she'd be clutching it pretty good when he returned.

He walked through the forest, keeping the river within hearing range so he wouldn't get lost. Despite his crash course in wilderness survival, which he didn't pay as much attention to as he probably should have, this was new to him—the terrain, the climate, the entire forest experience.

Home couldn't be more opposite to this vast and unending landscape that made him feel dizzy and inconsequential. In Gomeda, the vast sprawling city he called home, he couldn't take two steps without tripping over someone. Out here, there was nothing but trees and rocks, rocks and trees, and more zhanging trees. It made him appreciate the zillion-to-one chance that he and Cleo could show up at the same waterfall on the same evening. Almost too bizarre to wrap his head around.

At one point during the endless night of staring at Cleo, it occurred to him it that it might be a trap of the joke's-on-me variety. Nah. Achan couldn't be *that* cruel. The old man busted him out of hard-labor camp. If he wanted him good and truly punished for stealing those medical supplies out from under his rich, wrinkled ass, gramps would have left him there for the duration of his sentence.

Libra looked down at the raw skin on his palms, imagining what they would look like with nine more years of handling toxic waste. Nah, this was a much better gig.

How did these people survive without buildings and buzz trains and...civilization? Survival amongst the eleven million people of Gomeda was an every-day challenge, but all you really needed was a bad-ass attitude, a good knowledge of the rules, and enough coin to break them. Simple. And he had two out of the three.

This mission would give him the third, ensuring his survival and his freedom. That had been the deal-maker; sweet freedom, because money alone, even *that* much, couldn't motivate him enough to work for a bastard like Achan Cade.

When it was over, he'd live comfortably, something he hadn't known for a long time. There'd be no hunger, violence, or depravity. He could continue to do what he was passionate about, but in a smarter, more creative way. He could distribute the wealth of Gomeda as far as the slums of New Chicago and have the resources to cover his hide.

He smiled at the thought of delivering

Cleo in a tidy little package, days earlier than anyone expected. He could taste freedom on his tongue now, could taste it in his mouth even as he'd pressed his lips to hers and tried to revive her.

He'd saved her.

Now Cleo Rush would save him.

FOUR

WHAT KIND OF IDIOT MADE *camp so close to a waterfall?*

Cleo strained to hear over the incessant thrum. She gave another visual sweep of her surroundings before closing her eyes and tapping into her years of training to achieve a focused state. She concentrated on the movement of her diaphragm as her lungs filled and emptied, pushed the oxygen lower into her belly before letting it out slowly. Each cycle took her deeper into a state of intense meditation. She tuned into the suck and push of blood through her heart and mentally slowed her system until she felt centered. When she entered the zone, she filtered the sensory input of her surroundings, listened with an acute awareness.

She felt every molecule of air that

entered her ear canal, vibrated the tympanic membrane, and sent a burst of energy through the cochlear nerve. Her cerebral cortex took over, comparing what she heard with her mental inventory.

Unlike hearing, which was mechanical, sight, smell, and taste were harder to amplify because those senses depended on a chemical reaction.

But she could. It was her gift. Learning to maximize her senses had taken her years of intense training, but she mastered it in time for the Leadership Challenge. In the singular darkness of her mind, Cleo was able to filter through the distractions and become one with her environment.

Snake, slithering into a rock pile, twenty-five feet to the west of the clearing.

Four chipmunks, chattering while they ran up and down the spruce trees in the grove between the camp and the river. Nope, five.

Branch snapping—

Chickadees, sparrows, a lone female cardinal, red-breasted sapsuckers, and the familiar sounds of Canada Geese flying at approximately one hundred and twenty feet, two miles to the east.

Splashing, downstream, a couple of otters. Her nose picked this up even before her ears. Cute little critters, but otters had a distinct pungency.

Cleo switched her focus to smell as she continued to inhale deeply. The air around their campsite was permeated with spruce and pine, the earthy smell of composting foliage—a sure sign of autumn's fast approach, and something else. Something else out there stirred her senses, tugged at her concentration.

Raccoons—burrowed somewhere upwind.

As mischievous as they were, raccoons wouldn't make the hair on the back of Cleo's neck tingle. No, there was something else.

Wolverine scat. Days old, no threat. And...

Cleo took a final breath and tensed as a rush of adrenaline flooded her system.

Alphacat.

"Pay attention to the rocks. You know all about rocks, don't you, boy?"

"Yeah, I know about rocks. They're big, heavy, and hot." Libra flashed the old man his acid-burned hands.

"Never mind those kind. You need to look for peculiar patterns or formations, evidence of mining, tapping a vein, or stripping. I'll want a full report."

Libra almost forgot that part of the conversation. At the time, he'd reckoned Achan was giving him a personal dig about the way the inmates were clearing contaminated rubble and debris from the Dead Zone, but now, surrounded by the unfamiliar geography of the Ameradan Shield, he understood. Tons of zhanging rock, everywhere he looked, everywhere he stepped. But what constituted an odd formation? He had no clue.

He stared at the outcropping stone two times his height that blocked the path ahead. It had an angled peak, like it had been driven upward through the soil. Instead of navigating around it, he took a running leap and caught the toe of his boot about a third of the way up, then used his hands to spring his body up sideways, twisting in mid-air to give him upward momentum, scoring a perfect landing on the uneven cap. Anyone watching would have been impressed. He let one corner of his mouth slide up and did a mock bow.

And thinking of Cleo, because that's exactly who he had in mind when he bowed, he realized that he had three options. He had enough ampoules of psychoactive drug to have her willingly walk out of here with him, but he had serious reservations about using it. The side effects could permanently warp her mind, and Libra didn't want to zhang-up her brain, savage or not.

Especially now that he'd met her.

Since she wasn't the undomesticated ape-woman he'd expected, he loathed the thought of a bag-and-drag approach. To be cautious, he had injected the implant, so knocking her unconscious wouldn't be a problem if it became necessary.

But a third, more satisfying scenario—and one that would make the mission go faster and smoother, with less complication—would be if she simply went with him, crossed the Cut Road of her own volition.

Question was, how would he get her to go?

Seduction was worth a thought. He wasn't completely without charm and looks. Could he make a woman fall in love and drop everything when she didn't know him, didn't trust him? From the way she spit out the water he'd given her, he knew he had a way to go. He hadn't thought twice before adding the vitamin supplement to the cup, never considered that she'd never had one before. *Zhang hell*, what did they do for nutrient-deprivation out here? Once he took a gulp to prove it wasn't poisoned, she took a tentative sip, but her suspicious brown eyes stayed locked on his face the entire time. Maybe she knew about Zenwater, the poison they ladled out in Gomeda to keep everyone calm and controllable?

The trees thinned out as he approached the edge of what looked to be a sharp drop. He scanned the area following the line of the distant horizon. Nothing but rocks and trees, miles and miles of nothing. Why would anyone choose to live here?

There didn't appear to be any easy routes through this zhang-damned country. No roads, rails, or hover paths, just endless, winding trails through ridiculously difficult terrain. How the hell did these people move?

He stopped on the edge of a stout cliff and looked down. There, at the bottom, just what Cleo ordered: yellow spiked plants.

Cleo.

She reminded him of a cat, the way her eyes tilted up in the corners, the way she tracked his every move, intently and with suspicion. She never looked relaxed or at ease, even when she slept. Her limbs were tight, like over-wound springs. He had no doubt she'd put up a good fight if he tried to physically subdue her. But oh man, a part of him would like to try.

He was told that she was some kind of warrior. He laughed at the thought. She was a bitty thing. He was six two, and the top of her head barely came to his chin.

And how would one fight with all those curves?

He shook his head to clear the image of her that was stuck in his mind so he could properly assess the series of shallow ledges between him and the yellow spike below. He leaped off the edge with the agility of a cougar, bouncing from ledge to ledge. The shale was jagged around the edges but slippery on the flat surfaces, so he was as careful as possible considering the speed at which he descended.

Time was of the essence. The quicker down, the quicker back, and the more time he had for his plan. He would use the sound of the waterfall to mask his approach. He wanted to learn more about the mysterious Cleo Rush, and, just like he had learned at the poker table, the best way to learn was to observe the subject. In this case, it was preferable to do it unseen, see how she acted in her natural habitat.

FIVE

L ONG HABIT HAD HER GRASPING for the throwing knives in the harness she always wore across her torso, but of course, they were gone, lost to the river. Fight or flight time.

Running, climbing a tree, both out of the question thanks to her mashed-up leg. Besides, the cat could do both far better than a human. She scanned the campsite, looking for a tool, a stick, anything she could use as a weapon.

With options running out, she fervently hoped her nasal passages had been damaged during the drowning and she was wrong about this. But that smell was unmistakable.

Definitely alphacat.

Flesh eaters had an entirely different aroma than herbivores. And alphacats— genetic hybrids gone wrong—were anything but benign. They were rare in the Taiga, and Cleo had never encountered one alive, but she'd heard the stories. The Heron Clan lost two hunters and countless arrows bringing down the one whose black-and-gray-spotted pelt lay on her father's bedroom floor.

She could hear it now, even in her less heightened state, getting closer, zeroing in on her scent. Fresh meat. Breakfast. The fresh blood in her wound beckoning to it. She, the injured prey.

For the second day in a row, Cleo's survival was being tested. The second time in as many days when her heart rate climbed well beyond the zone in which she could think rationally. A second dance with death.

Damn waterfall! She would have heard the cats approach sooner if *he* hadn't made camp so close to the damn water.

Just the thought of her companion sparked an idea. He'd left his backpack behind, hanging on a tree. She prayed it would have something useful in it. Acid spray was a staple of sightseers, was it not? In case they had to defend themselves from itty-bitty squirrels. Maybe she could temporarily blind the cat and give her a small chance to escape.

If she didn't get slashed to death first.

Knees bent, she positioned her left foot a few inches off the ground, rocked her body back and thrust forward, hands out, using the momentum of her body and the muscles of her right leg to get herself upright.

Fighting a wave of head-spinning nausea, she hobbled forward, eyes on her goal. She flinched and stumbled as pain radiated out of her wound. Another wave of dizziness threatened to knock her down. Lack of food, blood loss... hardly her fighting best. Cleo dropped her head to her chest and inhaled deeply. She couldn't afford to pass out now. Not while she was being stalked for breakfast. And after it was finished with her, it would follow the urbanite's scent—her savior would be dessert.

The bag hung twelve feet away. Her head still throbbing, she didn't dare risk hopping the distance in case she lost her balance and toppled. If she fell, it would be The End.

She tugged the protruding end of a two-foot log from the smoldering fire, a thick-headed, dead tree branch that he'd not bothered to break up. Gripping it from the cool end, she smacked it on the ground to dislodge the loose embers that encased the bottom. Holding it out at arm's distance, she leaned on it and jumped forward with her left foot.

Jump, grunt, breathe and repeat, eye on the bag.

The leaves rustled from the shadows beyond the clearing, branches crackling under the weight of her hunter.

Almost there. One more jump, maybe two. Holding her right leg bent, she again placed the log in front of her and, with her teeth clenched tightly, she coiled the muscles of her left leg and sprang forward. The burned end of her cane shattered under the weight. Smoldering embers scattered everywhere. Cleo gasped as the ball of her right foot slammed down. She fought to gain her balance, to keep going, to get to that sack.

A quick glance down confirmed what she feared. Her throbbing wound dripped with fresh blood. The animal would be opening his mouth, flicking his tongue between the long, razor-sharp cuspids to taste her blood in the air.

Nausea roiled her guts, more from terror than pain.

Cleo dove the last few feet and ripped the bag off the branch as her body slammed into the ground. She rolled into a sitting position and, with trembling fingers, tore through his possessions.

It approached slowly, stealthily.

Clothes, a pathetically inadequate first aid pouch, packs of powdered food, a shiny black disc that she shook, hoping a blade or something deadly would appear. She threw it to the ground. Useless, all useless.

He must have something! People just didn't wander around the damn Taiga without some means of defense—spray, gun, laser... *oh come on, urbanite, you saved me once, please do it again.*

She almost wished he'd not found her last night. She'd be dead already, her soul in limbo, or heaven or wherever souls went when they had no body to inhabit. As bad as drowning was, and it was horrific, the thought of her flesh being ripped apart by sharp teeth... well, that was too much.

Cleo's pulse hammered in her ears, muting all other sounds.

All except the steady chuff-chuff-chuff of the alphacat's breath.

Her skin prickled. She knew it was sizing her up from the dark foliage, smelling her blood, her fear. She imagined the slits of its predatory eyes narrowing and widening, focusing on her, its next meal.

They always paused before the attack, confusing their prey into thinking they had time to flee, and it was the moment Cleo needed to collect herself. She held her breath, her arm buried in the backpack, her hand moving methodically through its contents, searching.

Cree-ack. A branch broke under its weight. It was settling back on its haunches, waiting for her to move. To scurry for cover. To run for her life.

Too scared to breathe, she imagined its tail, held low for balance, flick once, twice in anticipation of the pounce, the leap, the kill.

She let out a small whimper as her fingers reached the bottom of the bag. Her leg muscles tensed, prepared to run, when her fingers slipped under the reinforced bottom and landed on something long, hard, sheathed. A handle.

If lucky, she'd be able to rip the knife from its encasement before the cat emerged through the foliage. If she wasn't lucky, she would die.

A deep growl crescendoed in Cleo's throat as a burst of adrenaline guided her through the next few seconds. Her thumb snapped the release just as something exploded into the perimeter of camp, sending twigs, leaves, and a cloud of grit through the air.

SIX

IT TOOK LIBRA LONGER THAN he intended to get back to camp. He circled too far and probably would have kept going if he hadn't run smack into a familiar-looking rock wall. Though around here, every zhang-damn rock was beginning to look the same. He followed the escarpment eastward and sure enough, it came out at the waterfall. He gave his head a shake, glad his auto-tutor hadn't seen that gaffe. He'd never known a computer program so capable of sarcasm.

Fumbling around in the bushes made him lose precious time. He couldn't stay away too much longer for fear of amplifying her suspicion.

The closer he drew to the clearing, the more care he took placing his steps, sticking to the hard-packed soil and rock, avoiding the crunch of foliage. He scanned the vicinity until he found an ideal observation spot: two large rocks, boulders half as tall as he was, surrounded by brush. There would be just enough space to wiggle between them and crouch down, completely camouflaged, and still be able to see into their camp.

He barely took a step toward it when he heard her voice.

"I don't know your name."

Zhang hell!

"Libra," he called back, fighting his way through low branches of prickling trees. "I'm Libra."

"Why are you sneaking up on me, Libra?" Her tone was flat, accusatory.

"I...I wasn't. I just didn't want to disturb you if you were sleeping," he said. "And I got turned around, went too far that way and had to double back."

She sat on the ground a few feet from the fire, staring up at him with widened, untrusting eyes. He emerged, brushing twigs and pokey green needles from his hair. "What happened to your leg?" he asked, noticing her shin, slick with fresh blood.

Something in his peripheral vision caught his attention, made him stumble back. "What the—"

"I had a visitor while you were gone."

He felt his jaw moving, but no sound came

out. He stepped closer, eyes darting between the beast and Cleo. She seemed unruffled as he circled the cat tentatively, assuring himself that yes, it was indeed dead—that much was obvious, even for a city boy. He moved cautiously, not believing what he saw and knowing that on some level, he was losing serious man-credits.

The holograms on his auto-tutor did nothing to prepare him for the reality of seeing an alphacat up close and personal. Its thick short fur mimicked the colors of the rocky outcroppings he'd just leapt across. He could have jumped right over one and not known unless it snagged him.

The animal's mouth sagged open to reveal a double row of unnervingly pointed teeth. He reckoned it weighed three or four hundred pounds easily.

Guilt twisted in his gut. He'd left her alone. He'd left an injured, helpless girl, *alone.* He'd taken the DEL, left her helpless.

He looked to her again. She sat calmly, unfazed.

The paws were as big as his hands, with un-retractable claws sharp as curved scimitars, yet Cleo didn't have a scratch on her.

How in zhang hell did she—

Libra turned so she couldn't see his face and swallowed the bile that crept up his throat. He pivoted, an apology filling his mouth, but she stopped him with a raise of an eyebrow that seemed to say, "What? I do this every day." In fact, she appeared a good deal more composed than he felt. What kind of person could do that? Kill an animal and look so composed?

Though, her fingers were wrapped tightly around her pendant. And her complexion seemed waxier than it had been.

"You okay?" he asked.

"Better than him."

"You need a hug, a high-five, a shot of hooch?"

"Nah, I'm good."

Cleo's lip quivered when she attempted to smile, giving him a glimmer of reassurance that it wasn't commonplace to slaughter a living creature before lunch, and that under that tough Taiga façade lay a girl.

A girl he should *never* turn his back on.

"Well hell, darlin', you sent me out for salad while you slayed us some grill." He meant it to say it lightly, to salvage his compromised Y chromosome, but his voice wavered. He backed away from the dead animal, from between the hunter and the prey, and plopped to the ground in a spot from which he could keep an eye on both of them.

Zhang hell. He was supposed to hate her, her people, her way of life. But how could he not admire a woman who could take down a wild cat five times her size?

They sat in silence, staring at the alphacat with seven inches of blade firmly embedded between its lifeless, green eyes.

SEVEN

THE SUN HAD CRAWLED TO its apex, turning
long shadows to short when Cleo finally
broke the silence. Without taking her eyes off
the kill, without turning her head, she asked,
"How did you know my name?"

"Excuse me?"

"My name. You said it, earlier, when I had
my wobbly moment. How did you know it?"

Libra gave her a blank look. "Well, you told
me. Last night. But you were pretty out of it,
so it's no wonder you don't recall. And I *did*
tell you mine."

She eyed him a moment, unsure if she
should believe him, but without reason not to.
Cleo stuck out her hand, which had thankfully
steadied since facing the cross-breeding
disaster designed by misguided scientists
who were desperately trying to save any and

all species that were near extinction after the Polar War. "Let's do this again, shall we?"

Libra hesitated before inching closer to take her hand, but did, per the old customs. Hand shaking went out with the viral outbreaks in the last century, but it was a good way to gauge his grip, his strength.

As he pressed his dry palm to hers, her ability to assess disappeared faster than the morning mist. Libra's grip was sturdy, his fingers long and tapered, his hand big enough to engulf her own. Again, the odd texture of the skin on his hands struck her with curiosity. She would ask, but as his pale eyes locked on hers, a fission of electricity passed between them, confusing her thoughts and startling her with its underlying complexity.

If she had any sense, she'd pull him forward and get him into a headlock and demand answers. But sense had fled when she began enjoying the warmth of their connection.

"I almost forgot," he said, snatching his hand back before she could sort the conflicting signals. He reached into his pocket, pulled out a handful of small, bright green stems, and placed them in her open palm. "Nice to formally meet you, Cleo."

"You found chamomile!"

"I think I found everything you asked for," he said, dumping the small bag of leaves on the ground between them. "I grabbed anything that looked like hairy green spades, figuring that one of them had to be right."

Cleo separated out the ones she wanted and added them to a shallow plate of water that she'd heated over the embers of the fire.

"What's it all for?" he asked.

"The chamomile, which I'll make into tea, has antibacterial qualities so I won't get an infection. It also is a relaxant, which is important in the healing process. And this," she said, holding up the spade, "we call Indian Tobacco. It's good for healing, encourages cell regeneration."

She laid them in the water, waited a moment for them to soften, then layered them across her wound, wincing as each made contact. "They also act as a pain reliever, so I hope you remembered where you got them. I might need more."

"Or you could just ask me for some acetaminophen," he said with his half smile. "I do have a basic first aid kit with me."

Yeah, I know. "Really? What else do you have?" His mouth was fascinating to watch, the way his well-shaped lips formed words. Others she'd come across during her travels through Taiga country usually had dry, cracked lips and a dullness about them that spoke of poor nutrition. But Libra's looked soft and lush.

"What do you need?"

Your lips, pressed against mine—no, no, no! What she really needed, besides a hard cuff upside the head, was a good fighting knife and a couple for throwing. But she could hardly tell him that. She swallowed. "We're going to need food—"

"I've got Nutripacks—"

"Yuk, no!" Cleo shook her head and couldn't stop her mouth from puckering. "I'd rather starve. How about another weapon? Do you have a gun, or just *that*," she asked, looking toward the handle that protruded from the alphacat's skull.

"Just *that*."

"You really shouldn't come to the Taiga so ill prepared," she scolded. "It's a wonder you tourists survive your little holidays."

"Next time," he said with a shrug.

"Well, it'll do for a start, but we'll need something to hunt with, like a wire for a snare or a strap of leather for a slingshot."

"You're kidding, right? I've got steak and potatoes. Why would we need to kill—?"

"No, you have tough, dehydrated little cakes that are *called* steak and potatoes, but it's all chemicals. Not good."

"Beats spending all day stalking some poor animal."

"Why are you here?"

His shoulders hitched. "What do you mean?"

"I mean, you're an urbanite. Why are you

68

here? What brought you to the tribe lands?"

"I'm on vacation, trying something new."

"You brought your own food. That doesn't sound like such an adventure."

"I wanted to see trees and birds and water that you can touch without having to climb fences."

"Yeah, but why the Shield?" she probed. Of all the places in Upper Amerada, the area known as the Old Canada Shield was by far the roughest, most unfriendly terrain to those untrained to deal with its challenges. "I've heard about parklands, protected pockets around the city. Why not go there?"

"Not much of a hiking opportunity in three square miles of scrubby bush, and the Guard will arrest you for so much as snapping a branch."

She studied his expression. Tight facial muscles, tense around the neck and shoulders... He was lying.

Don't trust outsiders.

"And I wanted more of a challenge. A man-climbs-mountain-because-it's-there experience."

He sounded just like Jaegar, who'd do anything because... why not?

"Sightseers usually stay pretty close to the Cut Road," she said. "How'd you get all the way up here?"

"Hiked."

"By yourself?" She glanced at his feet. "Your boots are barely dirty."

"Okay, you got me." He pushed his hands through his hair and tilted his face to the sky. "I was with some buddies but wanted a bit more excitement than the Trading Post. The guys brought me up this far on their solar scooters and I'm going to boot it back to them."

His words were clipped, the warmth gone from his mouth.

"Well, don't let me delay you. If you need to go, go. I'll be fine here."

"Leave an injured woman alone in the hostile forest? Forget it. I'd lose all my Ranger Boy badges." His attempt at humor fell flat. He wore no smile, and there wasn't an ounce of mischief in his pale eyes. "Besides, I figure it's only a three or four-day hike and they're giving me a week to make my way back. If I don't show up by then, they'll know I'm either lost or dead."

"You can do it in two if you stay on course, but it's a hard walk."

"Is that where you were headed? The Trading Post?"

"Mmmm," she said, neither denying nor confirming.

"Tried to take a shortcut over the falls?"

"Something like that," she said.

Libra cocked his eyebrows and flicked his fingers in a gimme prompt.

Cleo felt her cheeks heat and looked away. "It's too embarrassing."

"Come on, darlin'. It's just you, me, and the pussycat. 'Fess up." The way he growled *darlin'* softened her.

She couldn't tell him the truth. He'd think she was completely out of her head. Her mouth opened and she started talking, hoping that whatever she managed to spew would sound convincing. She gave a pretend laugh. "It's quite funny, really. I was taking a pee in the stream—"

"Cleo," he said with a charming smirk.

The way her name sounded from his mouth shot straight through her. She put a hand over her belly to halt the bizarre pulling sensation.

"Okay, fine." At least she'd bought a few moments to come up with something plausible. "I was upstream catching fish for dinner and I slipped and got carried away in the current." She looked him in the eye while she lied. Jaegar taught her that. When they were little, Grandma would pump them for information about their dad. Cleo always looked at her feet and stayed quiet, but Jag would boldly look Gram right in the eyes and say, "He's great, happy all the time."

It was for Gram's own good, Jag said, otherwise she'd fret and worry. And Cleo trusted him. Jag was smart that way, about other people's feelings. Cleo would have just blurted out, "No, Gram. Dad's always sad. He hides in his work house. He never looks at me, never tucks me in or kisses me goodnight, and never, ever talks about Mom."

But lying never came easy for her, even to this strange man before her, this handsome urbanite, so she looked between his pale eyes and focused on the top of his straight nose. "It was getting dark and I couldn't find anything to grab onto. I tried to swim to the side, but the fall rains have made the water so high and fast that I couldn't make it."

It wasn't all made up. After a solid week of torrential rain, the water really was high and fast. But she and Jag had portaged through this area enough in the past that she knew she should have gotten out of the river before the rapids. Her impatience to make the Cut Road by the following day had her pushing downstream, thinking she'd be able to navigate the killer current and get out well before the plunge.

And she would have been just fine had the flash in the sky not distracted her.

Libra's eyes narrowed, almost imperceptibly, making her wonder if he believed any of it.

"Nothing to be embarrassed about," he said dismissively. "Could have happened to anyone."

"Not where I come from," she said, trying to validate his suspicion by admitting it was a complete gaff on her part.

"Where do you come from?"

"Shield Tribe, Wolverine Clan."

"You're the tough bunch. They were talking about you at the Post."

"I'm sure our reputations have been greatly exaggerated."

"Or you're just being modest. I've heard some stories. Wolverine Clan... You guys are practically legendary."

"Rubbish. We're a gentle people, as are all the Taiga tribes. We're an agricultural-based community that exists to survive, like everyone else on this ravaged planet, so whatever overblown myths you've heard are nonsense, I assure you."

"What I *heard* is..." He vaulted to his feet with the agility of a cougar. He took a moment to brush dirt from his butt before looking down, directly into her face. "You don't *fuck* with the Shield Tribe."

He turned and strode off, missing the shiver that crawled up her spine and made her body quiver. Was he teasing her, mocking the tribes, or did he seriously believe it?

"If we're so terrible, why do you people keep sending recruiters?" she called to his retreating back. Just the thought of those smarmy leeches that hung around the Cut Road, looking for young people to lure to Gomeda made her angry.

He turned and extended his arms, palms up. "Hey, I don't know anything about that. I just live a peaceful existence and mind my own business."

"What is your business?"

Libra picked up his sleep sack, shook it out, and laid it next to her. He squatted next to her and scooped her up as if she were weightless. "You mean besides saving damsels in distress?"

Cleo was about to protest, but his mouth tilted up in one corner and the glint of mischief returned to his pale eyes. Face to face, his lips inches from her own, she was afraid to speak, afraid her voice would crack and betray her vulnerability. Afraid that if she opened her mouth, butterflies would escape.

She caught her breath and, with it, his sun-kissed flesh, the citrus scent of his hair. For the love of horny bunnies, she wanted to reach up and wrap her arms around that thick column of neck. She wanted to nuzzle him, run her tongue along the underside of his jaw.

It went completely against her nature to be handled this way, but for the first time in forever, she didn't mind playing the helpless female, didn't mind being attended to, and didn't mind having this strapping example of virility set her down on the cushiony softness of the sleepsack. She found her voice as he released her, but it came out wispy, breathy. "Yes, besides that."

"I'm a pencil pusher, an office drone," he said, gathering his canteen from the ground beside the fire. "No cliffs to fall from, no menacing alphacats wandering the corridors. All very boring."

Cleo felt everything inside of her soften. If he dipped his head to kiss her, she wouldn't fight him, wouldn't push him away.

He's an outsider, not to be trusted.

And charming. He exuded charisma with that half-smile of his.

He's a liar.

His body, with long, rangy muscles, broad back and chest, shoulders she wanted to grab and hang on to...didn't develop from sitting behind any desk all day. His skin, healthy from sunshine and fresh air, didn't come from sitting under artificial lighting all day long. Physically, he looked more like a Taigan than a Gomedan.

Before she could wheedle more details about his pretend boring job, he continued, "And now, if you don't mind me saying so, you look exhausted. Lie down, relax, take a nap." He emptied the last few drops of water from his canteen. "After I refill this, I'll take care of our guest before he starts to stink up the place."

She lay back but didn't relax. Her gaze

remained on Libra's side until he was out of sight, thinking what a shame for such a gorgeous male specimen to house a deceptive soul. Cleo had no doubt that he was not what he said he was.

Who are you, Libra from Gomeda? For the love of skunks, she hoped he wasn't a recruiter, hoped they weren't becoming emboldened after years of skulking around the Cut, hoped, for their own sakes, that they knew better than to mess with the clans of the Shield Tribe or her father would take them on a long, slow tour of the Arctic in the dead of winter.

Recruiters, sent by the Restoration Movement, had been coming north since before Cleo was born. They lured the restless, disenchanted youth from their tribal communities with promises of riches and an easy life in the urban zone. She didn't know if that was true or not—that life could be anything but a fight to survive from season to season—but once they left, they never came back.

Her tribe had been untouched due largely in part to the reputation of her father, but for other parts of the Taiga, the Prairie and Acadian Tribes especially, it had become a hellish problem.

Cleo opened her palms and examined the small calluses at the base of each finger.

Taiga life was hard, but staying alive was a tough business. The original inhabitants, the survivalists who fled the dying and violent cities, settled in the vast emptiness of Old Canada. The wastelands, left desecrated and scarred after decades of war, offered very little in terms of comfort, so they were left alone with their rocks and emptiness and peace. Only when the forests grew back, when the animal life returned in abundance, and when everyone who was left on the planet decided they deserved a piece of it, then, and only then, were the Taiga people forced to become warriors.

They did what needed to be done to survive—it was imprinted in their DNA. Her ancestors on both maternal and paternal sides were leaders back then, instrumental in gathering the scattered settlers, setting up a governmental structure. As the value of the Taiga lands became apparent, they brought their charter to the United World Council and demanded protected status.

Meanwhile, they trained, arming themselves and fighting against those who sought to once more rape the lands of the north for her resources, just as the Restoration Movement fought for their ideals: to return to the mighty civilizations of the past, to build mega cities that nurtured greatness.

Cleo didn't generally enjoy schooling,

but the history module kept her endlessly fascinated, and though she couldn't admit it to anyone for the shame it would bring, she found herself excited by the mega-cities of the past—the art, the architecture, the bizarre customs and dress. She'd fight to the death with anybody who threatened her precious Taiga, but lying alone in bed each night, she dreamt of travelling back to the Nineteenth and Twentieth centuries to paddle the canals of Amsterdam, to walk the lamp-lit streets of Paris, to see the bright skyline of New York.

But they were gone. Nothing left but dust, rubble, and in some cases, oceans.

The Polar Wars, instigated by President Zhang, ended it all. Neighboring nations fought for every last drop of fuel. Allies became enemies. Death, annihilation, bombs: none of it mattered when a new fuel source was needed.

Polar melt and refreeze times were manipulated to keep the rigs and shipping channels operable all year around, while governments of the day promised their people that the end of the crises was imminent. But their manipulations backfired as they passed the tipping point. Melting continued, unstoppable, eating away the sea ice then, finally, the land ice. Coastal cities flooded, low-lying lands, entire countries, disappeared. Survivors, what few there were, fled inland, filling the interior cities that were already stretched to capacity. Eventually, they cut down every tree and ravaged the countryside of every natural resource she had, never anticipating the dire outcome.

Until it was gone.

Those who weren't claimed by death either walled themselves into small communities—literally hoarding everything from seeds to animals, killing those who threatened, dispatching those who didn't fit in—or they disbanded, wandered the devastation in isolated units looking for a new place to settle, to rebuild, or to die.

The last of old North America's corporate and political elite joined together to form the Restoration Movement. They knew about economics, understood that wealth begat wealth, that in order to have power, you had to have a population. They lured people with promises of rebuilding a new city just like things used to be—bright lights and big dreams, unreachable ideals.

Gomeda rose like a beacon of hope.

Lachlan Cade began the Restoration Movement. When he died, his son—and eventually his grandson, the formidable Achan Cade—took over. They made good on some promises and certainly brought those sad souls who made it through the ransacking of their country to a better place, but Gomeda remained plagued with problems.

At least, that's what she learned in her Taiga school from her Taiga teachers. None of them had ever seen it, so she wondered whether to believe them. None of them had hands as smooth as Libra.

But the stuff she'd overheard at Elder Council and the gossip whispered at potlach, scared her more than the records.

Gomedans couldn't have babies, they said. That's why the recruiters came north, for healthy, strapping young men and solid female breeding machines. The Ministry of Opportunity lured them so they could populate their great city.

The recruiters, who set up camps south of the Cut Road, were good at their jobs, offering a new, easier way of life, enticing them with gifts, showing them the glory of civilization and promising them leadership positions in the Restoration Movement—without having to win a competition!

The Elder Councils accused the Ministry of dosing their recruits with neuro-pharm, but the UWC dismissed their complaints and then the Elders got strangely quiet about it. She asked her father once, about why they didn't fight harder to make the UWC investigate, but he gave her an angry look and walked away. Whatever method they used, she just hoped that Jaegar wasn't too far gone by the time she got to him.

If she could find him. She didn't know what to do beyond *get there*. Knock on the door of the Ministry of Opportunity and ask for him? For someone deemed wise by the Elder Council, she sure had her stupid moments. The second she'd learned her brother had been spotted at the recruitment camp, she'd done nothing but make hasty, brainless decisions.

Cleo's eyes drifted shut, but that didn't bring sleep. How could she nap when she needed solutions, needed to figure out how to get back on track since her original plan was scattered at the bottom of the river? All the supplies that she'd carefully packed into the storage hatch of her kayak were gone.

There wasn't room for error, no time for mistakes, and, for the love of her people, she had to restore Jag to his rightful place in the tribe. Despite what it meant for her, she must transfer leadership to him or die trying. But how the hell was she supposed to do all this in her current state—no weapons, no transportation, no food, no shelter, not even a change of clothes? She was trained to use her surroundings to survive, to take advantage of what was close at hand, what nature offered. But would nature offer her anything useful enough to take to Gomeda?

She opened her lids a crack and spied Libra returning, wiping sweat from his brow with the sleeve of his shirt. Wide shoulders tapered to a lean, narrow waist, the picture of health and capability. She smiled to herself.

Nature did indeed deliver, in the form of a six-foot-something package of sinew with blond hair and an urban address. Cleo just needed to figure out how to use him to her advantage.

EIGHT

SHE STOOD NEAR THE EDGE of their small clearing, the thrum of falling water practically imperceptible now that the autumn wind had shifted. Using the trunk of a maple tree for balance, Cleo carefully applied more of her body weight to her injured leg, gauging the amount of pressure it would take. The tobacco-leaf poultice had done an admirable job. Aside from a bit of tightness from the swelling, it didn't feel bad at all. Certainly not as painful as it looked, ringed in an angry, purple-blue welt. And if she kept it bound and free of infection, she wouldn't have to alter her plans to tail the outsider. A little flesh wound wasn't going to stop her from using what the fates so kindly provided—a guide to the urban zone.

Libra still hadn't moved from his sleep

sack, hadn't made a sound to indicate he was even awake, but Cleo could feel his eyes on her back, feel the heat of his stare in every cell of her body. She knew he'd watched her half the night, but what he didn't know was that she had watched him the other half.

She had used the dark hours to search the night sky for signs of what she'd seen before. And she had formulated a plan. By morning, she'd had it worked out. Before she and Libra parted ways, she'd rustle up a few supplies like berries and some edible weeds, then she'd strip and sharpen a few good spikes of wood with his knife to use as weapons, and after he'd had a solid head start, she track him all the way to Gomeda. He'd never even know she was there.

She didn't doubt that she'd eventually find her way to the city on her own, but why bother with uncertainty if she could simply play follow the leader, surreptitiously?

She'd thought about simply asking him to take her, but her gut was telling her not to trust him, not to spend any more time with him than she absolutely had to.

This whole situation—him showing up when he did, his lame backstory—struck her as off. As a child, she loved the spot-the-hidden-picture books her grandmother used to give her. At first glance, it appeared to be a simple drawing of a village, but when examined closely, you'd see that the knot in the bark was really the outline of a polar grizzly, or that the branches of a tree formed a mother and child. It reminded her of Libra; benign at a glance, but Cleo knew if she looked hard enough, she'd eventually find the hidden images.

He seemed fairly capable, though ignorantly comfortable, like he didn't fully understand the dangers of the Taiga. His open and casual body language was at odds with his guarded nature. Perhaps it was natural for urbanites. She had to admit, his actions were not overtly suspicious, but her intuition about people was seldom wrong.

And her instincts were wreaking havoc.

Perhaps it was the way he studied her, sometimes with such intensity that *she* felt like a spot-the-hidden-picture. But when he spoke in that rumbly bass, his words came smoothly, unrushed, almost...flirty.

Men of the Taiga did not treat her as an object of desire. A few feared her, most respected her as a member of her tribe—a warrior and leader, *so says the council*—but those qualities didn't win her dates. In fact, Jag had told her on more than a hundred occasions that if she wanted a husband, she'd have to tone down her testosterone.

Whatever that meant.

It didn't help that Cleo avoided socializing

with other people her age. Unlike Jag, she avoided gatherings whenever she could, or at least stuck to the fringe. She didn't feel comfortable in groups, making conversation and pretending to care about who was walking with whom or who made the best moose sausage.

Cleo preferred the forest—the solitude, the beauty, the challenges. She loved to hunt, to follow the maintenance crews as they surveyed the rock channels, though they always shooed her away. Happiest when she could spend days on end discovering new plant life, she simply couldn't care less about her social status within the tribe.

Which was why it was critical to find Jaegar *before* he was indoctrinated into urban life. She was stunned when she'd learned he was headed to the recruitment station over the Cut. First they lost Simon, now her brother. Idiots!

But it didn't change that fact that Jag was the true leader, not her. *He* was the people person, not her. So why did she have to prove herself by winning the competition? What streak of sheer foolishness made her enter the leadership race in the first place? Had she really convinced herself she wanted it? Did she hate Jaegar so much that her sole purpose for the past two years was to best him?

Yes and no.

She adored her big brother, and she

certainly hadn't meant to humiliate him. Not really. But it seemed the only way to show them that she was worthy. She never gave a thought to what would happen after winning, or what would happen to her brother if he lost.

Cleo swallowed against the lump that formed in her throat, rubbed her chest to ease the tightness that formed beneath her skin. She pictured her heart forming into a piece of tough gristle.

The need to get moving, get to Jag, fired her into action.

In spite of a restless night, she felt back to her old strength, ready for action. The fact that she'd napped on and off for most of the previous day probably had a great deal to do with her restored vigor.

"You'd better head out, Libra. Soon, if you want a full day of hiking."

"Are you trying to get rid of me?"

"Just concerned about your deadline," she replied.

Cleo turned to see him crawl from his bed wearing only a pair of form-hugging shorts. He groaned as he stretched, muscles twitching and rippling as they lengthened. For the love of ducks, the urbanite was a fine sight.

She grabbed her lower lip between her teeth to keep her jaw from disengaging.

His leg muscles were larger, longer, and a good bit more defined than she'd expected for an urbanite. She wondered how simulated protein products could possibly put that much definition on a man's thigh, not to mention his gluteal assets.

She bit down harder to keep her from licking her lips salaciously, to stop a sigh building in her lungs.

He stopped mid-stretch. "You alright? You look in pain. You oughtn't be moving around."

"Circulation is important for healing," Cleo replied, forcing her gaze away. She rotated her ankle first one way, then another.

Satisfied that her leg would take the weight, she turned her back to him and headed toward the river. She had to get out of the clearing, away from him. Away from his silvery-blue stare and away from his half-naked body before she did something she'd regret, like blush.

"Wait up. I'll help."

He caught up, tugging a shirt over his head, and surprised her by snaking an arm around her middle. When his warm palm pressed against the flesh at her waist, she gasped.

"You okay, darlin'?"

"Mm-hm. I, uh, it's the...pain."

"Just as I thought," he said, taking more of her body weight. She wanted to protest but couldn't form words. His touch, his warmth, his strength left her breathless.

And annoyed.

She felt silly clinging to the fabric of his shirt, but it was her only choice. His muscles bunched and tensed under her touch, forcing heat into her cheeks.

She imagined trailing her fingers across his bare flesh, scraping her nails—

A rabbit bolted into the underbrush next to her, jarring her from her lascivious thoughts. Cleo stumbled, almost bringing them both down.

"Whoa. Steady now," he said, gripping tighter.

And she let him. For the love of ducks, she even leaned into him for support, though it was entirely unnecessary. As her muscles warmed up, they were gaining agility. But she limped on for show.

"Where are we going?" he asked.

"I don't know about you," she said, her voice a hoarse whisper, "but I need to freshen up at the river."

Libra stuck his nose in the air and sniffed around like an alphacat sensing wounded prey. He dipped his head closer, closer, until she felt his cheek against her hair.

"Yeah, I was wondering about that rank smell." He squeezed her side as his words flowed dangerously close to her ear.

"It's you, actually." She tried to match his playful tone but her voice came out dry, breathy.

"Oh yeah? That intoxicating manly scent is me? You must be ready to swoon."

"I'm practically drunk on it."

Flirty banter? She had never done flirty banter. This type of behavior usually made Cleo roll her eyes in disgust.

"Well, try not to fall in the river in your state of inebriation."

Cleo giggled—spontaneous and careless, and maybe a wee bit silly. And it felt good. "Will you pull me out if I do?"

"Sorry, darlin'," he chuckled. His breath fanned the hair at her temple, re-igniting the weird pulling feeling in her lower abdomen. "But you've spent your get-out-of-the-water-free card."

"I only get one?"

"Just one. You'll have to pick another life-threatening situation next time you want my help. But be original—volcano, quicksand, giant mutant snake." He grunted like a caveman. "Something challenging. Give me a chance to show off my bad-ass manliness."

"Other than your smell?"

He threw his head back and laughed, rich and low, sending a tingle through her that ended in a smile of girlish delight.

Truth be told, he smelled delicious, like a late-summer breeze mixed with pine, citrus, and a whiff of wood smoke. She wanted to bury her face in his chest, fill her nostrils until his scent was burned into her membranes.

Don't trust outsiders.

Her father's voice hummed in her head, though not as loud, not as urgent as before.

"How about an alphacat attack?" she suggested.

"That's woman's work."

Cleo slapped him with an open-hand to the middle of his rock-hard abdomen and instantly regretted it. His skin was hot, too hot. He'd burned her palm, she was sure of it. She swallowed and cleared her throat. Her eyes flitted up to his profile. "So you're up for a real challenge, something to get the adrenaline pumping?"

He glanced down. "Bring it on, darlin'," he growled.

For the first time in her life, Cleo wished she'd brushed her hair. Damn, she didn't know she was even capable of such nauseating girliness.

Way to crush on the enemy. Shake it off, damn it. Shake it off!

She didn't want to.

She should run, fast, in the opposite direction. Instead, she looked up from underneath her lashes and beamed.

They'd made it to the edge of the riverbank, downstream from the falls. He released his hold, the playfulness gone from his eyes. "I was thinking... Maybe I'll hang around here for one more day."

Yes, yes, please do, but no, that would ruin everything! Oh, for the love of skunks. She swallowed her impatience before answering, "Oh, really? Why?"

"I'd feel bad leaving you." He glanced down at her leg. "Despite that thing with the cat, you're still shaky. I just wouldn't feel right."

Way to undermine the plan, girly-girl.

"I'll be fine," she began, but when he reached up and swept a thumb across the top edge of her cheekbone, the rest of her argument lodged in her throat.

"This bruise here looks much better." His voice, as tender as his touch, turned her knees to water. "Still a bit yellow around the edges, but the purple has faded into a lovely shade of green."

She wanted to turn her face into his palm and nuzzle it. Their eyes met, and Cleo felt as if she were looking directly into his soul. She saw integrity and loyalty, but she also saw shadows and pain and...something else, something dark. She wanted to avert her eyes to get away from whatever blackness haunted him, but she couldn't. He held her as if by spell.

His gaze shifted to the ragged pink line in the hollow of her cheek and his expression became shuttered. "What beast left this mark?"

She pushed his hand away and palmed the

hideous scar. She pivoted toward the river. "Doesn't matter. It's old." Limping, she made it to the water's edge.

"It doesn't matter... Doesn't make you any less...beautiful."

His voice dropped on the last word, as if he forced it out.

"Scars aren't beautiful. They're nothing but reminders of past hurts."

The air felt thicker and she waited for a breeze to dry the moisture that beaded on her forehead.

"I'll go downstream a bit, give you some privacy," he said.

She listened to his steps crunch in the pebbles.

"Unless you need help?" he asked suggestively.

Her mouth softened and she cocked her head in his direction. "I'll be fine. Give me fifteen."

Cleo started mentally berating herself before he'd left her line of sight. He was getting to her with that charming *I care* act. And she was silly enough to be letting him.

But he called me beautiful.

With a series of frustrated tugs, she liberated herself from her leathers. In hindsight, playing up her limp was a spectacularly stupid move. Cleo couldn't catch one bit of luck on this fool's quest.

No use hesitating at the water's edge; it would be frigid, and she knew it. Three quick steps, she figured, would take her knee-deep. But one step in, the water barely at her ankle, and a rush of panic, bone-deep clawing fear, struck her. Cleo had been a swimmer her entire life, a strong one at that, but suddenly the thought of submerging into the very substance that almost killed her had her paralyzed with fright.

For the love of ducks, it's only water!

Hesitantly, she took another step. A gasp caught in her throat. Her chest felt squeezed, making it impossible to inhale. She focused on the smooth pebbles that surrounded her toes and tried to calm herself.

She counted to ten, then twenty, until her breathing returned to normal, until the phantom taste of river mud left her mouth, and took another step forward. The water sluiced around her calf, pulling at her. Her heart raced. She paused to wipe the dampness from her upper lip.

I can't do it.

I can do it. I can do it, damn it. I will do it.

Cleo managed another step, bringing the water level to her knees. Again, she counted to ten, then twenty.

Come on! Don't be a ninny.

Nope. She could count all day, but there was no way in hell she was going deeper.

She bent over and splashed herself, hung her head low enough to soak her hair but not touch her scalp.

Using tentative movements, she shuffled backward. At the edge, with only her feet in the water, she felt brave enough to crouch. She dug under the pebbles and scooped out handfuls of mud, rubbing it over her goose-fleshed skin, one limb at a time, using it to slough off the grime and sweat.

Her skin felt alive and tingly, her wound stopped throbbing, and she felt overall much better but for the curious ache in her belly, an uncharacteristic yearning for the touch of a male body.

Cleopatra Rush, she whispered to her rippling reflection, *has dying made you addled?*

She looked downstream but there was still no sign of Libra, so she stood on the riverbank and faced the wind to let the autumn breeze dry her skin.

Go with the wind, her father would often say. In other words, go with the way of things, not against as she often did, bucking trends, ignoring rules.

Go with the wind.

What if she were honest with him, told him she needed to get to Gomeda? Would he take her? Would he be sympathetic to her cause and maybe even help rescue Jag?

Don't trust outsiders!

No, she couldn't risk telling him why she was going—she'd keep that to herself—but it would certainly save time if she had someone along who knew the way. And it solved the problem with the Trading Post. She couldn't be seen there... but he could! She could send him in with a list of supplies, a new harness, a few blades, just to begin. And her father would never find out she'd crossed the Cut.

Cleo began to dress while she deliberated the pros and cons, just as she'd been taught to do about any important decision regarding tribe matters.

She still didn't know much about him and certainly didn't want to make any hasty judgements. But she didn't feel threatened by him, a big plus in the pro column. Perhaps she should let him stay one more day, if only to get a better handle on him. She could test him to see if he proved trustworthy. If he passed, she'd approach the topic of tagging along.

Yes. Yes, yes, yes!

She had a plan.

She was so lost in thought that her normally acute senses didn't flicker, didn't register any alarm over the man who stood a few dozen feet away, in the deep shadows of the forest, watching.

NINE

"TREVAYNE?" ACHAN CADE'S VOICE WHISPER-HISSED in his inner ear, making him stand straighter. Never mind that he didn't address him by his title. It was Mr. Cade's privilege.

"Yes, sir."

"Have we heard from the boy yet?"

"No voice communications yet, sir."

Trevayne tapped the com-plant nodule behind his ear, adjusting the volume so he wouldn't miss a syllable of his commander-in-chief's words. The man was deceptively soft-spoken.

"Why not?"

"If he's made contact with his subject, he may not be free to speak." Trevayne ran his hand over his bristled head and kept his tone firm but patient. His boss knew damn well the risks in using any form of open-channel communication in the Taiga. The boy was told to use his satcom device judiciously and put the mission completion above all else. They could not afford to draw attention. Being stuck on a roasting spit and devoured by the dirty tribal bastards was *not acceptable.* Besides, he didn't want the pansy-ass boy to think he could whine to his unit about the conditions twenty-four-seven.

"Location?" Cade grilled.

"The last time he activated his com, his positioning signal indicated he was still in the drop zone."

"Could he be dead?" The old man's icy tone could have triggered a glacial age. That was why he respected the old man; Cade never let his personal feelings get in the way of a mission.

"No, sir. His vital readings at dawn yesterday showed a slight increase in heart rate, blood pressure, and adrenal surges. All normal for an operative recruit."

Higher than normal, actually, but Trevayne chalked that up to fear. That's what you got when you sent a pussy to do a man's job.

"I want to know the moment he checks in."

"Of course, sir. You'll be informed as soon as I hear. Did you manage to get further intel that could aid in bringing her in?"

"Nothing you don't already know. One

source is dry, the other uncooperative. But we're working on it. Don't fail me, Trevayne."

"Failure is unacceptable, sir."

Colonel Leon Trevayne of the seventh division, Ameradan Army, Gomedan Guard unit, tapped the com-plant volume back down and loosened the breastplate of his dragon-skin armor. The lightweight body protector looked nothing like the regular army-issue equipment, but Cade's private security force, Achan's Elite, had access to the most innovative gear. Easily camouflaged by a loose-fitting flannel shirt, he blended in effortlessly with the other sightseers around the Cut. And that was important, not so much to him, but to the old man.

Achan Cade, CEO of DynaCade, the most powerful independently owned company in Amerada, also held the esteemed title of Minister of the Energy Collective, the controlling arm of the Restoration Party. The good people of Gomeda believed their city a democracy, but those in the know were fully aware that Achan Cade pulled every string and controlled the politicians and citizens like puppets. That said, he couldn't afford to incite a high-alert situation by breaching the United World Council's inane preservation treaty. The more those soft-bellied liberals in the UWC got involved, the more difficult their mission. Therefore, it was critical that this mission be kept low key and off of everyone's radar. Exactly why Trevayne was sent in to run the last-minute operation. Nobody screwed up when he was in charge. Failure was *not acceptable*.

He was to arrange transport from the Cut to Gomeda for the operative and the prisoner. Simple. Too simple.

A Private fresh out of basic training could have run this mission, yet Cade chose him. Made his gears turn, his skin itch. He knew Cade was acting outside of protocol—nothing new there—but he suspected he didn't know everything he should about this little jaunt up to the edge of wilderness.

A test of his loyalty?

He'd seen it happen to others, lesser men than himself. He witnessed firsthand what happened to those who fell on the wrong side of Cade's temper. They were sent back to the ranks of the general army, back to patrolling Lower Amerada, back to bashing heads of Drifters and breaking up the occasional skirmish between the human slime that populated the outlands.

Wasn't going to happen to him. No way was he giving up the unsanctioned pay packets Cade so generously issued. Or the perks.

So why play the zhanging boy? It was like throwing a pansy into a cactus garden. Libra, unproven and uncontrollable, was a big fat X in the equation, and Trevayne loathed unknowns. But he didn't get to the top of Achan's Elite because he was stupid. He had a Plan B, and as he rendezvoused with his men at the boat, he went over the details in his head. He knew how to deal with the pup and was prepared to subdue the enemy as soon as she was within his sights. He doubted he'd have any trouble taking down a mere girl. Even if she could chuck a spear.

TEN

"I T'S STARTING TO SMELL," LIBRA said as they made their way back to camp. "I dragged it as far as I could beyond the clearing, but that thing weighs a metric zhang-ton."

"I heard a few critters getting close during the night. Last thing we need is a wolverine or a pack of coyotes near camp."

"We should think about moving." He glanced down at the gash at the bottom of her pant leg before taking a decidedly longer time skimming up her body. "Though it would be better for you to stay put and let that leg heal." When his eyes finally met hers, his tone became entirely seductive. "I could carry you." Libra's mouth curled into his signature half-smile so she couldn't tell if he was being serious or cheeky. Or both.

He weakened her resolve, her fortitude, and

she couldn't risk being around him too long lest she forget about her primary objective and do something completely foolish, like fall for this outsider. For the next day and night, she'd have to give him reasons to leave the camp, to leave her alone. Which made no sense... How could she determine his motives, separate lies from truth, if she didn't watch him, converse with him?

"I'll show you how to make a travois."

"A what?"

"A travois, a stretcher," she explained. "Then I can stay put while you get the carcass farther away. And it's going to have to go a good distance so the scavengers don't bother us."

"Can it wait until after breakfast?" His silver-blue gaze caught hers. "I'm starved."

For the love of skunks, her knees wobbled and her head felt like the vortex that her kayak had been sucked into, spinning around and around with no way out. Logic melted into irrationality, sense became stupidity. She couldn't think rationally with Libra around.

"Looks like we'll need more firewood," she blurted.

"I'll see what I can find."

Cleo tried to concentrate on other tasks for his to-do list while he ate a press-formed bar he called "Good, filling protein." It looked like a particle board to her.

"How can you eat that?"

"What? It's good. Want some?"

"I'd rather starve, thanks."

"You will if you don't eat soon."

"I picked a wild gooseberry bush clean while you were getting the firewood," she said. "Hey, if I made a few snares, could you set them? It would be nice to have some real food for supper."

"Nutrifood *is* rea—"

Cleo's palm shot up. "Don't. Start."

"If you wanted fresh meat so bad, why didn't you roast the cat?"

Cleo made a face. "It's a meat eater."

"So?"

"So, meat eaters are *gross.*"

"You don't eat polar grizzly?"

"Some do, but not this Taiga girl. I stick to the vegans. Duck, deer, moose—"

"And you plan on snaring a *moose*?"

"No!" Cleo laughed. "But that rabbit we saw earlier would be nice."

"That's *gross.*"

"Says the boy who's never had a succulent rabbit stew."

"Are you trying to make me gag?"

"Pah. Your gag reflexes must be dead if you can eat that dried-out stick," Cleo said, wrinkling her nose. "Please, set me some snares and I'll cook you a decent meal. And trust me when I tell you that I don't offer to cook for just anyone."

"We'll see," he said, unwilling to disguise his skepticism. "But first I need to get that cat moved before it gets too hot."

While Cleo rested, she directed Libra on the construction of a travois using his sleep sack, two long, sturdy branches, and some polycord. She heard his grunts from deep in the bush as he maneuvred the stiff carcass into position.

He returned only to press the hilt of his knife into her palm. "I'm gone, darlin'. Try not to slaughter anything before I get back."

———

Cleo stood and stretched, her belly satisfied from the berries and roots she nibbled with her juniper tea, and watched Libra bury his biodegradable Nutripack container from dinner. The sun fell below the horizon, and she moved closer to the fire for warmth as the air quickly cooled.

"So handy that you could eat right out the package," she'd teased. "But what I'd like to know is how could you tell if you're eating the food or the packaging?"

"How could you tell if you were eating a root or a mouthful of dirt?" he answered back.

"If you could set a snare properly—"

"If you could eat like a civilized human being."

That last comment would have earned

him a kick to the gut if Cleo had been paying attention, but she was busy scanning the dusky sky—almost identical conditions to those of two nights ago, when she crashed her kayak. Chin tilted to the heavens, she searched for any dark shapes or bright flashes, any signs of that—

"Can't really use this, can I?" Libra said, interrupting her thoughts.

Nothing, not a sign. Did I imagine it?

She looked over to see him hold up the tattered and smelly remains of his sleep sack. After towing the alphacat over every bump and rock in the forest, its durability was sorely tested. It failed. He threw it into the fire and stepped back as sparks lit up the dusky evening air.

"You can take the air cushion and blanket," Cleo said from the other side of the bonfire. "I'll be okay on the ground."

"That wouldn't be very gentlemanly of me."

"I don't need a feather pillow to get a good night's sleep," Cleo shrugged.

"Good, since I don't even have one to offer you."

"They're overrated. Only good for pillow fighting." She laughed at some half-formed memory of childhood. "I'll just lay a few pine boughs down."

"Be awfully prickly." He was staring at her above the fire, his eyes glowing pale in the reflected flames, like twin moons in a misty night.

"Not if I cover them up with some moss."

One corner of his mouth curved up. "What about bugs?"

"Yum. Midnight snack."

"That's disgusting. Tell me you're joking."

"Tell me that you didn't swallow one single bug as you whizzed up here on your solar board, and I'll call you a damn liar."

Libra pitched his hands into his hair, defeated. "*You* have an answer for everything."

"Yeah, it's one of my more lovable qualities."

"Do you have any others?"

"Nope, that about covers it. What you see is what you get."

His gaze touched her shoulders, her breasts, her hips, before sliding lazily back to meet her eyes. "Surely your boyfriend finds something *alluring* about you?"

Alluring. The husky way he drew it out sent a gorgeous little shiver from the backs of her knees to the top of her scalp.

"No boyfriend," she replied, burying a hand in her hair.

"Really? A strong woman like you, who can take down a big cat with a little old knife in a single throw?" He shook his head with mock surprise. "You'd make someone a great husband."

Cleo crossed her arms and cocked her

hip. Squinting through the curtain of smoke that blew between them, she challenged him. "How does your girlfriend feel about your sexist attitude?"

"You'll be surprised to learn that I don't have one."

"And yet... I'm not so surprised."

"Ouch," he winced.

"Just returning the compliment."

"You misread me. Mine *was* a compliment. I've nothing but admiration for you."

His unwavering stare trapped her like bluebottle fly in a garden spider's web. Her temperature began to rise from the inside out.

"Ha." She rubbed her palms on her upper arms, wondering how goose bumps could form on skin that felt afire.

"No, really. The Taiga obviously breeds you gals tough."

"I suppose a city girl would have screamed until a big strapping man like you came along to save her?"

"Doubt a cat would stalk a city girl." He surveyed her again, trailing his gaze down her body, sending waves of heat over her. "Not enough meat on their bones."

She took a step back from the intensity of the fire, then laughed nervously at the absurdity of his comment. "And you want me to let you sleep on the ground? Your sensitive little city ass wouldn't last a minute."

Libra smiled. A full mouth one, not just a half. She had to lock her knees to keep the joints from folding.

"Really?" He walked around the fire, his eyes not leaving hers, until there were only inches between them.

Cleo's heart felt like it did when he touched her by the river earlier; livelier and a bit scared. "And what would you know about my ass?"

I know I'd like to run my hands over it, squeeze it, feel the muscles clench—

Cleo cleared her throat and swallowed. He was standing too close, and she couldn't find one damn pithy reply in her vast repertoire of sarcastic comebacks. Nothing. She continued to look at him like a deer caught in the shine of a camp light. And the look on his face, the bemused smile, told her he knew exactly what she was thinking.

"What's the matter? Swallow a bug?"

"The only bug around here, urbanite, is you."

"You're right. I am a city boy, used to creature comforts like soft beds. But I also was raised with manners," he said. "You take the bed."

"Absolutely not." She could be stubborn all night if she had to.

"Fine. We'll share."

"I... uh..." *Oh for the love of quivering*

porcupines! "I... uh..." She closed her mouth and swallowed, an embarrassing, audible gulp that made her eyes slam shut.

He leaned in close, so close she could feel his body heat. "Another bug?"

She inhaled sharply, catching his sent. Libra-saturated oxygen zipped through nasal passages, setting off tiny atomic explosions in her head and causing butterfly tingles to shoot back through her limbs.

"Fine." Her mouth said the word before her mind could filter her response. "We'll share."

ELEVEN

LIBRA BREACHED THE SURFACE OF the deep pool with a gasp. He dove again, under the pounding spray of waterfall, as far into the icy depths as he could stand. It was just what was needed to clear his muddled head. He couldn't dawdle much longer but couldn't leave before retrieving the item he came for. He floated on his back for a moment to catch his breath and watched the sky turn from deep purple to indigo. The sky was identical to the night he'd jumped. It felt like forever ago, but only a couple of days had passed.

The cascade of water calmed him, its steady tempo reminiscent of the wind turbines back home. He never gave a conscious thought to the low-level thrum that accompanied his life in the city, but when he was thrown into the isolation cell his first night at the prison, he would have a given a small fortune to have it back. He wasn't used to the quiet.

Silence, the complete absence of sound, was terrifying.

The Taiga was cacophonous in comparison—the wind in the leaves, birds chirping, fire crackling. All the noise made it hard to think. But the biggest distraction was Cleo.

Watching her by the river had been a mistake. A *zhang*-up of major proportions. He meant to observe her behavior, get-to-know-an-animal-in-its-natural-habitat type surveillance. He learned about watching in the penal colony. It became a valuable survival tool, especially in the beginning. The faster you pegged a man's weakness or were able to predict his next move, the easier it was to prevent a *situation*. He'd had a few altercations in the first few months and it cost him food, privileges, and the worst penalty: twenty-hour shifts. The normal twelve hours of physical labor, six days a week, was bad enough, but Punishers—that's what the inmates called them—turned grown men into whimpering idiots.

Nothing had grown in the Dead Zone since the Polar Wars, when the Euro-Asian Alliance decided that a massive dump of radioactive chemicals between Canada and the United States would stop the North American army from advancing, stop the allies from cooperating. Just south of the famed forty-ninth parallel, from the eastern shores of Lake Superior, west to the Rocky Mountains, millions of acres of forests were sacrificed, border cities and towns razed in a flash of heat that annihilated every living thing. Not even Superior, the deepest, freshest lake on the continent, survived. The runoff from infected shorelines eventually killed every living thing—including algae—and left nothing but crystal-clear poison.

If you were sent to the colony—one of hundreds of camps set up along the DZ—your only job was to clean it all up. There were over nine thousand men in the Gomedan Penal Colony, ranging from hard-ass murderers to hard-working men who did nothing more than piss some government official off. At any given time, there were hundreds on Punisher shifts, and you knew it by the deadness in their eyes, the desperation on their faces.

Punishers were doled in four-day cycles, the guards letting you sleep for one hour out of every six. By the fortieth or fiftieth soul-crushing hour, you wanted to eat handfuls of contaminated rubble just to stop the madness. He'd heard about it happening, seen guys with burn scars in and around their mouths, unable to eat solid foods.

Libra coped by making lists in his head—people he'd visit, things he'd eat, songs he'd listen to, warehouses he'd rob. In the bad moments, he began questioning his decision to sacrifice himself so the rest of his crew could escape. And his worst moments were spent swallowing the skin-splitting panic at the thought of the next ten years in hell.

One Punisher was all it took for Libra to become a watcher.

Still, he regretted watching her, invading her private moment. All he saw was unguarded fear and it made him feel lower than scum.

What did he expect—for her to pull a fish from the stream and gnaw it raw, or grunt and dance around like an ape?

The people of the Taiga *were* savages, he had no doubt about that, but not in the way he imagined. Their savagery was different. It was an intelligent savagery, cunning and manipulative, a deeply entrenched and unstoppable survival instinct, which is probably why his father couldn't spot it. Libra needed to remember that, to learn from his father's tragically naïve oversight.

He had to stay on mission, though his head was clouded with Cleo's every breath and every sigh. He couldn't let himself slip, had to keep reminding himself not to fall stupid.

Libra backstroked to the opposite bank and hauled himself out. He found the mound of rocks he'd used to cover his stash. It had been no easy feat trying to conceal his equipment—

the parachute, oxygen equipment, harness, and jump suit—while wet and shivering. It was fortuitous that Cleo passed out before noticing the gear.

From the pocket of his jump suit, encased in a hard tecton shell, he withdrew a small glass ampoule and inspected the vial for cracks or flaws. He should have used it on her the first night, as soon she started talking in her sleep, as soon as he'd made positive identification.

Should have, but didn't.

As fascinating a creature Cleo was, he had a job to do. He wanted to know her, wanted to find out what made her tick, how deep the savagery ran, but time was running out, his freedom was at stake, and four billion cashpoints were four billion cashpoints. He needed it to survive. He needed to help other people survive. So he would focus on what was important, and that was getting the mission done, getting his money, getting free of prison once and forever, and cutting his ties with Achan Cade.

He'd do it before this night was over, before she awoke at dawn. He'd break open the vial next to her, give her just a little whiff, not a full dose, nothing that could cause permanent damage but just enough to make her mind sufficiently malleable for him to walk her out of the forest.

Libra rubbed the ache from his jaw. He

palmed the ampoule before wading back into the river.

Cleo would understand. It was all about survival, a concept her people knew well.

And why, *why* should he care what she thought of him? He reminded himself that he'd always loathed everything about the Taiga—the inhabitants, the land, the pathetic and desperate way of life. He was glad that the snares came up empty because he wasn't about to eat some fluffy rabbit. The thought made bile rise in his throat. What the hell kind of people ate animals?

But Cleo...

Libra sighed, a small part of him wishing he could have witnessed her take down that cat.

As her image filled his mind, the determination in those tawny brown eyes, the curves accentuated by her leathers, he could feel the blood rush to his groin. Zhang damn him but she was distractingly gorgeous. This mission would have been much easier if she had excess body hair and facial growths. He couldn't stop looking at her.

Maybe she was using some kind of voodoo witchcraft on him.

Libra swam back across the pool, glad for the icy water to temper his raging lust. It was imperative he stop thinking of her like that. The only way to get through this was to tap back into his need for revenge and use his hatred as emotional impetus.

TWELVE

A S HER GRANDMOTHER USED TO say, something in the milk wasn't clean, and before Cleo could trust Libra with her life, she had to see what he was hiding. She waited for a few minutes after he'd left, then went straight for his backpack.

Don't trust outsiders.

But she had to. Trusting Libra might be the quickest and best option for getting to Jaegar, but she wouldn't be foolish about it. If she found anything suspect, anything that would give her pause, she'd rethink her plan.

She opened every compartment, patted every piece of clothing, and examined the Nutripacks and other supplies. Everything looked like the typical gear a tourist would have, with the exception of the black, palm-sized disk she'd stumbled upon during the alphacat situation. She didn't know what it was then, and she still didn't. She held it by the edges and turned it over and around, but there were no markings or buttons, no switches, sliders, dials, or knobs. So what the hell was it? Cleo held it up, fascinated but leery. Not a seam or screw marred the reflective surface. She ran her thumb across the top, startled when an electric blue light radiated from around the edge. She clutched it to her breast, concealing the glow, and glanced into the trees to ensure Libra wasn't returning before looking back down. In the same eerie blue, two words flashed over and over:

UNAUTHORIZED BIORHYTHM

Skunk dung. Cleo shook it, hoping the warning would disappear, but the light didn't go off. She slapped the screen, covered it with her palm, tapped it on top and bottom, ran her finger around the blue edging, but nothing made the words go away.

"For the love of ducks, please stop!" she hissed as the incessant blinking triggered a bead of sweat to trickle down her temple. Maybe it was voice controlled? She brought it close to her mouth and whispered, "Off."

UNAUTHORIZED BIORHYTHM

"Off, *please*?"

UNAUTHORIZED BIORHYTHM

"Power down... Power off... Sleep... *Turn off!*"

UNAUTHORIZED BIORHYTHM

She could bury it. Or throw it deep into the forest. Smash it with a rock.

She hadn't seen Libra use it in their two days together, so maybe it wasn't important. He probably wouldn't even know it was gone.

Movement in the trees alerted her to his approach. She turned one way, then the other, panicked, unsure of what to do. She thrust it into the bottom of his pack and smothered it with his clothes.

That was stupid! His things were neatly organized; he'd be able to tell for sure.

Too late to change course. He was almost at the clearing. Cleo zipped the compartment and plopped down in front of the fire, striking as casual pose as she could muster, and prayed the blue light wouldn't show through the lightweight weave of the material.

Libra strolled into the campsite wearing only a pair of shorts. His wet hair, so fair by the light of day, was dark and slicked back, making the angular planes of his face appear leaner, harsher. Or maybe it was the grim set of his jaw...

Heart racing, she tracked him across the clearing and watched out of the corner of her eye as he bent down to stow his things. Cleo held her breath as he opened the flap. He pushed the tight bundle of clothes into his pack without looking inside—so unlike him to not roll them neatly. She exhaled a prayer of thanks to the heavens.

As he pivoted toward her, she masked her face and stared into the fire, afraid he'd see the deviousness in eyes.

"I filled the canteen," he said.

"Ah, no thanks." Her eyes flicked toward him before settling back on the fire. It was now or never. Cleo took a deep breath and blurted, "I'll take you to the Cut."

Do not trust outsiders.

Libra froze, the canteen halfway to his lips, and looked at her through half-mast lids.

DO NOT TRUST OUTSIDERS!!

She ignored the voice in her head—her father's voice, so clear, he could have been shouting in her ear.

No, Daddy. I've got to get to Jaegar, and this is the quickest way.

Blue letters flashed in her mind's eye. She blinked them away. The black disk couldn't be a weapon... It wasn't even heavy enough to throw at someone.

"That's where you're headed, right?" she said, watching while he recapped the water without taking a drink. "I know which paths are the quickest."

He shrugged and looked away. "Sure."

"I'm going that way anyway. We might as well travel together." But the look on his face—startled, perplexed—almost made her wish she'd stuck to her original plan. Had she completely misread their friendly banter? Did he think she'd slow him down because of her bum leg, which wasn't as bum as she'd let him believe? "If you'd prefer to go it alone—"

"No," he said quickly. "That would be great. In fact, it's a big relief."

"A relief?"

He closed his eyes and forced a laugh. "Oh man, this is horrible to admit, but aside from 'go south,' I have no idea how to get back. And I didn't want to beg, so I've been racking my brains trying to figure out how to lure you away. I hadn't ruled out kidnapping."

"Like you'd have a half a chance," she said, imitating his half-smile. "We go at dawn. Better get some sleep."

He let her crawl into the air cushion first.

She moved as close to the edge as possible. He did the same on his side.

She felt winded, as if she'd been running. Her heartbeat pounded in her ears. Could he hear it? She needed to shift his attention.

Cleo pointed skyward. "Orion, the warrior."

"All I see are stars."

"No kidding. But the three brightest stars in a line, there, there, and there? That's his belt. And those two hovering above the line mark his shoulders, the one below marks the tip of his sword."

"Oh yeah, I can see him now," he said thoughtfully. "We don't see stars over the city.

There's too much light and too many turbs to obstruct our view."

"What are those?"

"Lights? They're an ancient invention credited to Thomas Edison."

A sharp elbow to the ribs said she didn't appreciate his lame humor.

"Wind turbines. They feed the power grid. The blades make annoying flicking shadows that make my head throb. There's not enough wind to make them go fast—not like there used to be—and the slow rotations are the worst. Like a dying man's pulse."

Cleo turned to ask him a question, but he'd rolled his head toward her at the same moment, bringing their noses only inches apart. The words caught in her throat. She looked back toward Orion and prayed her fellow warrior would give her the strength to get through the night.

She felt jittery—nerves probably—and longed to stretch, to move, but kept her arms rigid at her sides so she wouldn't bump him by accident. The paper-thin solar blanket suddenly felt too hot, too constricting.

"Hey, is that the North Star?" he asked, pointing.

"No," she said craning her neck for a better angle. "That one, behind and to the right."

He "mmm'd" and lowered his arm. The back of his hand brushed hers as he settled, and he left it there. She never imagined that there could be so many nerve endings on the side of her pinky finger, but for the love of all things furry, she could feel charged ions popping in every single molecule. And if the most un-sexual part of her body could be so affected, how would it feel to roll over and press her mouth against his? To kiss him and kiss him and kiss him until her lips throbbed.

"So, you have a birthday coming up?" she said, doing her best to dislodge kissing from her brain.

"Not for long time, no."

"But October is only days away."

"I wasn't born in October," he said. "My birthday is the thirteenth of December."

"But that makes you a Sagittarius."

"That's what my astrologist tells me."

"So Libra is your nickname?"

"Nope. It's the name my parents gave me."

"Why would someone name a child Libra when they're a Sagittarian?" she asked before her manners could stop her.

He shrugged, his shoulder bumping up against hers. "Nothing to do with my birth month. It actually means fair and impartial. Balanced," he explained.

"And are you?"

"Sometimes," he said. "Not always. How 'bout you? What's Cleo all about?"

"Short for Cleopatra," she said, suddenly

sorry she started this topic. She waited for the jokes.

"No kidding?" he said with no trace of mockery. "That name sounds familiar."

"Gee, you think? Maybe an Egyptian Pharaoh? Mark Antony's main squeeze?"

"No, no. Besides her," he replied. "It's a lovely name, anyway. Is it your mother's?"

"No, my mother was called Rose. That's my middle name." Cleo reached for the stone that lay warm against her skin. It made her feel connected to the woman she knew only from stories and pictures.

"You said 'was.' Is your mother—"

"Dead." *Please don't ask, please don't ask.*

"I'm sorry," he said softly.

"It was a long time ago. I never even knew her." Before he could press, she asked, "How about your mom?"

"Alive. But we don't see each other much."

She wanted to ask him why—it was inconceivable to her that someone *with* a mother would not embrace the relationship— but he seemed just as eager to change the subject. "So, Cleopatra. Where you really named for the Pharaoh?"

"No, but it's kind of a long story. The short version is, I'm named after my father's friend's wife." Cleo sighed. "He's dead, too."

"Your father?"

"No. My father's alive, but his friend was

killed. Which is why, I suppose, I was named after his wife. Like a tribute."

Just thinking about the tragedy that colored her family's past left an ache in her heart. She often wondered what her life would have been like if her mother hadn't died. Lewin Rush wasn't the kind of dad she longed for, but he was the kind of man that Taiga history books would someday revere as a great tribesman: a warrior and pioneer. His ancestry was renowned; both sets of grandparents had been instrumental in penning the Charter of Tribal Nations. At some point in their history, the leader of the wolverine clan, the most powerful and politically active of all the clans, became de facto leader of the Shield.

Her father, who embodied the tribal principals of peace, community, solidarity, even served as advisor to the Prarie and Acadian Tribes, and sometime the UWC.

But he was emotionally lost. Never to the outside world—oh no—he had always kept a pleasant but tough demeanour. Around his children, however, he let his mask drop. Underneath the façade was an empty soul. Witnessing the slaughter of your pregnant wife and your best friend could do that to an individual, no matter how tough.

Yet despite his unfortunate encounters with urbanites that cost him the lives of the people he loved, he still supported a cross-border system of trade, the ultimate example of generosity. Gomedans could outright purchase or trade for agricultural products like fruit preserves, grain flour, fresh meats, and whatever else the Taigans had.

Taiga citizens who were either too young or too old to work in the fields or hunt, spent their days making clothes, rugs, and blankets from animal skins and natural fibers, and crafting beautiful wooden furniture, figurines, and toys.

Despite their seemingly peaceful existence, Libra wasn't entirely incorrect when he said... *how did he put it?* "You don't *fuck* with the Shield Tribes."

At the age of sixteen, all tribe members, with few exceptions, went through Passage, a rite by which the individual reached maturity in the eyes of the tribe. If the trial was passed, the new adult was given voting privileges, independence, the right to choose a path of learning, the right to travel, the right to marry and bear children, the right to be a soldier of the Taiga.

Cleo's Passage took place in the winter, but she survived the week of isolation, sent out into the wilds of the Taiga to shelter and feed herself, with ease. In fact, she'd completely embraced the experience, repeating it many times for no other reason than the challenge. Some of her peers weren't so lucky. Some never came back. But those who did came back stronger. And strength was necessary for survival, especially in these times.

The climate heave, President Zhang's wrath, the Polar Wars, hunger, disease—none of it changed human nature. If one group of people achieved health and happiness, they were envied, brought down, even if they tried to be good and help the less fortunate. The past century saw humans, animals, and plants die, but not greed. Greed flourished.

So every member of the Shield Tribe wore a weapons harness when they left the community, and there wasn't one who made it through Passage that couldn't wield a knife or strike a bull's-eye with an arrow. They would, *they did*, attack if threatened. They were warriors. Their survival depended on it.

Libra's heavy sigh broke into her thoughts. "Who was this man who killed, this *best friend* of your father's?" His voice was hoarse and strangely accusitory. "Another tribe member?"

"No, one of your people, an urbanite," she said. "He was a doctor, a scientist, I think. He came to do research in the Shield but liked it so much, he decided to stay."

Libra's hand jerked away. Out of her peripheral vision, she could see him rake back his already raked-back hair. She could sense his muscles tense, his body become rigid. His hand came to rest over his eyes.

The air around them thickened perceptively.

Had she insulted him by implying an urbanite would choose life in the Taiga over the city?

"His name, Cleo. What was his name?"

Libra's harsh, impatient tone unnerved her. "I-I really don't remember."

"Try."

"Why? What do you care about the name of a guy who's been dead a really long time?"

There was a cottage at the outer edges of their settlement, away from the other homes. She knew it was where her mother was killed. Her father went to the cabin practically every day. They called it Dogby's place for the man for whom it was built.

"Nothing. Never mind. It's not important," he said. His exasperated sigh said otherwise.

"Well, it sure seems important."

"Never. Mind."

Cleo didn't want to *never mind*.

Dogby. Dogby's place, Dogby's cabin. No, not Dogby but Doc Bee.

She swivelled her head to tell him, but he'd rolled over, leaving Cleo to stare at his back.

For the love of ducks, what the hell got into him?

THIRTEEN

THE SKY REMAINED STARRY AND cloudless, but Trevayne could feel a storm coming, deep in the marrow of his bones. He steadied himself on the low ceiling of the boat's cabin as choppy waves slapped the hull, and used the toe of his boot to awaken the bunch of sorry slugs that made up his mobile unit.

He considered contacting Cade, but the old man would want answers he didn't have.

"Our boy has been compromised," the Colonel said, once he had their attention. He flipped his satcom in the air, the green line of text flashing in the dark bunker. Three UNAUTHORIZED BIORHYTHM messages meant someone other than the pup was tampering with the device.

"Savages probably got him," one of his

men grumbled.

Trevayne's lips peeled back across his teeth in anticipation. Finally, some action. "Suit up, pussies. We're going flower picking."

FOURTEEN

H E WAS ORION, STANDING ATOP Mount Olympus. He pushed his broad, star-tipped shoulders back, adjusted the sword sheathed at his belt, and took chase after the elusive Goddess of Light. He had to catch her, and though he didn't know why, he felt an urgency about it, as if his life hinged upon her capture.

Made entirely out of the golden pink clouds, the goddess flitted in and out of his vision. When he finally caught up to her, he buried himself in her vaporous wisps and inhaled deeply. The fresh scent of heaven filled his nose, his lungs, his soul. He wanted to stay wrapped in the goddess's entrancement forever...but he had an annoying tickle deep within his sinuses. Water filled his eyes and he blinked away a sneeze.

The morning light filtered through Libra's dream-lust haze, bringing him fully awake. With it came the realization that his body spooned Cleo's in a most intimate fashion. His face was buried in the silky tangle of her hair, and his arm was snugly wrapped around her midsection. Hers was on top, as if holding his limb in place.

But that wasn't the worst of it.

Libra's fingers rested against her breast, separated from her flesh only by the soft leather of her halter. His thumb lay on the bare skin at the curve of her cleavage and her pendant draped over the back of his hand, trapping him. The stone felt uncomfortably hot against his skin, burning him for his transgression.

That still wasn't the worst part.

Cleo's bottom was snuggled tightly against his rock-solid erection. The minutes that followed Libra into full wakefulness turned into a disturbing combination of discomfort and desire. Hell on earth.

He managed to breathe through the worst of it and was preparing to move when Cleo's derriere wriggled against him. Libra swallowed a gasp. It took every ounce of willpower to still his hips, fight the urge to grind. Sweat erupted on his brow as he concentrated on lying still. The pain was physical: sharp and urgent. It hurt to want something so bad. *So zhanging bad.*

How would she react if he slipped his fingers under the leather and rolled a delicate nipple between his fingers? Would she fight him, or give in? She couldn't deny that something hot and alive zinged between them when their eyes met. Last night, around the fire, their connection had gotten so intimate that simply looking at each other was practically fucking.

His thumb twitched, the tiniest movement against the skin of her breast, but it was enough to send another jolt of need straight to his groin.

This is wrong.

She was his prisoner, not his lover. He tried to dislike her, distrust her, but she was making his task very difficult. Zhang hell, it didn't help that she was beautiful, vulnerable, and so fucking hot. He should have used the ampoule.

In her sleep, Cleo released a breathy, contended sigh. The simple act of her lungs filling with air pushed her chest against his palm. Libra closed his eyes and gritted his teeth. The ache was exquisitely unbearable.

It would be so easy to nuzzle her neck, caress her, knead her warm flesh. She would murmur *mmm, don't stop*, urge him to untie the laces of her pants so he could slip his fingers into her sweet slick folds, make her—

"You awake?" she whispered.

Whoa, awkward.

"Hmm? What?" He pretended to rouse.

"Must have gotten cold during the night," she said without turning round.

Trying carefully not to grope her in the process, Libra pulled his arm from around her middle and pulled his hips back, breaking all physical contact. It was like being doused by a bucket of cold water. *No, go back*, his body screamed, but he kept rolling until he lay flat on his back.

"Yeah, must have," he said, his voice sounding as if he'd swallowed a handful of rocks. He lifted his head, tried to sit up, but the sight of the blanket propped up like a tent over his groin had him quickly rolling onto his other side.

Worse than zhanging grade school!

They'd followed a path that ran parallel to the river for six hours, mostly in comfortable silence, when her companion asked, "Are we stopping for lunch anytime soon?"

She spared him a brief glance over her shoulder before looking up at the sun, now at its apex in the blue, cloudless sky.

Cleo smiled to herself and pushed on. He wasn't having any trouble keeping up—an unexpected but very pleasant surprise. She didn't think her urbanite had the stamina to follow, but he seemed as determined to prove himself as she was.

"Why? Need a break?"

She'd lost valuable time already, and the need to get to Jaegar as quickly as possible chased her like a pack of rabid wolves.

But there was something else driving her at such a frenetic pace.

Cleo stole another glance back at Libra. His shirt was soaked with sweat, the side of his face smeared with dirt from the back of the arm that he'd been using to wipe the moisture from his face, and his hair was plastered against his skull. He was clearly pushed to maximum output yet, like always, Cleo felt the need to outperform, be the fastest, the most capable, the last one standing. Even with an injured leg, she couldn't let herself stop first, wouldn't be the first to suggest she needed a rest.

She wasn't trying to provoke the city dweller into declaring defeat, she just simply didn't know how to turn off her competitive spirit. Cleo thrived on being first at everything, at winning *everything.*

The very thought made her stop cold.

But it was this misplaced sense of competitiveness that ruined Jaegar.

As guilt snuffed the fire in her heels, she slowed. "There's a good spot to stop just ahead," she said as Libra closed the few feet between them. "Can you manage a bit more? I can take the backpack for awhile if you'd like."

He narrowed his eyes and gave her a slow half-smile. "Darlin', I can do another twelve hours if you give me a second to replenish my liquid." He held up his canteen and shook it, letting the few remaining droplets splash hollowly against the sides. He'd misread her concern for mockery, but before she could defend herself, he asked, "And how is it you're not drinking? You part camel?"

"Used to it, I guess," she said with a shrug and turned before he saw her smug grin.

Libra didn't mind the hike so much so long as he got to stay in the rear and watch her. This Taiga gal sure had stamina, he'd give her that. Her limp had vanished and her stride would have impressed the shit out of Taurus, who did everything in high speed.

T, his best friend and partner in crime, had no idea where he was. Didn't even know Libra was out of prison, let alone on a mission. He'd be all shades of green if he knew, too. That guy had been a Taiga lover for as long as he could remember.

But he didn't have time to think of Taurus or his bull-sized envy. Not now, not when he had the back end of Cleo to admire. She trekked on until they came to a shallow creek that branched from the main river.

The crystal clear water, barely a foot deep, meandered over smooth stones and pebbles. She tilted her chin skyward, one hand over her eyes to shield the glare of the sun. She did that a lot, almost as unconsciously as she held her pendant. He looked up, too, didn't see anything but a few wispy clouds and blue sky, but before he could ask what was so interesting up there, she did a twirl and declared the spot *perfect.*

"Perfect for what?" he asked, squatting to fill his canteen.

"Fishing."

"Fish? Why? I've got food."

"Nooo," she said, pressing her lips together and shaking her head. "You have chemicals pretending to be food." She picked up a few large stones from the banks and stacked them in a pile at the bottom of the creek. "I've had enough of that nasty stuff."

"Hey, stop knocking my Nutripacks. We'd be starving right now if we had to rely on those useless snares," Libra said. "And in case you haven't noticed, Princess, we left our fishing tackle back at the castle."

"They weren't useless snares. You just didn't set them properly," she said, building up the rocks until she'd made a dam in the middle of the stream. "And we don't need rods. Nature hath provided."

"NutriCorp hath provided this NutriBeef,

complete with all the protein found in real beef." He glanced down at the label. "And six other essential vitamins...which they don't actually name."

"And that brook trout swimming behind me has six times as much protein as beef, real or simulated," she said, tossing her head in the direction of the fish.

"And you're going to catch it with what? Your bare hands?"

"Watch and learn," she said, heading upstream, careful that her shadow didn't fall across the water.

"I'm too hungry to wait for you to tame nature, so if you don't mind, I'll stick to my NutriBeef."

"Fine. You start a fire, but I can guarantee you that I'll have this fish caught, cooked, and eaten in less time than it will take for you to boil water and choke down yours."

"Sounds like a challenge," he said.

"Well, let's call it one," she said, a smile creeping across her face.

A few feet beyond the oblivious trout, she built another rock dam, corralling the speckled fish into a tight pen. She picked up a few sticks, examined the ends, and chose the pointiest one, the corners of her mouth turned up like she was harboring a secret.

He watched her spear that zhanging fish, watched her clean it with his zhanging knife, watched her set the zhang damn fillets on a flat rock in the middle of the flames, all before he'd poured boiling water on his dehydrated beef.

"I'm first!" she declared when she nudged the opaque fish with the tip of his knife.

He made a face at the simmering bubbles clinging to the edges of his pot. If the water from the stream hadn't been so damn cold to begin with, he might have had a chance. "I refuse to concede."

"On what grounds?"

"On the fact that thing was alive, probably swimming back to his poor waiting family, moments ago. How in hell can you eat that disgusting creature?"

With a waggle of her eyebrows, Cleo popped it into her mouth. "De-licious. You have no idea what you're missing."

"Barbarian."

"Hypocrite."

"How am I a hypocrite?"

"How many NutriCows did they kill to put in that biodegradable package? Just because you didn't meet the cow first doesn't mean it didn't go into the final product."

"I...uh...don't think there's real animal meat in this," Libra said, sticking his utensil into the semi-moistened patty and holding it up for examination. He made a face, as if seeing the unappetizing texture for the first time. "Just...simulated."

"I will take that as your concession speech." Cleo said, slipping another hunk of the flaky fillet into her mouth.

During lunch, which he continued to choke down but with considerably less gusto than he had during previous meals, Cleo announced a change of route. "We need to head south for a bit, find the next rock line that'll take us to the Cut Road."

"What's a rock line?" Libra asked, licking his fingers. He looked up, hoping she'd explain but was given a look normally reserved for the stupidest beasts.

"The big rivers of rocks that you solar scooted over to get up this far?"

"Oh yeah," he said, bringing the canteen up to his lying lips. Of course he hadn't seen them. The plane was flying at such a high altitude that he saw nothing but a few clouds out the cockpit window of the otherwise windowless aircraft. "I was wondering what those were."

Libra had led a relatively guilt-free life of crime back in Gomeda. Redistributing the wealth had never particularly bothered him, so why he had an attack of the consciences when it came to misleading Cleo, he couldn't understand. She was nothing to him, less than nothing. Yet his lies left his mouth with a bitter tang. "I uh, didn't realize they had a name. What's the story?"

"You don't know?"

Libra shook his head. "Why would I?"

The corners of Cleo's mouth turned down. "I thought everyone learned about it in history."

"Not in Gomeda."

"They don't teach you about the President Zhang and the Polar Wars?"

"Only that we won."

"That's not true. *Nobody* won."

Libra bit his tongue. Arguing politics likely wouldn't make this mission easier.

"The army blew up half the Taiga back then. They blasted through this entire region so they could bring their equipment north. Afterward, all that was left were wide swathes of nothingness running up and down, leaving an ugly looking grid of transport channels, and the survivalists who resettled here decided to fill them all in. First, they pushed in all the debris; all the garbage the war left behind from vehicles to the rubble of destruction. Then they used the rocks, sand, and boulders from the blast sites to literally bury the detritus of war. It took them many generations to complete."

"Why didn't they just keep them as roads? Or why not let nature reclaim the land. Eventually, all those damaged areas would've just grown back in, right?"

"Two reasons. They wanted to discourage

the mass movement of anything. Especially people. We don't need roads up here. You can see that the Taiga is one big crisscross of trails and paths for foot travel, many wide enough for a horse team and wagons, solar scooters, and sleds, so logistically, inter-tribal travel isn't an issue."

It still didn't make sense to him. Filling in thousands of miles of roads was too labor intensive a task to justify the benefits.

"The second reason is more practical," she said, a hint of pride in her voice. "One of our biggest natural enemies is fire. During dry spells, a lightning strike can destroy hundreds of acres of forest. The rock channels are a barrier of sorts, so that a big blaze can never really take out more than a single area."

"That makes sense."

"We have dedicated maintenance crews that check each rock line a few times a year, just to make sure it doesn't get overgrown. And I guess, if you want to call this the third reason, they're a great navigation tool. They provide markers, map features, helps us figure out how far we have to go or how far we've come."

Or they could have put up signposts, which made more economical sense, but he kept quiet, opting for an acquiescent nod. It all felt like a colossal waste of time and money, but what did he expect from ignorant savages?

Except Cleo, of course. She was clearly on the intelligent spectrum of savage.

"You ready?" she asked, kicking loose dirt over the remaining embers of their cooking fire.

Libra secured his backpack to his shoulders. "When you are."

Cleo hopped across the creek and glanced above, scanning the sky before she re-entered the thick of the forest.

"You keep doing that," he said.

"Doing what?"

"Looking up."

She kept walking, but a misstep told Libra that he'd hit on something worth digging in to.

"I'm navigating by the sun."

"Bullshit," he said the moment she reached for her pendant.

"Pardon?" Her eyes were guarded, her knuckles white against the black stone.

"You've been searching the skies, *obsessively*, for the past few days."

"We're due for a storm."

"Is that right, now?" he pressed. "There hasn't been so much as a cloud up there for days."

"The wind shifted. I can smell rain coming."

"You're lying."

Her nostrils flared. "I am not!" She turned her back and resumed walking. "I'm looking for rain cl—"

"Cleo!" He shook his head and expelled

his breath. It was getting to him, the lies, the deception, and mostly the suspicion in her eyes... It was eroding his psyche. "Look at me." She turned with a harrumph, crossed her arms over her chest, and thrust her hip to the side. But she kept her eyes averted.

"Look. At. Me."

When she finally turned her brown eyes on him, her mouth was pursed in challenge. And he was quite certain she was staring at his nose, not into his eyes, but it would do. Someone around here needed to start telling the truth. And it couldn't be him.

"Why, Cleo?"

Her shoulders popped up in a petulant shrug. "You wouldn't believe me if I told you."

"Try me."

She regarded him for a moment, and Libra could see a play of un-translatable emotion in her eyes. Whatever it was she had to say was beginning to make him nervous.

"Come on, Cleo. What's up?"

"Have you ever seen a..." She toed the ground. "Do you know what aer-o-planes are?"

A tendril of dread unfurled in his gut as she pronounced the three distinct syllables. Libra didn't like where this was going. "Uh, ye-ah, of course." He'd tried to sound casual but his intention backfired and his tone dripped with sarcasm.

"They haven't flown in almost a hundred

years, since the Polar Wars," she said, refolding her arms. "How am *I* supposed to know if *you* know your history? You didn't know anything about the grid!"

As much as he wanted to end this conversation right here, right now, he had to know. It couldn't be a coincidence. "I'm sorry," he offered, tempering his agitation.

"Never mind," she said.

"No, go on."

She eyed him. Libra relaxed his facial muscles best he could. "Please."

"I know this sounds crazy, but... I saw one, Libra. A couple of nights ago."

The trees seemed to close in on him, turning his vision to green swirling specs. He looked toward his boots in hopes the ground would stop spinning. Cleo had just knocked the wind out of him.

FIFTEEN

"**Y**OU WHAT?"

Zhang hell! Here was the part where she told him she watched him jump out of that plane and knew exactly what he was up to, then took his knife, which he stupidly—*stupidly*—let her hang on to after lunch, and drove it through his skull before he took another breath.

"I know, I know what you're thinking," she said, reaching for...

Libra braced.

...her head to rap her knuckles against her skull. "You're thinking I'm a complete nutcase. I can tell just by your look."

"No, it's just..." He exhaled forcefully, unaware he'd been holding a lungful of air. "No, I don't."

Her shoulders deflated with a heavy sigh

as she dropped her arms. "The other night, just before I—I mean, the reason I—"

Cleo's head shook back and forth in a struggle to find the words to explain. It was so unlike her to stutter, to look unsure, that it gave him a paradoxical glimmer of hope.

"Okay, look," she finally said. "What I told you about falling in the river wasn't exactly true."

"I didn't think so."

Her eyebrows shot up.

"Who fishes at the top of a waterfall?" he said, his confidence recovered. "You just don't seem that incompetent."

"I'm not, normally! I was kayaking down river. I've shot those rapids a hundred times! I know how far I can go, how close I can get to the falls, *safely*, before hauling out. But I was in a hurry and the sun had already dipped behind the tree line, and I pushed on a little farther than I should have. And there's been a lot of rain lately, so the river is swollen and moving a lot faster than normal." She hesitated, her fingers toying with the leather string around her neck.

"Continue," he pressed. He fought his impatience, fought the urge to take her by the shoulders and shake her until she spewed every detail. Heart thumping, he had to find out how much of the truth she knew.

"I was just angling toward shore and that's

when I saw it—this weird flash in the sky. I looked up, as crazy as this sounds," she said, meeting him with an earnest stare, "I swear to you and the deities of our forefathers, I saw the sun reflecting off a giant metal bird. It was different than the history module images, but I know what I saw. An aer-o-plane!"

Libra's mouth filled with moisture. He turned and spit into the bush as a tendril of dread bloomed into a thick, choking vine that wrapped around his heart and lungs. He tried to relax but could feel his facial muscles tense up like a lock.

She must have taken his silence for shock.

"I couldn't believe it, either," she said, shaking her head. She became more animated, began using her hands to illustrate as she rushed to get the rest of the story out. "It was so big, I mean, so small, way up there, but it must have been so big for me to see it! And it was just a split second, but in that moment I took my eye off the river to look up, my bow slammed into a pile of rocks that I swear came out of nowhere. Before I could backpaddle, I got slammed sideways and was pinned against them. When I pushed off, I flipped the kayak, and because I was caught in an eddy, I couldn't right the damn thing before my breath ran out. I managed to release the cockpit cord and slide out, but the current got me. It was so fast and I was so tired from paddling all day that I just couldn't manage to swim against it. The rest, you know."

Yes, the rest he knew.

Libra fought against gravity, to remain upright when he really wanted to double over in pain. *He* was the reason she went over the falls. *He* was the reason she almost drowned. He was the reason she *did* drown. The image of her, limp and blue in his arms, swarmed his vision until he thought he'd lose his lunch. The gash on her leg, the bruised cheek, the scraped forehead... He looked at his hands, feeling like he had beat the shit out of her.

What are the chances that she would be out there, miles from any settlement, to witness that moment, that perfect alignment of altitude, sun, and wings. More amazing was the fact that she didn't see him floating through the air, though it would have been difficult considering his 'chute was made to blend with the twilight sky.

Libra reached up to wipe away a rivulet of sweat that rolled down his temple. Though Cleo stood in front of him, the picture of health, he couldn't get the sound of the painful retching as her body fought to expel the river water from ringing in his ears.

He blinked a few times, tried to focus on the here and now, tried to ignore the acid churning in his gut. *It's not supposed to be this way. I'm not supposed to give a zhang for this savage.*

He should never have agreed to this ridiculous mission. And now he had no choice. He needed to get it done, get it over with, get back to the city, get out of her life. Get *her* out of *his*. Why, for hell's sake, didn't he tell Achan to stick the money up his ass and do his time in the colony? Hard labor never killed anyone.

Though guilt could.

And Achan played on that too.

"These people killed your father, and by extension, your family. Libby may have survived if he'd been home to look after her. You're mother might not have turned into a dependant. We aren't savages, boy. We don't believe in that eye-for-an-eye crap, but you owe it to them to get revenge on the family who irrevocably damaged us."

Cleo looked up at him with those big, unsure, honeyed eyes, waiting for some kind of response. He wanted to blurt it all out—the lies, the truth, the entire zhanged-up situation.

Donning a mask of indifference, he glanced up and shrugged, falling back on what he did best. Bluff, lie, deceive...survive. "It was probably lightning."

"Libra," she said, twisting her fingers around her black stone. "I know lightning when I see it, and that was most definitely not lightning."

"Maybe it was a flare. Someone was lost," he said, pushing past her on the path. He couldn't stand the way she looked at him, couldn't get out of this godforsaken land fast enough. "But there's no fucking way it was an airplane."

"I know what I saw," she said quietly from behind him. He heard her disappointment, knew he'd let her down.

It was too much. The tight hold he'd had on his cover began to unravel and he couldn't deal with warring emotions pulling apart his guts.

"No, you don't know, Cleo," he said jabbing his finger toward her. "You've never even seen a zhang-damned *aer-o-plane* before, so how would you know?" he mocked. "There aren't any museums in the northern wild. You're living centuries in the past! You don't even have a transportation system, so what do you know about planes, about anything?"

"I've seen pictures," she shouted. "We're not dumb, *urbanite.* We have teachers, doctors, statesmen—" She pulled her shoulders back and added, "And *warriors*, who'd kick your ass for your insults."

"You're right, Cleo," he replied, his voice thick with condescension. "Nothing but a bunch of savages."

Murdering savages.

SIXTEEN

LIBRA CRASHED THROUGH THE FOREST like a hunted buck and, though she knew he didn't have a clue where he was going, she followed. As long as he went in the general direction of the nearest grid line, she'd let him satisfy his need to stomp and charge. He clearly thought she was an incompetent guide if she was seeing mythical planes in the air.

She thought about stopping, going her own way, but he wouldn't even notice.

She should. Leave him to make his own stupid way to the Cut. Maybe even detour right into the path of a hungry polar grizzly. Against her better judgement, she plowed on behind and tried to sort out what the hell just happened.

They'd been getting along so well, at least she thought so, and despite her niggling distrust, he was an overall decent guy. But his reaction to her plane story was a complete puzzle. It was so out of character, so over the top! Doubt and disbelief she expected, but the way he shouted, with his reddened face and jabbing finger, left her cold and feeling like an ignorant fool. If he'd told her he saw a woolly mammoth grazing in a field, she may have told him to stop snacking on fermented berries, but get angry and call his entire culture stupid?

Cleo couldn't understand why his reaction shook her so. Her chest felt so tight, even the clear Taiga air couldn't dislodge the stones sitting at the bottom of her lungs. Her eyes stung with unshed tears of...of... Not sad, weepy tears. Cleo Rush didn't cry. Ever. It was more a feeling of disappointment and betrayal.

Her heightened emotions were most likely the sum effect of the last few weeks—from the exhaustion and extreme high of winning the gruelling trials of the leadership competition to the depths of the lowest lows when she'd realized that Jaegar had to leave, not to mention where he damn well went. Then there was the whole drowning thing, getting tied up by an outsider, and lest she forget the most serious: breaking an indefensible tribal rule which was going to get in her in a shit-load of trouble with the elders. Perpetuating harm toward a leader, sitting or elect, was taken very seriously; hence the rule that the three runners-up in the leadership competition must undergo memory-death, thereby eliminating any threat.

Drugging her father's tea with a three-day sleeping potion was the only way to ensure her head start in getting to Jaegar. Technically, even though she committed the act as leader-elect, she could be sentenced to true death.

Death. Again. Seemed like a running theme for her. Been there, done that, and she wasn't eager to try it again for many years. For the love of ducks, no wonder she was a mess.

Cleo refused to credit her vacillating emotions to the man who walked forty paces ahead. She stuck her tongue out at his back.

Don't trust outsiders.

Thankfully, Lewin Rush would never learn of her stupidity. How naïve to think she could know someone, *trust someone,* after only a few days.

Urbanite. In this case, it was synonymous with idiot. Damn him, carrying on like a seal-starved polar grizzly. What a difference from yesterday, when he looked at her with such mind-blowing intensity, her nipples tightened into hard little diamonds. Or this morning when she awoke wrapped in his arms, their bodies pressed together. She'd dreamt of his kisses in her hair.

Libra was right... She was an ignorant,

stupid girl from the backward Taiga.

Lost in her own self-pity, Cleo didn't notice the root sticking out of the ground. She stumbled forward, throwing her hands out before her face connected with the dirt.

She leapt up, pride driving her fleetness. Her palms stung from the impact. She picked out the tiny imbedded sticks and pebbles, then spit on her hands and rubbed them against her thighs. It didn't help. Now they were sore *and* streaked with dirt.

He hadn't even turned around to see if she was okay. She could have bumped her head, been knocked unconscious, but did he once check his back? It was a damn good thing for him that she'd lost her knives. She mimed pulling a blade from her weapons harness, closed one eye, and locked on target. Drawing her arm back, she flung the blade forward, almost hearing the *whoosh* as it travelled through the air and embedded itself in the back of Libra's neck. Bull's-eye!

Now that he was imaginarily dead, Cleo looked down and concentrated on the tips of her sandals as they shuffled along the increasingly rocky path. She gave herself a mental cuff upside the head. She needed to keep her mind on task, not on him.

So why couldn't she cover ten feet without her thoughts eddying around him and only him, replaying every comment, every movement, every tidbit of personal information he'd shared since the moment they met. Libra, the oddly named Sagittarian.

"Not so 'fair and balanced' today, are you, *urbanite*?" she said, intending to flick eye-daggers and surprised that he no longer occupied her line of sight. Cleo found him halfway up Raccoon Ridge, a mountainous obstruction with a ridiculously steep incline, difficult and dangerous to climb. Which is why there was a perfectly good path that veered around it.

Libra had nothing to grip but a few misplaced saplings that found shallow life in the cracked stone—nothing to break his fall if he slipped.

If time wasn't of the essence, she'd enjoy watching him ascend, just to see him come back down when he realized the other side was a sheer cliff.

She growled with impatience, cupped her hands to her mouth, and yelled, "You can't go that way!" The rest she huffed to herself. "You dumb *outsider*."

Libra paused and turned slightly, acknowledging her warning. The dumb-bug ignored her and kept going.

Cleo let out a deep sigh and watched him try to gain a foothold on the angled slope. By the time she'd caught up, he was almost to the top, but the loose shale was severely inhibiting the climb.

"Be careful. It's slippery when it gets wet," she mumbled. He didn't believe her when she said it was going to rain, so why bother shouting the warning.

Feeling righteous, she stuck to the footpath as it forked west. Once he made it to the top and realized that he couldn't go down the front face, he'd figure out how to follow the ridge westerly until, lo and behold, it came out on the very same path she was already on. Only he'd be exhausted from clinging to shale and a good half hour behind her.

"I should have kept my damn mouth shut about the aer-o-plane," she mumbled. Of course he didn't believe her. Aer-o-planes hadn't flown since the fossil fuel depletion. By the middle of the Polar War, even combat flying had ground to a halt, reducing the war to a fierce and bloody ground operation that lasted for another decade.

But it *was* a plane she'd seen. It had to be! She'd only confided in him because she thought they shared...what? A journey, a friendship, a connection? And maybe a small part of her hoped he'd validate her claim, that maybe the urbanites had developed a new energy technology that made air travel a reality again.

Fool.

She assumed he broke contact the moment

he woke that morning because he was embarrassed that he was practically groping her in his sleep. Now she knew better; he was horrified at touching a Taiga woman, a *savage*.

How long had she lain, enjoying the feel of his body against hers, wishing she had the nerve, the confidence to turn in his arms, slip a knee between his legs, and sleepily bury her face in the crook of his neck? Thank goodness she hadn't. The humiliation would have been devastating.

Cleo's head perked up at the sound of a rumbling boom in the distance. Thunder. She couldn't help feel a little smug after he resolutely refused to believe her. Who was the fool now?

She walked and stewed, every distant rumble pushing her feelings of righteous victory.

What the hell did an *outsider* know about survival? Adventure, ha! Why do they even bother coming up here? They should stay in their precious cities with precious universities and corporations and choke on their Nutrishit.

Before she knew it, the better part of an hour had passed. Cleo looked up as she rounded the edge of the escarpment, just to make sure he'd found a path down from the ridge. She could feel an "I'm first!" bubbling to get out, *if* she decided to speak to him at all.

She scanned the side of Raccoon Ridge, but

there was no bobbing blond head in sight. Her heart tripped a little faster as her eyes swept the terrain again, more slowly, searching for some sign of him coming down, through the scrubby trees, some sign of him at the top.

Nothing. No Libra.

She really *didn't* want him to be ripped to shreds by a polar grizzly. Not until he got her to Gomeda, anyway.

Cleo squinted, a hand across her forehead to fight the nonexistent glare, but there were no signs of man nor sated beast.

She paced back and forth along the curving path, straining her neck, trying to see around the natural obstacles in her line of sight. Cleo swallowed, trying to prevent the frantic worry that made her jaw tighten and her mind bounce to horrible conclusions, all of them ending at Libra's broken body.

"Libra?" she called. An anxious echo mocked her.

This was ridiculous. Worrying was not productive and, by its very nature, counterintuitive to everything she'd been taught. She expelled her breath and, with it, her growing panic. Closing her eyes, she concentrated on breathing, letting the sounds of the forest consume her. She was searching for footsteps, his voice, that little clanking noise his pack made whenever his left foot came down.

Nothing. Nothing but another rumble of thunder, louder this time.

Her eyes snapped open and the panic rushed back like a tidal wave.

She should have insisted he take the path. Should have warned him shale and raindrops do not mix.

And what if he tried to get down the cliff? Could he be that stupid?

She placed her hands across her stomach, felt it roil like she'd eaten rancid squirrel.

"Libra!"

Imagining him lying at the bottom of the cliff face, broken, shattered, bloody, just for the sake of getting there ahead of her, Cleo ran.

SEVENTEEN

LIBRA SCANNED THE LANDSCAPE WHILE waiting for his breathing and heart rate to return to normal after an anger-fuelled climb. He'd completely forgotten to take note of rock formations as per Achan's request but frankly, all these rocks looked the same. Unless he meant the rock rivers Cleo mentioned earlier. But how big a secret could they be if they were visible from satellite? No, despite the vague instructions he'd been given, he was fairly confident that Achan was looking for something abnormal, like massive excavation or something that didn't jibe with the rest of the Taiga, and he'd witnessed nothing out of the ordinary thus far.

He'd climbed high enough to see one of the Dead Lakes to the south, a massive body of water so big, the far shore wasn't visible over the horizon. There wasn't a sign of life on or around the choppy water, not that he expected to see otherwise.

The canopy of trees surrounding the ridge took his breath away. A thousand shades of green, dots of yellow, snaking ridges of grey-green rock, all contained under a mostly bright blue sky. Angry grey storm clouds gathering in the northwest, offering contrast to an otherwise idyllic scene.

He was standing on top of the world.

So why did he feel like hell? He should be mentally planning the havoc he'd wreak on Gomeda when this shit job was over.

The first thing he'd do once he got his points accounts secured was get his crew back together, outfit them properly, and buy a safe place they could use as a home base; a little business in the fifth prefecture. Nothing ostentatious—just a small shop to front as a legit operation—nothing that would arouse the suspicious nature of the Gomedan Guard. They'd have to find something close to the tunnels or, ideally, right on top of them. They had work to do, wealth to redistribute. And this time, they'd do it smarter.

Libra stretched, took a deep breath of the fresh Taiga air, and turned in a circle. The angry bank of storm clouds rushed forward, quicker than he thought possible.

Cleo was right.

Cleo, again. *Get out of my zhanging head!*

He couldn't go three minutes without her image popping into his brain, making his belly clench and his balls ache.

She stood between him and his freedom. The faster he cut all ties, the better. Tonight, he'd use that damn ampoule, drug her into a docile bag of putty, make contact with Trevayne, and go the hell home.

Home. Those are the memories that should be consuming him, motivating him, driving him forward... not the sweet scent of Cleo's hair.

He needed to reconnect with his gang. They'd set his priorities straight in no time. He wouldn't tell anyone but Taurus about this mission. T was obsessed with the Taiga, though he tried to hide it from the rest of them. Libra had always rolled his eyes and tuned him out, never caring to hear about any of it. He walked away at any mention of the Taiga because it stirred memories, unearthed resentment. Now he'd wished he'd stayed to listen.

Had Taurus's father, who did a lot of business with the Trading Post, ever dragged his family this far into the interior? Had Taurus ever seen a vista like this, on the top of the great vast world, and if so, did he feel as conflicted as Libra...So insignificant but so overwhelmed with the beauty at the same time?

T would get a raging hard-on for Cleo—the outfit, the attitude, the knife skills. Yet the thought of Taurus ogling Cleo made his fists clench.

Zhang damn, she'd invaded his head space again. Surprise, surprise.

He'd acted like a total shit back on the trail, but really, what choice did he have? *"Oh yeah, a plane. Sure. I jumped out of one—a hydrogen-powered, orbital glider prototype that nobody was sure was going to even make it this far. It was very cool if you don't count being scared shitless."*

He used the bandana to wipe the sweat from his face before tying it around his forehead to keep his hair back, then looked down to examine the cliff face. Hundred and fifty feet, he reckoned, the first thirty of which dropped straight and smooth, as if the side of the hill had been sheared off. Below that, there was a two-foot ledge and then a combination of juts and angles, edged outcroppings and serrated protrusions that would take him to the ground below. Free-running had been the perfect training ground and though this jump was a good deal more dangerous than his familiar urban scene, it was do-able. He could use his rope to abseil down the top section, then use his *parkour* techniques, calculate his movements, compensate for the weight of his backpack, and use counterbalance to jump safely to the bottom.

He shot a look over his shoulder, to the path that brought him. Nope, not an option. Straight down the front was the only way. The risk was nothing compared to the thought of getting behind her, having to watch those leather-clad legs, that perfectly round little ass wiggle in front of him, the sum effect of which was far worse than plunging to his death. Nope, he'd rather worry about having a knife in his back than get stuck behind her again.

He secured the rope around his waist, found a good sturdy tree near the edge of the cliff to anchor it to, and planned his descent.

"Piece of cake," he reassured himself.

Thunder boomed in the distance as he dropped.

"Libra!"

Cleo, bent at the waist, her pulse ticking in her ears, stopped to catch her breath. She'd been sprinting at top speed, ignoring the throb in her lower leg and the burning stitch in her side, praying to all that was holy and feathered that Libra remained alive.

If he did fall, if he were hurt, she could help. With her training, there was no fracture she couldn't set, no flesh wound she couldn't patch. Internal injuries would be a problem, but she might be able to keep him alive until she ran to the Trading Post for help.

She straightened to resume her search, limp-jogging, ducking under the low branches that pulled her hair from the braid and scratched at her cheeks and arms. Her heartbeat whomped so loudly in her ears, she couldn't concentrate on the sounds of the forest—a potentially fatal distraction. Every few minutes, she looked up between the treetops, keeping track of the thickening thunderheads.

"Liii-bra!" she called in breathless desperation. She left the beaten path to get closer to the cliff face. If he'd fallen, was unconscious, unable to call out, then staying on the trail was useless, valuable time would be lost. "Lii-br—"

"Looking for me?"

He emerged from a copse of alders, dragging his pack on the ground next to him. Alive. Unharmed.

Shirtless. Sweaty. Smug.

Half-smiling, he said, "Looks like I'm first."

Cleo felt a wave of relief so deep, so complete, she almost wept. She doubled over, sucking cool, rain-scented air into her lungs, waiting for the searing in her oblique muscle to subside, for the tightness in her chest to loosen.

"I heard you calling," he continued. "Where have you been? I was starting to get worried."

She lifted her head, eyeing him from under her lashes. "Where have *I* been?" she asked, incredulously. She stood and planted her fists on her hips. "*Where have I been*? Where the hell have *you* been?"

Mother Nature underscored Cleo's questions with overlapping sheets of lightning.

"Up ahead," he said. "Waiting for you on the trail."

"What do you mean, on the trail? I've been watching, waiting for you to come down."

Thunder cracked overhead.

He gave her a deer-in-torchlight look and shrugged. "I've been down for a while now."

"But how?" Cleo asked, her gaze flicking between him and the cliff face.

Another shrug.

"Turn around."

"What?"

"Turn. Around. Make a circle. Do a pirouette."

Libra looked at her like she'd been bitten by a rabid wolf, but pivoted on his heel.

"Yeah, just as I thought," she said using the sarcastic voice she'd usually reserved for Jag. "Ain't no wings attached to your back, *darlin'*."

"Who needs wings, *darlin'*, when I can just hitch a ride on a magical aer-o-plane and fly down." He actually flapped pretend wings.

"You *bastard!*" The air temperature suddenly dropped as the heavens released a needle-like drizzle. Cleo stomped forward. "I waited. And when you didn't come, I...I..." *Worried and ached and fretted.* And he had the colossal nerve to mock her, the unmitigated gall to...to...stand there and look cocky and unapologetic. The audacity to stand there while cold droplets meandered down the planes and valleys of his muscled torso. Stand there with one eyebrow lifted, looking sexier and more smug than he had a damn right to. She wanted to smack him.

"I thought you'd fallen!" Cleo open-palm whacked him in the chest. "Or worse!" He didn't step away, didn't flinch, didn't make a move to stop her. So she used both her hands to smack him, again and again, until her dirt-smeared palms stung as they made contact with his solid, wet flesh. It was either get violent or cry, and she was not, for the love of all things carnivorous, going to shed a tear for this stupid, thoughtless, idiotic *outsider!*

"I thought you were lying in a bloody heap," she said, teeth clenched. His skin reddened beneath her fingers. "Hurting, dying..."

Libra encircled her wrists with two fingers pinning her hands in place against him, against his searing flesh, against his chest as it rose and fell with rapid breath. "Were you worried?" His voice was as rough and rasped as the cliff face.

"Worried? No." Cleo said, unable to meet his eyes. She concentrated on stilling the emotion that vibrated through her, telling her limbs to cease shivering, her knees to stop shaking. Her chest heaved in defiance.

When she absolutely could not stop herself, she looked up at him, just as a fat droplet hit his cheek. His pupils widened, his lips pressed together for a brief second, but he didn't speak, didn't let go of her hands.

Cleo shook her head to protest, shook her head so her eyes would unglue from the stare that might let him see her too deeply, might lead him to discover why her heart was still pounding as if in full run.

Libra's scent, his presence, his strength, everything about him radiated masculinity. The air changed, the lightning creating an unnatural charge between them, striking Cleo with a realization that was so ancient, so obvious, yet somehow obscured until this very moment.

She knew lots of men, but Libra was the only man who made her acutely aware of her own femininity, conscious of her hair, her face, her smell, her curves...her *sex*. He made her feel like a female in the most basic sense of the word, a woman standing next to a man, a Jane next to a Tarzan, a Romeo next to a

Juliet. Two halves of one whole, necessary components in the survival of a species. Yin and yang, dark and light, man and woman. The contrast was suddenly so clear, so biologically profound, it made her feel naked.

Naked. The tips of her fingers curled into his flesh, and she felt his muscles quiver beneath her touch.

"Why are you naked?" she asked, barely a whisper.

"I'm not naked."

"You're not wearing a shirt."

"Since when does a little bare chest offend your sensibilities?" He tugged her forward, into him.

Cleo bit back a gasp when her forearms made contact with the heat of his torso. Off balance, her jellied knees threatened collapse, but she refused to take a step closer.

Don't trust outsiders.

Thank you, Lewin Rush! She needed that voice in her head to remind her that Libra was a bastard. An outsider. Not to be trusted.

Narrowing her eyes, gathering her Taiga indignation, she met his stare. "What? You think just because I'm a triber, I don't have a moral code?"

Damn it! For all her intent to sound caustic, her voice was breathy and expectant. He parted his lips ever so slightly and his lids dropped to half-mast. "Do you think that we walk around n-n-naked, no better than animals?"

He pressed his thumb into the pulse point at her wrist.

She wished, no she *needed* him to say something jack-assly stupid to piss her off because her anger was being pushed aside by physical need stronger than the rushing current that had pulled her under the surface of the river. She didn't want to succumb again, didn't want to surrender to *him*.

But he didn't. He didn't speak at all. Hooded eyes remained fixed to her lips, lingered there long enough to make her nervously lick them. She felt his chest hitch, and when his silvery-blue orbs sought hers, her own lust reflected back.

"I don't know, darlin'," he rasped. "I've only been here for a few days, and I'm feeling some overwhelming animalistic tendencies."

EIGHTEEN

L IBRA'S MOUTH CAME DOWN JUST as an ear-splitting boom shook the ground under them. Oblivious to Mother Nature, oblivious to everything except a consuming need to be possessed, Cleo parted her lips and invited him deeper.

He dropped her wrists to bury his fingers in the loose braid, tilting her head further back. Tongues tangled, twisted, their teeth scraped and bumped, and still, they couldn't seem to get enough. Rising on her tiptoes, Cleo pressed herself into his rain-slicked chest and snaked her arms around his neck.

Don't trust—

He yanked her head back, breaking the kiss. He searched her face, puzzlement in his eyes.

A pang of fear tapped the fragile wall of

her heart. She waited...for him to focus on her scar, to see disgust cloud his eyes, for the glass to shatter and the pain to seep in. She waited for him to realize he was cavorting with a savage. But when he blinked, the only thing in his gaze was pure want.

He smoothed back the wet tendrils plastered to her face, his breath coming hot and uneven.

Libra pulled her into him and nibbled her bottom lip, sucked it into his mouth before plunging back into her mouth, moving his tongue slower, deeper, more controlled.

His taste filled her, awakened every nerve ending in her body. From head to toe, her skin bloomed and tingled, like a flash of heat after a gulp of corn whiskey.

Don't trust—

She'd never been kissed, not like this, not ever. Cleo leaned into him, her body forming against him so perfectly that not even the raindrops could get between them. They fit together like two parts of a whole and she felt her body vibrating like a tuning fork at perfect pitch.

Don't trust outsiders—

Shhh, Lewin. This one is different.

This one used the tip of his tongue to draw electric lines on the underside of her jaw.

He framed her face, turning her this way and that as his hungry mouth sampled her cheeks, her neck, her ear, and back to her lips...always back to her lips.

When he groaned for her, made his chest rumble like the thunder, she pulled him deeper, wrapped her arms tighter, pressed her body harder.

Libra gripped her ass and hauled her against him so she could feel his lust pushing into her abdomen.

Cleo's heart banged against her sternum, stealing blood from her limbs and sending it to her core. Her leg muscles faltered, unable to support her, while her head floated somewhere up in the trees.

Libra's kisses became more urgent, more intense. He used his tongue, teeth, and lips with bruising ferocity. His hands coasted up her hips and encircled her bare midriff. The touch of his fingers as they spanned her ribs made her quiver from the inside out.

She willed him to touch her breasts, to undo the straps of her halter and drag his thumbs across her bare nipples. Just imagining it made them tingle and tighten.

His breathing became erratic, as if he'd read her mind and conjured the same image. She felt his heart pound against her chest, matching her own crazy rushing blood. A moan, low and needy, came from deep in his throat—raw, primal, and erotic as hell.

He wants me.

I want you, too, her body answered, undulating against his. Unable to hold them in, unable to swallow them, she let escape the little mewls of pleasure.

She tunnelled her fingers into his damp, silky hair and concentrated on keeping them there. Because what she really wanted to do was explore every inch of him—scratch him, bite him, taste him, lick him...go savage on his ass.

He tore his mouth away from hers to rain kisses over her chin, down the column of her throat, and across the edge of her collarbone. Her lips throbbed, ached for him to come back, but Cleo dropped her head to the side to let him have his way.

"About before," he said between kisses.

"Forget it."

"I can't."

"Shh," she said. "Not now."

"I'm sorry," he whispered. "I believe you. I really do."

"It's okay—"

"No, you have to know something." He stopped and tongued the shell of her ear. He went very still and whispered, "I'm sorry." His breath was hot against her. "Whatever happens, please know that I'm sorry for today, sorry for—"

"For the love of ducks, Libra," Cleo groaned and opened her eyes. "Just shut up and kiss—"

Cleo's body tightened, every muscle, every sense on high alert. There was movement in her peripheral. She shoved Libra backward, thinking only to protect him.

Bangers. Two of them, and they were big. From the looks of them, they'd been living too close to the Dead Lakes. Bangers had a reputation for being dangerous sons-of-bitches, mostly because their mental capacity didn't reach much past finding their next meal.

These two were sneaking off with Libra's backpack.

"Stop!"

She launched herself onto the hunched back of the closest one while the other darted through the trees.

Cleo coiled her arm around the Banger's neck and pulled her forearm taut, compressing his windpipe. She used her knees to squeeze his torso until her inner thighs burned while he tried to buck her loose.

By the time Libra caught up, a dazed look about the eyes, the other Banger was a half-dozen yards away. "He's got your stuff!" Cleo grunted, thrusting her chin. He hesitated shifting from one foot to the other, not wanting to leave her, but not wanting to lose their only supplies. "Go!" she said as another crack of thunder shook the ground. "I've got this one."

The Banger clawed her arm, grunting and

gasping, his blunt fingers scratching Cleo's sweat-and-rain-slicked skin. He thrust his head back to knock her in the face, but she'd read his body language, predicted the move, and ducked sideways. He repeated the move twice more, swinging his blunt skull around like an angered bull. Cleo used it to her advantage, tightening her hold around his throat with each movement.

His hammy forearms punched against her legs; dirty, sharp fingernails tried to pry her knees from his middle, but without a supply of air to his lungs, his movements became uncoordinated, his strikes powerless. Cleo didn't relent. His sickly gasps and increasingly desperate whacks did nothing to deter her.

He stumbled backward and, with a surprising burst of strength, rammed Cleo into a tree trunk, hard enough to knock the air from her lungs. Her head snapped back against the rough bark, sending a vibration down her spine that threatened her tenacious hold. While Cleo gasped to refill her lungs, the Banger stumbled forward then lurched back again. Cleo braced for impact, pulling her head into her shoulders, but he faltered like a drunk and sideswiped her against the tree trunk, scraping a strip of skin from her upper arm.

"Bastard!" she wheezed, ears still ringing from the impact. She was going to squeeze this bugger until his eyeballs popped.

She could sense him drifting into oxygen-deprived unconsciousness. He dropped onto one knee, then fell forward onto the damp ground, taking Cleo, a living, breathing, hurting backpack, with him.

"'Bout time," she muttered as the muscles in her arm burned from exertion. She lay there for a moment to give her lungs a chance to fill to capacity.

For the love of skunks, *he reeked*. How did she not smell these things coming? She laid her fingers to the side of his throat and, satisfied she hadn't killed him, rolled off his back and rubbed her palms against her thighs, as if that would rid her of his stink.

"Let's go find your friend," she muttered and took off after Libra.

Cleo found them on the dirt trail, circling each other like two alphacats in a cage. This Banger was more disgusting than his friend, with patches of sparse hair on his head, a matted, patchy beard, and the visible flesh on his face and arms marred by lumpy tumors.

He was spitting and gnashing his blackened stumpy teeth, which probably accounted for the retch-inducing odor, though the animal-skin rags he wore could probably growl on their own.

One glance toward Libra confirmed that her city-boy had no clue what he was facing.

Bangers were single-minded when it came to survival and didn't know the concept of a fair fight. To them, it was kill or be killed. She wouldn't allow her urbanite to get snapped in two, couldn't allow him to be hurt on her watch, in her territory. Not before he could lead her to Lower Amerada. Especially not before she learned how that kiss would end. She had to think fast.

Cleo knew her best chance would be to take him from behind, like she'd done to the other, but now that she'd been spotted, it would be hard to get around him.

The Banger eyed her, his gaze extending into the forest at her back. When nothing moved in the bush, he narrowed his eyes and snarled a mouthful of garbled sounds, as if asking about the other Banger.

Interesting. These troglodytes almost never developed bonds with another, didn't have the capacity for social behavior, or so she thought. Maybe she could capitalize on that.

"Killed him," she replied nonchalantly. "Now, be a good little troll and hand over the bag."

He clutched it tighter, eyes darting left and right, trying to decide which way to run.

As soon as his attention flicked away, Cleo dove and, using the mud for added momentum, threw herself into a sliding scissor kick, taking his legs out from under him. Before the Banger could find his feet, Libra was over him, wrestling away the backpack.

Mistake. Going hand-to-hand with one of these guys was like getting between a mother bear and her cub. This guy wanted food. Bad.

He went right for the throat, digging his scabby fingers into Libra's windpipe. The urbanite clung to his bag with one arm while the other pummelled the Banger in the ribs, but they were matched in determination, and Libra still appeared confused by what he was up against. For every blow he landed, the Banger only squeezed harder.

Libra brought his knee up between them, but Cleo could see his face taking on an unhealthy purple tinge as his strength drained with his oxygen supply. The Banger leaned into a roll and if Cleo didn't intervene, he'd get on top of Libra, and that would be the end of the city boy. Libra's eyes started to bulge and his movements were becoming jerky and uncoordinated.

Cleo clamped down her back teeth, knowing what had to be done. To a Wolverine Clan warrior, even a third class one, stomping on a man's balls was a low and desperate move. She didn't want to do this, she really didn't, but Bangers fought dirty. With a huff, Cleo drove her heel into his man business and jumped back.

The Banger let out a keening wail, dropped

his vice-grip on Libra's neck, and folded into a fetal position. Libra crawled off him and fell to the ground a few feet away, coughing and clawing at his throat as if the Banger still had hold.

Cleo scooped up the backpack and dug out the knife, thinking she might never let it go. It felt good in her palm, like it belonged. She looked down at the pathetic, stinking Banger and shuddered.

She quickly emptied the satchel of all the Nutripacks.

Libra looked at her with confusion. "What are you doing?" he rasped, sounding like he'd swallowed broken glass.

"Just what it looks like," she replied, throwing the Nutripacks onto the ground next to the writhing Banger. "Hey," she shouted over his moans. "Add water. You hear me? *Not* from the Dead Lake. Use river water." She raised her voice. "*River water.* You understand?"

"But that's all our food!" Libra rasped, "You can't—"

She cut Libra off with a single sideways eye-cut. A combination of fear, relief, and physical exertion, topped with a heaping dose of sexual frustration, made Cleo pissy as a rabid badger. She was glad he got that from her look.

She toed the Banger with her foot. He looked up at her through slitted eyes. "It is food," she said, over pronouncing each syllable. She mimed the action of eating. "Num-num, good food. Make you strong."

The Banger grunted.

"Go back and get your friend and don't even think of following us." Cleo poked the tip of the knife into his neck, just enough to draw a bead of blood. "*Do. Not. Follow.* Get it?"

She thought of offering a hand to Libra, but at the last moment, stepped over him, pausing only to growl, "In case there's any further confusion, *that* is a savage. Get it?"

Taking for granted that Libra would follow, Cleo took off at a jog. She led them a fair distance down the path before slowing to ensure the Bangers didn't tail. The forest was silent except for the rain. Cleo was glad of it. It helped wash away the grimy feeling of disgust, the stench, and eased her headache. She felt uncharitable for hating Bangers, especially in the predicament she'd put herself in, but she couldn't help herself. Bangers weren't any more responsible for their actions than a wild animal, but because they were human, they were held accountable; loathed, shunned, and generally avoided, though it was that same humanistic need to survive that kept them alive.

Murder of humans was murder, no matter how brain-fried the subject, whereas killing an aggressive polar grizzly, an animal respected for its fierceness, was not. How could that be logical?

"Why did you give him all of our food?" Libra asked. She'd forgotten he was there, a safe ten feet behind her.

She turned around and walked backward. Ugly red welts marred his beautiful neck. She pivoted, unable to meet his eyes after what happened between them. Ashamed for what she'd done to the Banger.

"That's all he wanted from us," she said over her shoulder. "They were hungry."

"And we won't be?" His voice was still raspy. Probably would be for a few days. "Those Nutripacks are the only thing separating us from becoming like them."

She laughed at the absurdity. "We'll cope."

He caught up to her but kept to the far side of the path, leaving a few feet between them. Everything had changed since this morning when she woke up in his arms. What were they now? How were they supposed to relate? Friends, enemies, travel companions, almost-lovers, and now fighting partners. How did she talk to him, how should she act, how in hell could she stay in control?

Libra seemed just as disoriented, keeping his head slightly bowed as he walked.

They continued the journey in silence, the rain turning into a light shower before giving way to a brightening sky.

"Thanks," Libra said awhile later. "Guess we're even in the life-saving department."

"You're welcome."

"I don't get it," he said after a few more minutes. "How come you're so different from those other Taigans?"

"Other Taigans? You mean the Bangers?" she looked at him from the corner of her eye, could see how conflicted, how puzzled he appeared. He couldn't think...

Cleo ground to a halt in mid-step. "Those aren't my people, Libra. Those aren't Taigans. They're Bangers. Did you think— Oh for the love of ducks, no, no, and no."

Libra's eyebrows came together, clearly unable to process her denial.

"Bangers wander the Taiga, usually alone— in fact, that's the first time I've ever seen them in pairs," she said, glancing back. "They don't have the mental acuity for socialization or know better than to drink from the Dead Lakes. They're violent, aggressive, and singular-minded when it comes to food."

"Are there a lot of them?" he asked.

"No, not really. Scattered around here and there. I haven't encountered one in ages, and they generally stay far away from the villages. Even when we do run into them, we just give them space and avoid confrontation. Don't you have people like that in Gomeda?"

He shrugged. "We certainly have

individuals who can't cope with life, sure. But we institutionalize them and try to fix them."

"Oh." Cleo wasn't sure how to respond. Was he implying the Bangers could be fixed?

"Where do they come from?"

"I don't know. They just...are." That's what her father had told her once when she was very young. She never thought to question him and accepted them as part of the threat, like alphacats, polar grizzlies, and everything else scary and unexplainable.

"Why do you call them *Bangers*?"

"It's how they eat. They catch small animals—squirrels, mice, rabbits if they're lucky—and pound the carcass with a rock until it's pulp. Then they slit the skin and drink...well, I think you can figure out the rest. You could see for yourself that they don't have the dental capacity for chewing tough meat. Or the mental capacity to care."

Libra winkled his nose. "That is the *vilest* thing I have ever heard. Just...*disgusting.* They don't even *cook* it first?"

Cleo shook her head. "Bangers and fire don't mix."

Libra put his hand over his stomach. "I don't even care that you gave away my food. I can't see my appetite returning for weeks. Maybe months."

"It is kind of gross." Cleo laughed and met his gaze. Their kiss came rushing back into memory, the way his mouth moved across her lips and neck, so vivid, she felt heat rush into her cheeks and a pull of longing in her abdomen that made her shiver. She averted her eyes, embarrassed.

"You must be freezing," he said, misunderstanding. "I've got some dry clothes in my pack. You can take your pick."

"Why don't you find something for me."

While Libra rummaged, Cleo was struck by another shiver, complete with goose bumps, and realized she really was chilly, especially now that they'd stopped jogging. The rain had kicked the temperature down to an uncomfortable level. They'd been lucky with the weather 'til now, but September nights could drop the mercury into low double digits and Cleo had no intention, after surviving drowning, a hungry alpha-cat attack, and a pair of thieving Bangers, of succumbing to pneumonia.

"These will have to do for now," Libra said, tossing her a ribbed sleeveless shirt and pair of black thermal leggings. "My apologies for the wifebeater, but it's the only thing I have that's both dry and clean. The pants are some kind of special material that I'm supposed to wear under my clothes if it gets cold, so they should warm you up." Libra turned his back to give her privacy and peeled off his wet shirt. "Tell me when you're done."

"These are perfect, thanks." She lingered a moment to gawp at his physique. She'd almost forgotten how marvelous his back was; broad with well-defined muscles across his shoulder blades. *Definitely not a malnourished desk jockey.* "Why are wives beaten for these flimsy little tops?"

He chuckled, low and chesty, the damage to his vocal chords only enhancing the sexiness of his rumble. "It's just an expression."

"We'll have to find some dry wood to make a fire tonight," she said, fighting with the swollen laces of her halter and wishing she'd chosen a different outfit at the start of her journey, like the practical woven-thread tunic that was at the bottom of the river with the rest of her things. "Oh, for the love of wet cows."

"That's a new one. What's wrong?"

"Ever try to peel off drippy animal hide?"

"Need help?"

Yes. "No, but this could take awhile."

The rumble again, heavy with implication, struck her midsection like a ball of fire.

"Hey, when we were back there, you told the Banger you killed his friend," Libra said. "But later you told him to share the food."

"Mmm-hmm?"

"How could he share with a dead guy?"

"Ghosts get hungry too," Cleo joked.

Libra remained silent.

She glanced over her shoulder. "You don't

really believe I killed that Banger, do you?"

Silence. Stillness. He remained focused in the other direction.

"Libra?"

"I don't know. Did you?"

"No!" Cleo pulled so hard on the leather cord, it snapped. "Damn it." She pulled the laces through and tugged the wet garment off her body with a huff. "How could you even think such a thing?"

"I don't know. Nothing about this territory is what I thought. Everything's a surprise. Especially you."

"Me?"

"Yeah, you."

"How could I be a surprise? You didn't know I existed until a few days ago."

"I don't mean you as an individual, but you as a girl from a tribe in the Taiga. I expected you people to be more like...them. Bangers."

She wished she could see his face, read his expression, his body language. Words alone gave no hints as to how to interpret these revelations. "But that's ridiculous. Whatever gave you that idea?"

"Talk, stories, personal accounts. I think Gomedans have a load of misconceptions about the tribal way of life."

"Clearly," she huffed, discarding her wet leather for the comfy leggings. She rolled the waistband over a few times so they wouldn't drop off her hips. "But for the record, I've never killed another human being, not even a Banger." Cleo turned. "There hasn't been a murder in my clan since the day I was born," she said, unable to cover the malice in her voice. "Hope that convinces you we're not some kind of animals."

Libra spun round to face her. "I wasn't implying—"

"Yes, you were. Did," she said matter-of-factly. "Many times."

"No, I wasn't. It's just that..." Libra blew out a breath and shrugged. "The way you had him in that strangle hold, then how you took down the other one... how was I supposed to... I mean, I've never seen a girl fight like that."

"Well, let's get this out in the open, then. I'm a Wolverine Clan warrior, third-class. Do you have a problem with that?"

"I never said that!"

"Did my *savagery* shock you?"

"What? No!" he said. Libra turned on his heel and walked a few steps. He pushed his hands through his wet hair before pivoting abruptly and marching back to where she stood.

She stood her ground, hands on hips, shoulders back, and chin up, ready to face whatever bullshit misconception he had. Perhaps she'd flatten his ass to the ground for good measure.

"Fact is..." His Adam's apple bobbed. He reached up to remove a leaf from her hair then scanned her face, his gaze lingering on her mouth. "Fact is..." He brushed his thumb across her mouth, making Cleo's breath catch. His eyes locked on hers and his voice seemed to take on an even raspier tone. "I was completely turned on."

NINETEEN

TURNED ON.

Did he really say that? Cleo wondered if her cheeks were as bright as they felt.

"We'd better get moving." Her voice sounded disembodied as she concentrated on putting one foot in front of the other.

Turned on. *By her fighting.*

She was damn proud of her skills, but the guys in her tribe either challenged her or avoided her. Group A had the cocky I'll-show-her-who's-boss mentality, then went away bitter, tails between their legs, when she put them in their place. Group B were the opposite—completely intimidated, scared to ask her to go walking with them, terrified when caught staring.

Now the urbanite went and added a new category, Group C—*turned on.*

For the love of all things... Damn, she couldn't come up with an appropriate ending to that one, but at least she felt a little better about letting him take up so much of her headspace. At least he appreciated her kick-assness. She might even forgive him for that other shit.

He cut into her reverie. "Can we make it to the post tonight?"

Cleo glanced at the dimming sky. "Not a chance. There's not much daylight left. But it's all pretty easy from here. Once we hit the grid line, we'll go south until we get to the Dead Lake."

Cleo bent to pick up a broken branch, snapping away the few skinny twigs protruding from the sides. It made a perfect walking stick, and she was a little sore. "I know a good spot to stop for the night. From there, it's only another couple hours to the Trading Post. If we get up with the sun, we can make it in time for breakfast. And believe me when I tell you Miss Valentina makes bread that will make your mouth water. Oh, and fresh bacon! I can practically smell it. Don't you love the smell of thick applewood-smoked bacon, frying in the skillet?"

When he didn't answer right away, she caught him staring at her backside like *it* was a side of bacon. "Did you even hear what I said?"

"What? Oh, sorry. Bacon. Never had it."

"You've never had bacon? You poor, deprived soul!"

"Yeah, well, there aren't an abundance of farm animals wandering around Gomeda."

"So, besides Nutrishit, what's on a typical menu?"

"Ha! Nutrishit...because I've never heard that one before," he derided. "We get the occasional fruits and vegetables from the hydroponic farms; whatever the Ministry of Food and Agriculture deems there's an overage of. For instance, if they have an inventory excess of tomatoes, they're sold in open market, albeit at an exorbitant price."

"What do you mean *excess*? What happens to the original inventory?"

"It goes to the NutriCorp. Oh, don't give me that icky face, please. Nutrifood *is* made up of some real food, you know. It's not *all* chemicals. At least nobody has to bang it with a rock," he said with a shudder. "But realize that they have eleven million mouths to feed on a limited supply, so they hydroponically grow perfect specimens that NutriCorp then uses to mass produce balanced meals for everyone, so even folks that can't afford to supplement their diets with fresh ingredients... Well, at least they're getting some kind of nutrition."

"Like the Stone Soup fable?"

"Yes, exactly. Except there's not quite

enough of the good stuff, so they do have to bulk it up with fillers and such."

"It's the 'and such' I'd be worried about."

"Yeah well, there *are* nutrition issues in Gomeda," he said quietly. "I can't deny that. But people aren't starving anymore, not like they did after the collapse, but some do suffer from certain...deficiencies. Lots of disease still lingers about, far too much chronic illness affects the young, the poor, et cetera. I guess *healthy* is a relative term for us."

She craved to ask him about his past, about his life in the city, but bit her tongue. It was sure to lead to comparisons, then to a Gomeda versus Taiga competition, and though part of her still itched for a fight, she didn't like how Libra's face tightened up when they argued. She wanted the warm-fuzzy feeling to come back to their conversation. She wanted that half-smile that made her insides feel squishy.

"You don't look too deprived." Cleo reached out to give his upper arm a squeeze. "Or *feel* too deprived."

"All the better to save young damsels who throw themselves over waterfalls," he said, flashing his half-smile.

"But seriously, how..." she let the question trail off, unsure of how to word it.

"How come I'm the picture of health?"

Cleo nodded thinking "picture of health" barely described his toned physique.

"I was born healthy." He sighed as if it were a burden. "And was lucky to have access to potable water, vitamins, and a fully stocked food consolidator."

"But no bacon."

"Alas, no bacon."

Cleo gave her head a slow dramatic shake. "That is just so wrong. Don't think I could survive without bacon. Or want to. I'd probably throw myself over a waterfall."

"Oh, is that what happened?" Libra smiled and reached out to tuck a loose strand of hair behind her ear. "We had other meat-like things that don't bear scrutiny, so we won't discuss them. How about you? It's obvious you don't subsist on grubs and rodents—"

"—that we catch with our bare hands and eat raw?"

"You mean *drink* raw?" He crinkled his nose. "And you're correct. I admit, and you may flog me later, but I had some pretty heinous misconceptions about the people of the Taiga, especially the—"

"Oh, we're here," Cleo interrupted as they rounded a bend in the path. She pointed to the wall of stone that cut through the trees.

"Zhang hell!" Libra started agape at what lay ahead, then flicked his eyes back to Cleo. "I mean, it didn't look as big when I came up on a solar scooter, you know?"

There was no other way to describe the

grid but a river of boulders; rocks of every shape and size, piled ten to fifteen feet high and fifty feet wide.

"How do you traverse these with wagons and horses—you do still use those, right?"

"And solar scooters, sometimes," she said, hating herself for caring what he thought of their lifestyle. "There are all kinds of passes on the inter-tribal trails, and bridges or tunnels, depending the landscape. The trails that run a direct route from village to trading post are simple to navigate. We're a bit off the beaten track here."

"What about animals?"

She was surprised he would have considered migration routes. "They climb over," she explained, but Libra looked sceptical. Cleo laughed. "Moose can cross rocks, you know. They're far more agile than their spindly legs let on. The smaller critters go between the gaps and spaces. That said, lots of snake nests in there, so be careful."

Cleo hoisted herself onto a three-foot-high boulder—the biggest in the wall in front of her—but if a little kick-ass action got him turned on, maybe fleet-footing it over the channel would heat him up, too.

She peeked over her shoulder to see Libra's eyes darting from rock to rock.

"You're not afraid of snakes, are you?"

"Hmm? No. Take this," he said, throwing

his pack up toward her.

"Yeah, sure," Cleo said, swinging it onto her back, wondering why he looked so charmingly distracted.

"These rocks are pretty solid, yeah? No loose bits or booby traps I should know about?"

Cleo hoisted herself up to the next level of rocks and looked down from her perch. "No, they've been jammed in here for decades, so they're pretty stable. But you should be careful anyway."

To her amusement, Libra did two deep knee bends, rotated each ankle, and then backed up a dozen paces.

"Not sure a few rocks warrant such Olympian preparation, Libra," she laughed. "This has nothing on the escarpment you managed to scale."

Instead of answering, he puffed his breath a few times and took off at a sprint. Just before he got to the first row of rocks, he leapt— not just jumped, but leapt like a freaking alphacat—into the air. Arms out, Libra hand-sprang off the three-footer she just came from, his body twisted in a full upside down circle, and landed on the row above her. The rest happened in a blur of movement—hands, feet, bouncing, somersaulting, flying over the channel until he was out of sight on the other side. The entire performance couldn't have taken any more than ten or fifteen seconds.

"For the love of tap dancing ducks, what *the hell* was that?"

Cleo, who had always thought of herself as nimble, scrambled across the rocks, shaking her head with disbelief, shock, and most annoyingly, a touch of envy.

"Gravity..." she huffed as he came within her view. "Got something against it?" She tossed the backpack down at him.

"Hell no," he said, beaming like a wolf in a field of sheep. "It's essential to what I do."

"And what is it you do, *exactly*, Mr. I'm-just-a-pencil-pusher?" Cleo demanded, ignoring his proffered hand as she jumped to the ground from the highest boulder on the edge. "You got a cape and mask I should know about?"

"No. And no wings, either." He did a repeat of his earlier pirouette to satisfy her. "It's just a hobby. Ever heard of PK or free running?"

"Nope."

"PK is short for parkour. It's a sport that people do in the city, a way to get from one place to another using a combination of running, jumping, flipping, twisting, basically using your body in an acrobatic way to get around obstacles."

"And you're a PKer in Gomeda?"

"People who do it are called *traceurs*, and yes, I do it all the time."

"The escarpment?" That's how he did it.

Cheater. He could have mentioned...

"You got it. Between the roots jutting out from the rocks, the ledges, bumps, and slopes, it really wasn't that much of a challenge."

"Really," she said, thinking it was probably a good deal more challenging than he'd admit. But as this new information simmered, she couldn't help feeling a bit pole-axed, torn between being impressed and feeling a little like she'd been duped.

"And I did have a good length of polycord."

He hadn't mentioned this PK skill. Should he have? Did the opportunity come up before now? Probably not, but her suspicion vibes tingled nonetheless.

"Why didn't you tell me?"

"Never came up. Why didn't you tell me you could fight like that?"

"Never came up."

"Guess we're even."

"No. We're not," Cleo said, tightening her jaw. "Why didn't you tell me, you know, back there, when I flipped out, imagining you dead?"

"I...I don't know," he said, reaching for her hand. She didn't pull away, but neither did she curl her fingers around his. "I guess I was shocked that you actually seemed to care. And you were so wound up, angry..." Libra's eyes darkened as he tugged her toward him, "...and hot. You looked so mussed, like you just tumbled out of bed after an especially athletic night," he said, dipping his head, getting closer with each word, "so damn sexy that I just wanted to eat you up."

Libra's lips brushed against hers, not with the hungry punishing force like before, but affectionately, softly, making her eyelids flutter down, completely surrendering to the tenderness of the moment, the tenderness of his touch.

Cleo sighed and pulled back before he had a chance to deepen the kiss, before she could get lost in him again. "That little handspring move was kind of cool."

"Kong," he said.

"Excuse me?"

"It's called a kong."

Cleo smiled and raised on her tiptoes to plant a kiss on the corner of his mouth, on the side that always curled up. "You're good," she whispered. Cleo loved that he had this amazing talent, yet hated that it was something that made her feel completely lacking. "Could you teach me?"

"A few moves, sure. Tomorrow. Right now, we need to focus on priorities," he said. He pulled her close and placed a kiss on her forehead. Affection, apology, friendship, she wasn't sure until he said, "Fire, food and...bed."

Bed. His voice was low and suggestive. *Bed*, he said, not sleep.

TWENTY

LIBRA HUNCHED OVER THE SMALL pile of tinder, the driest collection of forest debris he could find, and blew the sparks until a flame appeared. Cleo had left him in charge of making camp while she hunted for something to eat. He had no idea what manner of beast she'd return with, considering she had nothing but his K-Bar knife and the net bag, but having witnessed her unique capabilities, he wouldn't be surprised if she brought back a four-course meal.

After a hard day of physical exertion, he should feel hungry, but his appetite couldn't compete with the germ of anxiety that settled in his gut during the airplane conversation and spread throughout him like a virus with every step that took them closer to the Cut, toward the inevitable end of his mission.

Throughout their journey, as guilt, lust, and honest-to-goodness admiration for Cleo tipped his moral scales, his mind turned over every possible alternative scenario to avoid doing what had to be done. It was either drop her into unconsciousness with the implant just before they got to the Trading Post and carry her out, or make use of that damn ampoule, nestled deep in the pocket of his pants. Either way, the self-loathing felt like a black hole in his soul.

He may have only known her a matter of days, but she'd impacted his life, his views and attitudes. He was split between resenting her and admiring her, wanting to throttle her and wanting to kiss her. Never had a woman, or anyone, made him feel so two-faced, so unsure of himself. He'd always been a righteous bastard—he'd gone to prison for his convictions—but Cleo had turned his black and white axioms to murky gray.

What would she think if she knew the real reason he was here—the points, the personal revenge? Worse, what would she think of him and his group of shit-disturbers back in Gomeda?

The faintest glimmer of an idea began to form as he built a fancy tepee with sticks and twigs around the crackling tinder. He stood to crack a few larger branches across his knee when he heard her come up behind him.

"Let me guess," he said without turning. "Buffalo steaks?"

"Buffalo have been extinct for a century."

"Yeah, but if anyone could find one, I've no doubt it would be you." Libra began to pivot when she draped something around his neck.

Snake.

He barely caught himself from committing an unmanly jolt, instead pretending nonchalance at the headless reptile across his shoulders.

"Time for your cooking lesson," she said. "Taiga survival for beginners."

She had to be kidding. With two fingers, he yanked the snake to the ground. At least it wasn't as slimy as he'd imagined. Wasn't slimy at all. "Think I'll watch, if you don't mind."

Libra had no intention of doing even that. If he had to partake in the barbaric practice of eating something that had been alive less than five minutes ago, he preferred to ignore the process. He returned to fire tending, but by the time Cleo had washed, gutted, and skinned it, and threaded the pieces onto a sharpened stick to roast it on the fire, fascination replaced his revulsion.

Didn't smell horrible, either.

"Okay, hand over a piece."

Without trying to hide her smug smile, she passed him a morsel.

The meat was flaky and looked a bit like

her fish from earlier. The rib bones made him pause—there may have even been a gag—but if his little warrior could take down two Bangers, he could be man enough to choke down a little fresh-cooked kill.

All the same, he was glad it was dark enough that she wouldn't be able to see his complexion pale at the thought of putting it in his mouth. Not that he was squeamish.

"Well? Will you live?"

"It's...it's not bad, actually."

"It's better when it's battered and deep fried with a side of butter sauce."

While he helped himself to more, Cleo threw together a second course of dandelion leaf salad, flavored with a handful of nutty-tasting berries she'd picked along the trail. She added a bonus education lesson while he ate, so he knew that were he ever stuck and starving in the Taiga, he should only eat berries if they had a little crown because it meant they weren't poisonous. If she could throw a decent meal together out of snake and berries, imagine what she could do with real ingredients. She babbled on about roots and mushrooms unprompted, allowing his mind to tumble over other things.

There it was again...that glimmer. An idea so thread-thin, so ungraspable, too insane to even contemplate... but what if?

She could always say no.

And since the perfect segue presented itself, he decided to dip his toes in the water. "Y'know Cleo," he said, pouring water from his canteen over the empty plate, "Maybe you should join me in Gomeda. We could open an authentic Taiga restaurant. First of its kind."

"I'm glad I've impressed you," she said, smiling, "but if I've given you the impression that cooking, or spending any time in a kitchen, is appealing to me, I've misled you."

"Aw come on," he joked. "We could serve bacon."

She grew very quiet and a serious furrow formed in her brow. Libra wasn't sure how to continue since cajoling hadn't taken him in the direction he needed.

"Actually, I wanted to ask you about that," she said, staring at her feet.

"Bacon?"

"No," Cleo said, shaking her head. "Something else."

She fidgeted and paused as if she were unsure how to approach the question. When she finally spoke, her voice thin and vulnerable, he wished he'd been mentally prepared.

"Can I trust you?"

"Trust me?" *No! Absolutely not. Run.* "Have I given you reason not to?"

She contemplated that for a moment, eyes on the stone she'd been toeing out of the ground. Her gaze flicked up for a second—too quickly for him to read her expression, too quick to prepare himself for what she would say next. "I need to go to Gomeda. Will you take me?"

Libra's jaw unhinged. If he didn't believe in a spiritual overseer before, he was all kinds of devoted now. "You want to go to the city? With me?"

"Not *with you,* with you. Not like a stray dog that won't leave you alone. Just 'with you,' like a travelling companion."

Libra couldn't find words fast enough.

"Because that's kind of where I was headed when I, you know...when I had the incident in the river."

Libra set down his plate and faced her across the circle of fire. This was getting interesting, and he didn't want to miss a single detail.

"You were going to Gomeda?"

"Yes."

"Why?"

She picked up the stone she'd unearthed and turned it over in her hand. "I need to find my brother."

"And he's in the city?"

"That's where he was going, yes." She brushed the dirt from the rock, revealing a shiny, almost crystalline surface. She toyed with it, turned it between her thumb and forefinger, hypnotized by the reflection of the flame in the facets. "I've got to get to him before he gets inducted or drugged, or whatever it is your Ministry of Opportunity does to keep my people there. I need to bring him home." She flung the rock deep into the bushes and watched it, as if she could see it land in the dark foliage. "Will you help me find him?"

Libra dug his fingers into his scalp to stop his brain from exploding. They wanted her, she happened to be going there. Coincidence? And why didn't she just tell him that in the first place and save him days of planning, days of emotional tug of war? Why the big secret? There was something more going on, and he had a feeling he was a pawn in much larger game. If they already had Jaegar, what did they need his sister for? But while his mental cogs spun, he needed to answer her.

"What if he doesn't want to come back?" he asked. "He must have had a reason for leaving."

Cleo's face blanched. Last time it had gone that pale, he had to catch her from fainting. She clutched her necklace, her lifeline, before answering. "Yes, there was a reason, but it was a stupid one."

He let silence fill the space, hoping she'd continue.

Cleo rose and went to the stack of sticks and branches he'd assembled to feed the fire during the night. She grabbed a dried-out chunk of dead timber and threw it haphazardly onto the pile of embers. "I have to set things right. And I'm the only one who can."

He tracked her as she sought something to do, some task, other than sit and face him across the fire.

"Of course I'll take you," he said, realizing she was waiting for his answer. "I'll even help you locate your brother."

She stilled. Her shoulders dropped and her face drained of tension. Her look of pure gratitude unravelled him.

He wouldn't need Trevayne's help after all. Or the ampoule. Or the implant. He waited for a sense of relief to hit, but his fingers curled into tight balls and the muscles up his back wound like a constricting spring around his spine.

Lies aside, his mission had gone from a potential violent kidnapping to that of a simple escort service. Take her to Gomeda, find Jaegar, politely suggest they stop by DynaCade to visit Achan, and put them both on the transport back over the Cut Road.

The truth would eventually come out, but not yet. He couldn't compromise her trust so far into the end game. Better to wait until they were in Gomeda. Or on the way *out* of Gomeda.

"Thank you, Libra. That means a lot to me. I...I...don't know why the fates are suddenly taking pity on me because I don't deserve it, but thank you. For...everything."

The irony made him laugh. "Why don't you deserve it?"

"I just don't."

Interesting. Cleo Rush had more secrets. "What will you do if he doesn't want to come back?"

She stared into the fire.

"Cleo? What if your brother likes the city, doesn't want to come back up here?"

"He has to come back," she said, her voice revealing no hint of emotion. "He's supposed to be the leader-elect of our tribe."

Libra's mind spun the new facts into those he already knew, which wasn't much. It explained why Achan wanted Jaegar Rush— the leader-elect would hold as much power as the sitting leader. If mining agreements needed to be made, they could be done with Jaegar alone.

So why the last-minute change in his mission directive? If Jaegar already made it to Gomeda and Achan knew that, why send Libra to get Cleo? Why not just cancel the mission and send Libra back to the penal colony? What could Achan possibly want with them both?

Though he was barely old enough to remember his father, the story of how Lewin Rush killed Bronson Cade, Libra's father, in cold blood, was dinner-table conversation. It was a given that Achan hated the tribers for taking his only son away from him, but he never once spoke of vengeance. He only used his anger and loathing to enforce his convictions about the savages of the northern wild.

No. His grandfather was a single-minded bastard whose purpose often shadowed his motivations, but Libra never knew him to be violent. The old man didn't even like dirt under his nails. Achan was a brains-over-brawn kind of director. If he couldn't use logic to get his way, he used manipulation. But violence? Never.

Was he being manipulated? Of course, but only in the sense he was performing an unsavory task for money.

Libra still felt as though he was missing critical information, but what? Cleo was holding back, he could feel it, but he didn't dare poke too hard lest she pulled a quid pro quo. So far, the less either of them asked, the less they had to answer. Like a silent game with unspoken rules...but they were both definitely playing.

Tonight, after she fell asleep, he'd sneak out of camp with his satcom and call off Trevayne. That much, he could do.

His attention returned to Cleo, who busied herself turning over the wet cloths that were drying on a rock. He was completely unprepared for that rush of light-headedness he got whenever he looked at her.

Did she have any conception of how gorgeous she was? How sexy? How his entire body hummed to life when she spoke? Just watching her luscious lips form words made him ache.

Like an addict, he needed to hear her speak. "I don't know anything about your politics, Cleo, but do you think he took off because he doesn't want to be the leader? I mean, that's a lot of pressure for someone to face, isn't it?"

"Yes. It is. Too much. But he has no choice. It's tribe law." Her movements were jerky, repetitive, and unsettled. "It's...complicated."

He hadn't seen her agitated like this since she woke up naked and bound. Not even after she killed the alphacat. Another thought nagged him. Why was Cleo sent after Jaegar, alone? If her brother was that important, why wouldn't they send a delegation or an army? "Why don't you try to explain?"

She threw more wood on the fire, which was already flaring too bright and using up what they'd need to stoke it during the night.

"Cleo?"

"Because I drove him away, okay?" She dropped a heavy chunk of rotten tree stump in the center of the flames. "*I'm* the stupid reason he took off, and *I'm* the one who must get him back." She stared at the flames, her face shiny with sweat, her breast heaving.

Libra circled the fire, kicking the embers that had bounced out back into the shallow pit. "Okay, darlin'. Whatever you did isn't worth burning down the Taiga for." He made his way around to her and slid an arm around her shoulders. "Just... Take a deep breath and..."

She turned and threw herself into his arms. He rubbed her back and thought he felt her shoulders tremble. Crying? No, she couldn't be. Cleo Rush was the strongest woman he'd ever met. He looked down, but her face was buried in his shirt.

"Don't worry, Cleo. I'll find him. I promise. Everything will be fine."

"Thank you," she said, her voice muffled.

He smoothed her hair, tangling his fingers in its silky length, until he felt her muscles relax. Until he felt his own muscles relax. Holding her like this felt so right, so damn perfect, he didn't think he could let her go.

"Will your friends mind?" she asked, peeking up.

"My friends?" *Shit, his cover story!* He stepped back.

"My camping buddies? Hell no. And if they do, we'll just head out alone, right? We can double on my solar scooter. It's a biggie, and brand new..." he babbled, telling her they'd go east and shoot over the St. Mary's Dam, avoiding the longer but safer Dead Zone route. He prattled about their journey while his mind worked out other things, like how to communicate all this to Trevayne, and how he could pull this charade off without her catching on. How could he have forgotten his camping buddies?

"I'm going to wash up," she said, taking the lantern and heading toward the bank of the stream. "Coming?"

He nodded and went to untie the lantern from the back of his pack.

"Leave it," she said. "It'll only attract bugs."

Libra shrugged and followed her into the blackness of the forest. "Why didn't we just make camp on the bank?" He asked as he blindly followed.

"Because animals come during the night to drink and we don't want to disturb them, nor do we want to be disturbed."

"Good point—ouch!" He walked straight into copse of pines. Turning to backtrack, he got another face full of branches. "It's like they're attacking me!"

"Watch where you're going," she laughed.

"How can I watch where I'm going when I can't see for shit?"

As if to illustrate his point, he ran straight into Cleo, who had stopped, turned, and put her hand out, anticipating that he'd find it with his chest. "Close your eyes," she instructed.

"Why?"

"Just do it. Or I'll go Banger on your ass."

Libra chuckled and complied. "Now what?"

"Just wait a sec."

"What am I waiting for?"

"For your eyes to adjust. You've been staring into that fire, so your pupils are dilated. Now open."

He could see. Not much, but he could make out silhouettes and solid objects, like the few trees that stood between him and the river. And Cleo, who put her hand in the air to wave. On impulse, he caught her by the wrist and brought her palm to his lips.

"Thanks," he whispered, the word laced with more meaning than she could ever understand. "Shall I wait here? Give you some privacy," he said.

"Yes," she said, tugging her hand from his grasp and disappearing into the night.

A fresh ache grew in his gut at the thought of lying next to her all night. If she let him. She did last night, so he hoped... But things had changed since then. A whole zhang-load of complicated happened since then.

It would be wiser to make a bed clear on the other side of the fire so he could mull over the new information he'd learned, but his need to lay next to her, touch her, smell her overwhelmed his cogitation chip. Like an all-out battle between his mind and body.

How would she react if he pounced on her, ravished her like he wanted to?

What would he do about Trevayne? Could he convince the old soldier to playact?

Just do it. Ravage her senseless.

Could Trevayne be relied upon to play pretend? Probably not. He practically screamed Gomeda Guard.

By the time she'd returned, Libra's imagination had taken him so far as to wonder if she'd moan his name when she came, or if he could he make her scream until he could hear his name echoing back off the rocks.

TWENTY-ONE

CLEO STIFLED A GIGGLE WHEN Libra bent over to tidy the mess she'd made of the fire during her tantrum. "You got some...uh...bits on you."

"Huh?"

"From your tangle with those aggressive pines. Stand still," she said, picking the tiny green needles from the tops of his shoulders.

The whole world felt lighter now that he'd agreed to take her to Gomeda. She had every confidence Libra would fulfill his promise, and having an ally in a strange and scary urban center made her want to weep with relief. She almost had, earlier, but managed to stop any real tears from spilling. Warriors did not cry, even when overjoyed.

She picked and plucked the detritus from his back, most real, some imaginary, following the contours of his spine until she came to the narrows of his waist. There wasn't a speck of foliage, but she couldn't resist. Without hesitation, without a thought to the consequences, she pinched his butt.

"Are you trying to start something?" he said, peering over his shoulder.

"Me? Never. Pine needle stuck right here," she said, pinching again, "and here—"

"Fine, have your fun, but keep in mind, I get to do you next," he said with a sexy chuckle.

"But I didn't get attacked by nature."

For a trained warrior, third class, she didn't anticipate his lightning speed turn, so when her legs were swept out from under her and she landed on the ground, his hand cradling her head, she squealed.

"No, but you were attacked by the rare and dangerous Gomedan He-Man, which were previously thought to be extinct, and now you have dirt on your ass." He hoisted her up with the same speed and strength he used to drop her. His palm slid down the center of her back and over the curve of her ass. "Which I will obligingly brush off."

Cleo stayed perfectly still, letting the arm that encircled her waist take her weight. She could feel the tension of the last week pour out of her like water from a draining tub. Libra's eyes were shadowed, but she could feel their heat. "Are you sure you don't mind?"

"I consider it my duty." He dipped his head and, with feather lightness, brushed his lips against the corner of her mouth. "Wouldn't want you to make your city debut with a smudge."

"I meant, are you sure you don't mind taking me to Gomeda?" she clarified.

He tipped her chin up with his thumb so their faces were aligned, eye-to-eye, mouth-to-mouth. "Darlin', I'll take you anywhere you want to go," he said, his breath mingling with her own. "I'll take you places so high, you'll think you're flying."

Libra brushed against her lips again. His kisses were soft, not as demanding as earlier. She liked it, liked it just fine, but they made her feel vulnerable, left more room for thought. She preferred the other way, when there wasn't thinking involved, just moving, filling each other's senses. She angled her head and parted her mouth slightly.

He took the bait, dipping into her, teasing her with his taste.

But she wanted more.

She wanted him to lay her down, to touch her, everywhere, without modesty, without caution. She wanted to feel his bare flesh against hers, his lips on her shoulder, her breast, her thighs. Such primal need; it felt as if every human aspect about her disappeared and she was reduced to a rutting animal, as if he were essential to her very survival and if she didn't get it, get *him*, she would die. She wanted to taste his neck, to run her teeth along the corded flesh, lick a line down the centre of his chest. Perhaps there was a kernel of truth to his misconceptions because she felt every bit the savage when it came to him.

She wanted to fly.

The next time his tongue breached the border of her lips, she grabbed it between her teeth and sucked the tip until she felt a groan rumble deep in his chest. When she released it, he plunged into her, thrusting and winding his way into her like before.

Her fingers curled into his shirt, gripping the material tightly to keep herself from touching him in places she so badly wanted to touch.

Fear mingled with desire, muddying the experience.

She'd never done this before. She knew the technical aspects, obviously, but what if they did things differently in Gomeda? What if there were rituals she was unaware of? What if she did something that offended him, turned him off?

He grabbed her ass and pulled her into him, hard, so that her abdomen crashed into his erection. She wiggled against it and felt his stomach go taut. So she did it again, this time rolling her pelvis against him. His groan vibrated through him and into her.

He ripped his mouth away from hers and tugged the strap of her tank down with his teeth, nibbling the cap of her shoulder as he went.

Knuckles skimmed her ribs, pushing her shirt up. It had to go. Their hands tangled as they both tried to pull it over her head.

Libra placed his palms on the sides of her face, and gently tilted her chin up so he could look into her face. He placed a tender kiss on her forehead, the act so gentle, she had to blink away the sting trapped in the corner of her eyes.

Sliding his hands from her shoulders down her arms until his fingers entwined with hers, he stopped. He was giving her a moment, or perhaps he was taking one for himself. Cleo's lids, heavy, languid, dropped to half mast as she watched him, watched his face as his gaze drifted to her bared breasts, heard his ragged breath hitch.

Somehow, through the lump in her throat, she managed to whisper, "Touch me."

Okay, Studly, that was your cue—move! Kiss, pounce, ravage.

But Libra couldn't move, couldn't speak. The only thing he could hear was the blood pounding in his ears, rushing through his veins like a freaking buzz train.

He felt like he'd been given the biggest, shiniest box under the Christmas tree—the one present that everyone admired and hoped would be theirs. That moment of wonder, of awe that you should be so lucky, and that everyone around you was waiting, expectantly, to see how you'd react to whatever was inside.

Her exquisiteness overwhelmed him, froze him in time between breaths. She was a goddess and he a mere mortal. He didn't want to simply grab those luscious globes. Well, he did, *badly*, but he wanted to worship, not grope, so he steadied himself before moving his hands to the flare of her hips. He wanted to pull her into him, but then he couldn't look at her, so he moved her back.

He skimmed his fingers across the satin-soft skin of her torso and felt her muscles quiver under his touch. She squeaked as he grazed the underside of her breasts, trembled for him. It pleased him that she was as tightly strung as he was. As close to losing control as he was.

He brushed the pad of his thumb across her nipple, heard her broken sigh, just for him. He dropped to his knee and wrapped his hands around her waist, encircling her, holding her steady while he dragged his nose across her skin and inhaled her. He was transported right back to Mount Olympus, and his Goddess of Light smelled like heaven.

He captured her breast with his mouth, feeling the peak harden into a little pearl between his lips. He flicked it with his tongue, suckled it, let her fill his mouth. He felt her chest rise and fall with each breath, its rhythm quickening the harder he pulled her in. He backed off and blew on the wet skin before leaving it for the other. She tasted like she had in his dream, like the clouds, like the heavens. He couldn't get enough.

Cleo knit her fingers into his hair and muttered his name over and over, her husky chorus making his blood boil, making his cock so hard, it was painful. She moved to his shoulders, kneading and grasping, moaning low and deep so he could feel the vibrations under his mouth. If only his heart would stop pounding so hard in his ears because he wanted to hear every catch of her breath.

While his mouth drifted back and forth across her ribcage, devouring every inch of exposed flesh, he tried to tug her pants down, but they caught on her hip bones and the luscious curve of her ass. Her fingers pressed into his muscles with urgency, as anxious as he was to get to the next step.

As he mapped her torso with kisses, laved the silken skin around her belly button, he searched for the drawstring, but she'd rolled the waistband over and over and he couldn't find the zhanging ties and he was losing his patience, and he wanted more of her, immediately, this instant, *now*. Off, he needed them off. He needed her, needed to be *inside* her, *thrusting* into her. *Now*.

Gripping the banded material, he tried to snap the ties, but they wouldn't give. He wanted to squeeze the bare flesh of her ass, he wanted to feel the slick wetness of her pussy and if he had to tear the ridiculous pants off her, he damn well would.

Abruptly, she knocked his hands away.

He looked up between the valley of her breasts, past her swollen lips, her dewy-skinned cheeks, and met her half-closed eyes.

God, no. Don't make me stop, not now, I can't do it...

His heart pounded, on the verge of implosion, and the pain in his groin was practically unbearable.

"Too slow," she mumbled, pulling the leggings off herself.

Libra hadn't thought it possible to get any harder, but those two little words made his cock swell so big, he feared he'd split his own skin. Cleo had no idea what she did to him, had no idea that he hadn't been with a woman since before his incarceration, had no zhanging clue how much effort he was spending trying to maintain control.

Libra pulled his shirt off in a swift, one-handed move while she stepped out of her clothes. He didn't even stop to admire the view, just pounced on her, swept her legs out from under her, and lowered her to the air cushion. She didn't protest.

Nor did she when he pushed her legs open and nestled in the cradle of her hips. She wrapped her body around him and kissed him with a frantic urgency that matched his own.

Brushing her hair aside, he ran the flat of his tongue down and across the blade of her collarbone as she undulated beneath him. It took great willpower not to bite her, sink his teeth into her flesh, taste her, all of her, her essence, her blood, her muscle. Who was the savage now?

He rolled them onto their sides, his touch roaming freely down her back and over her ass. He trailed his finger up the smooth flesh of her inner thigh. She responded to his every touch with a mew or a quiver, propelling his need like no one had ever done, but he didn't want to take her higher yet. As close to the edge of control he was, he wanted to tease her, drag out the pleasure. This might be his only chance with her, and he wanted this to last.

He pulled her knee up high onto his hip and reached between them, fingering the soft damp curls at her apex. She whimpered into his neck when he breached her folds, already creamy and warm and so ready for him. He toyed with her, knowing exactly where to touch, how to tease the tight bundle of nerves to make her crazy. She was so intent on being first all the time, he'd make sure she came first tonight.

Cleo arched like a cat when he slid his middle finger deep into her tight, slick channel. She was so small, so snug.

"Please," she whispered. "More."

He added a finger, easing into her, stretching her so he wouldn't hurt her later. When her muscles contracted around him, he almost passed out as every drop of blood in his body converged in his cock.

Cleo Rush, with her tilty eyes and pillowy lips, rounded hips and deliciously curved ass—how they worked him, seduced him, entranced him. She made him lose his footing, made him dizzy. Made him hungry. He wanted to cause the same frenzy in her that he was feeling. Make her cells vibrate. He wanted to make her scream his name while she writhed beneath him, make her forget every other man she'd ever known.

He withdrew his fingers, slick with her essence, and trailed a creamy path over a breast and down to her navel, quickly following with his tongue before the night air could dry her skin. It was a heady preview of what was to come.

Libra traveled down her body, kissing and

laving a meandering line south. Her muscles tensed when he pushed her knees up and spread her thighs apart, but the breathy gasps were all the permission he needed to dip his tongue into her.

She tasted like the rain, fresh and pure, electric and uncontrollable.

"Yes, oh Libra, yes," she begged as he increased the pressure. He slid two fingers deep into her, hooking the tips. The other hand, he splayed over her pelvis to hold her steady as his concentrated on her hooded nub. He sucked, used the hard tip of his tongue to flick and stroke her until she panted his name, until her body grew taut, then quivered with release. He stayed there until the muscles of her abdomen stopped clenching, lapping up everything she had to offer.

He slid up her length and buried his face in her neck. "I want to be inside you."

"Yes," she whispered, dragging her fingers through his hair. "Yes, please, urbanite. I want you inside me."

Her voice was tinged with a sexy rasp that made her sound eager and reckless, a combination that shot though him like a strong aphrodisiac. Could he have stopped himself if she said no, pushed him away? No zhanging way.

Together, they managed to rid him of his shorts.

Cleo locked her arms around his neck and her ankles around his back.

He slid his cock up her slick seam and pressed the head against her clit, just to hear her gasp. He positioned himself at her entrance and pushed into her a few inches.

Cleo cried out softly and screwed her eyes shut.

"You okay, darlin'? Am I hurting you?" he asked. She was so hot and tight, he eased back to give her a moment to adjust.

Her breaths were quick and uncontrolled. "Fine, fine, I'm fine." She tightened her legs, coaxing him forward.

In one slow thrust, he was in heaven. He stayed, unmoving and buried deep, while Cleo's body pulsed around him. Libra sucked in his lower lip and bit down, fighting for control.

He withdrew slowly and thrust his hips again, deeper, harder, up to his balls. He found her mouth and swiped his lips across hers. "Stop wiggling," he whispered. If she kept it up, he wouldn't last another ten seconds.

"Can't help it," she said, nipping his lips. "My hips have a mind of their own."

She reached down and grabbed his ass, pulling him deeper still. Without withdrawing, he tilted his hips back and thrust forward again, grinding against her clit.

Cleo bit his shoulder, so he did it again.

Her fingernails scored his back, digging and gripping, begging him for more, giving him a distraction of pain with his pleasure. Urged by her moans, Libra surrendered. He drove into her until they matched one another pant for pant, grunt for grunt. Sweat trickled down his forehead as his blood turned to lava.

He dropped onto his forearms and slowed his pace, circling his hips with every grind. Cleo's eyes were wild, her pupils wide open. Her cheeks were aflame with heat, her lips puffy from the abuse he'd dealt. He reached between their bodies and barely grazed her swollen nub when she arched and dropped her head back, the muscles of her inner walls milking him. Whimpered cries of release sliced through the night.

One final thrust was all it took to set off his own blast of pleasure. The waves of release were so powerfully consuming, he'd decided, definitively, that Cleo Rush was the most sinfully wonderful creature on earth.

He collapsed onto her and rolled them onto their sides so he wouldn't crush her. Legs and arms entangled, they kissed, lazy, languidly, until they'd recovered enough to speak.

"Say it."

"Say what?" she asked.

"You know what. That you were first to orgasm."

"First and second," she replied. She

scraped her fingers over his forehead, down his nose and traced his lips. "But I don't think it works that way. You made it happen, so it's your win."

"Good point," he chuckled. "I'm first." He caught the tip of her index finger and sucked it to the first knuckle.

"In more ways than one," she whispered.

TWENTY-TWO

LIBRA'S FINGERS MADE SLOW CIRCLES at the small of her back while she relaxed in the afterglow. She couldn't make the line of her mouth straighten from the satisfied smile it had curled into, and she tingled in places she didn't know could tingle.

He didn't get it. She could tell by his lack of reaction that he didn't understand what she'd meant, that she was trying to tell him he was the first man she'd lain with. But it didn't bother her, not a bit. If he couldn't tell, it meant she hadn't done anything obviously wrong. Truthfully, after a certain point, she stopped thinking and just *did*. She let her body react without thought, without calculation, without caution. It hadn't hurt, much.

"Tell me more about you, Cleo Rush," he said, pushing his fingers through her hair before resuming the patterns on her back.

"What would you like to know?" she asked, willing to tell him anything, everything.

"I dunno. Tell me about growing up in the Taiga. What did you do for fun?" He dropped a playful kiss on her nose. "Besides terrorize your brother?"

"Actually, it was the other way around."

"I don't believe it for a second."

"Really? Where do you think I got my competitiveness from, who do you think I learned *first* from? Big brother won every race, every game of hide-and-seek, was the first to complete his homework, first to eat his vegetables... It was a never-ending fight to the finish between him and me."

"But it was all in fun, right?"

"Most of the time. Sometimes it got a little more serious." And sometimes it got downright ugly. She wanted to win so badly and to hear her father say, "Good job," like he'd say to Jaegar, but when she started winning, that little phrase seemed to have disappeared from his vocabulary, making her victories seem small and inconsequential. It made her feel dirty, like she'd cheated or played unfairly. Which wasn't true... most of the time.

"I imagine you had to be pretty clever to beat an older and presumably stronger big brother."

"Oh, Jag tops me by a foot so thanks for

recognizing that I had to put some brains behind my wins."

"Tell me more," he asked drowsily. He'd moved from her back to drag his fingers up and down the length of her arm. His touch was unnerving and sensual all at once. She wanted him to stop so she could concentrate on their conversation, but she never wanted him to stop. Ever.

Aside from the occasional sucker punch from Jaegar, she'd been denied any kind of meaningful physicality for so long that she wasn't used to it. She couldn't recall ever having a hug from her father and her Gram had been dead for years. Suddenly, she couldn't bear the thought of never having it again and it was crucial that she to earn Libra's touch, his continued affection.

"There was this one time, we were in a competition," Cleo began, wondering how much to reveal about the leadership race. "Think of it as a combined hunting-survival skills sort of thing. But we went into it blind, with absolutely no idea what the challenge would entail. They dump this bag of supplies out, and we, the five of us—I'm the only girl left by this point—have to run across an obstacle course to get to the stash, and we can only take two things from the pile. I'm fast, but these guys have a long-leg advantage, so I get there in the middle of the pack. By then,

Jag has the rope and machete. Simon and I both go for the axe, but that nasty-ass badger snatches it right out of my hand—see that pink line on the inside of my thumb? Never mind, it's too dark. I'll show you in the morning. But it's from the blade sliding through my fingers, the dirty bastard."

He held her hand up so he could see by firelight. "Looks pretty fresh," he said, bringing her hand to his lips as if a kiss could erase it.

"Because it only happened last month," she whispered, swallowing the emotion his action invoked. "Anyway, I take a can of bear grease and a small throwing knife and leave the wire, fish hooks, and moose jerky for the other two."

"Bear grease? I don't even want to know what that is."

"Just what you think it is. Bear fat."

"Odd choice."

"You'd think, but I had a hunch, so I grabbed it."

"So what was your task?" he asked, propping up on one elbow.

"We had three days to make it to a rendezvous point on the shore of the Dead Lake. Once there, we'd be given further instruction. So the first part was simply survival and transportation. Jag was laughing. He had the rope and machete so spent half a day making a raft, another half day hiking it to the river, and managed to make it to the lake in two days. Simon tried—he had the axe, after all, but couldn't bind the logs together well enough with vine, so it kept falling apart. Everything was too green and tender, so it kept snapping. Fibrous vines work best once they've dried out—every idiot knows that—but he kept at it, cursing and swearing enough to offend the elder council overseer. Meanwhile, me and the other two head out on foot, so it takes the full three days at a half-run."

"How did you survive three days in the forest with no supplies?"

"Are you kidding? It's me... Remember how I caught that trout? And there were berries, roots, all kinds of things."

"What about fire, shelter, protection from wild animals?"

"Can you see my eyes rolling in this light?" she laughed. "Please, Libra. I've been surviving in this forest since I was old enough to walk."

He pushed her hair from her forehead, as if to get a better view of her eyes, then continued to finger-comb her tresses away from her face. She would purr if she could. "Where was I?"

"You, conquering nature."

"Right. So I get to the rendezvous a couple of hours ahead of the other three to see Jag wearing an expression so smug, I wanted to smack it off him."

"Did he *first* you."

"You know he did," she replied. "He'd spent his extra day repairing the raft from the journey downriver, except now, he'd coated it with pine resin because—and here comes the good part, so pay very close attention. Our task is to open a huge wooden trunk that looked as if it had been washed ashore. It's banded with steel and sealed with a metal padlock the size of my fist. And the key is sunk in twenty feet of water."

"In the Dead Lake? But it's acid!"

"Exactly!" she said, unable to keep the excitement out of her voice.

"So Jag has the raft. All he has to do is fish for it," Libra said.

"Yes, but he doesn't have the hooks or wire, so he's trying to make a tiny lasso out of frayed rope, but he doesn't have enough, so he's got to trim some from his raft, which compromises the structure. Simon shows up with his axe and starts hacking at the trunk, which is ludicrous because this thing is huge and solid as a brick and he practically wipes himself out trying to break into the thing."

"So the guy with the wire wins, right? He can fashion a hook, throw it into the water, and snag the key."

"You'd think. But he decided he was going to try and pick the lock, and the other one, the one with the fish hook, sat there dumfounded, twirling his little hook around in his finger and bashing his head with his fist."

"Why didn't he team up with wire-guy?"

"Couldn't. Against the rules."

"And what was my clever Cleo doing?"

"*Cleo* had stripped down to her skin and was coating herself in gobs of bear grease."

"I'm turned on and repulsed all at once." Libra gave her hair a playful tug. "Why would you do that?"

"With the exception of Jag, the others stopped what they were doing to watch, which was part of my evil plan to buy myself some time," she chuckled. "And the grease protected my skin from the water."

"You... Oh no, you didn't. Please tell me you didn't go in."

"I did. I swam to where the flag was floating above the skeleton key, shut my eyes tight, and dove. It took me about three tries, but I finally got that sucker."

"And you didn't burn?"

"Nah. It's not quite as bad as everyone thinks."

He rubbed her arms and back, as if brushing away the harmful toxins. "It's acid, darlin'. It's as bad as everyone thinks."

"When I was little, my father, Jag and I were on the river a bit up from the Dead Lakes. I guess they were busy doing whatever they were doing and didn't notice that I'd waded down to the mouth of the stream, right where it flows into the lake. They heard me crying. I'd been standing in the lake for a few minutes before they pulled me out. I had mild burns on my skin, but the flesh didn't bubble and melt off like they tell us it will. The water was diluted enough by the stream water that I didn't notice at first, but I do remember feeling a tingling the further I went out. Then it started to prickle, like when you step into water that's really hot."

He squeezed her closer, as if protecting the little crying girl. "So what happened after you got the key?"

"I waded back onto the beach—"

"Wait. I need a mental picture. Are you still naked?"

Cleo laughed. "Very, but I'm covered in thick yellow grease, so whatever your man-brain is thinking, it's not like that."

"My man-brain can see through that yellow goop. Don't you worry."

"Are you going to let me finish?"

"Kiss me first."

Cleo leaned in and pressed her lips on his, then pulled back before he could deepen in. "So I stick that key in the lock, open the trunk, and yell—"

"First!" They said it simultaneously.

"Yes, I figured," he chuckled. "Then

what happened?"

"Then I spent the next week trying to wash the bear grease out of my hair."

"You're ingenious and brave."

"I know," Cleo said with a satisfied smile. Despite what happened afterwards, that was a great day. She felt so good, so confident, that she worked up the nerve to explore him. She started by tracing the contours of his bicep and shoulder.

"You seem pretty competitive, yourself," she said. "Do you have any siblings to spar with?"

"I had an older sister. Libby. She died."

"I'm sorry," Cleo said, stopping to cup his cheek.

"It was a long time ago. She was ten."

"What happened?"

"To be honest, I don't remember it all that well. I don't even remember *her* that well. I was only six when she died, and we didn't do much together. She couldn't play with me because she would tire easily, spent most of her days confined to bed."

"Poor little girl. She must have hated that."

"Her skin was so pale that I would trace the bluish veins on her jaw when she read to me. I remember thinking she was a ghost, or an angel."

"What was wrong with her?"

"Her lungs were weak. She caught a

virus when she was a baby, and it left permanent damage."

"So tragic," Cleo said, pushing back the lock of hair that had fallen across his forehead. She continued raking her fingers through the mess of thick blond tangles while inside, her heart twisted for the little boy who lost his angel.

"I've never told anyone this before," he said, holding her gaze, "but I think I resented her because we couldn't do the things that other families did. It was always 'poor Libby can't manage it' or 'it's not good for Libby'."

Libra averted his eyes. "And after Libby died, things were worse. My mother couldn't cope with it all. She withdrew so much that talking to her was like trying to communicate with...with a...a piece of toast. She didn't say no, didn't say yes, so I sort of did whatever I wanted."

"What about your father? How did he cope with Libby's death?"

She felt his muscles tense. "He died. Before Libby."

"That must have been horrible for your mom."

"Yeah. It's probably why she was so protective of Lib. Though I didn't understand that at the time." He shrugged as if to shake the memories. It must have been painful to discuss, but she wanted to know if it turned out okay, how that hurting little Libra turned into this big, charming, lovable, gentle man.

The lump in Cleo's throat made it hard to speak. "Do...do you remember what he was like?"

"Not really. He was gone a lot."

"Oh." The tightness in her chest prevented her from saying anything else. She could feel his pain as if it were her own. His father gone, his mother's love used up on his sick sister who eventually left, too. And a mom who emotionally abandoned him. As the sadness seeped from her heart into her bones, she shivered.

"You cold?" he asked. She nodded against him, too afraid to speak as she fought tears. Warriors didn't cry. Except maybe for little boys. She bit the inside of her lip and blinked the sting out of her eyes as he cuddled her closer.

"Your turn," he said, his voice understandably a bit rough. "Tell me about your father."

Cleo pressed her fingers into his muscles, trying to massage the tension out of them. He clearly was only being polite in asking, as this was an obvious sore topic for him. Maybe she should tell him the truth? That having a father could be just as damaging as not having one. Maybe not. No use killing the dream.

"His name is Lewin and he's... he's...an

amazing leader. Everyone loves him, respects him, especially other Taiga leaders. Did you know that he's responsible for the trading post system on the Cut Road?"

His eyes were closed, but he gave his head a shake, so she knew he wasn't sleeping.

"His motto is 'Need, Not Greed,' so he's big on sharing our resources, and he discourages excess and waste. He's generous and kind to everyone and gives every issue, every problem, every decision considerable thought. And he's usually very fair, except when he deems it petty, like who tossed the rock furthest in the slingshot competition, when I clearly had a height disadvantage of at least a foot... but *never mind*."

She felt the vibrations in his chest as he chuckled. "Not one you agreed with, I take it?"

"Well, come on. It wasn't like I was asking for a distance handicap. I just wanted to stand on a stump for the tie-breaker."

"Okay, so he's the perfect leader? What about as a father?"

Cleo pressed her lips together. He tapped her backside as if to prompt her, but she didn't know what to say without appearing disloyal.

"Much like your mother, I suppose," she said softly. "I never knew him before...before my mother died, you know, so I can't really compare. But my grandmother said he used to be different. Warm, jovial, the life of a potlatch—more like how my brother is now. There are a lot of pictures of him smiling and laughing, but I don't think, in my whole life, I've ever seen him smile." Cleo felt Libra's arms tighten around her, and that little show of support made her want to go on. Spill the hurtful truth.

"No matter how hard I tried—I got good grades, won competitions, learned to play an instrument—but nothing made him happy. He'd just give a nod without even looking at me. God, Libra. I tried so hard to be everything to him—perfect daughter, cook, seamstress— but it was all for naught. Everything Jag did was rewarded, so I figured he just didn't know how to treat me because I was a girl, so I decided to be a boy. Cut my hair off and started hunting and fishing with Jag, tried to learn everything he knew. But still I didn't get taken on the father-son trips to the post or to tribal meetings. It was always just him and Jag while I got left with my grandma."

Libra was quietly regarding her, his face intent, empathetic. Whatever it was, she felt like he cared, like he wanted to know. So she told him.

She bit the inside of her cheek. "He never looked at me. Never. He looks past me, over me, behind me, but my own father has never looked at me, in my face." The pressure in her chest grew to an unbearable level, but she couldn't stop, couldn't *not* tell this man her deepest, ugliest secret. "Because of this," she said, scrubbing her cheek with her knuckles as if she could erase the scar. "This hideous thing."

Cleo felt tears prick the corners of her eyes, hot and unwelcome, but couldn't stop them, couldn't stop until she got the words out. "I look like her, like my mother, except for *this*, and he can't take it. I'm a repulsive version of her."

Libra held her face in his hands and placed the most tender and precious kisses on her forehead, on each her eyelid, on her nose. His lips fell softly, like butterfly wings, a balm for her wounded inner child. He took her hand away from her cheek and traced the length of the marred line with his finger before following it with his lips, right to the notch on the shell of her ear. She hadn't realized he'd seen it under her hair, but somehow he did. No words could penetrate her self-consciousness, her self-loathing, like his kisses did.

He wiped her tears with the pad of his thumb, then put it to his mouth to lick the salt off. And when her chin finally stopped quivering, he kissed her mouth, deepening it until a welcomed longing stirred in her belly, until she didn't care about her father, or her scar, or her childhood, or Jag, or anything but the unendurable heat between them.

Libra reached behind her knee and pulled her leg up over his hip, never breaking contact with her mouth. She assumed he'd roll her onto her back, but he held her in place, on their sides, face to face. He tucked his length into her in an agonizingly slow thrust that sent a wave of tingling heat radiating through her.

Cleo tilted her hips and rocked into him. Physically and emotionally, they were synched. There was no awkwardness, no fumbling, no nervousness, almost as if they'd been together forever; they were effortlessly in tune.

Libra stopped their lazy play of tongues to trace the line of her jaw with his teeth, sending a new set of vibrations to her core. Her nerve endings sang under his touch.

They explored each other with fingertips, unhurried, uninhibited. He drew patterns on her shoulder, her neck, her breasts, as if he were writing secret messages all over her body. Slipping his hand between them, he touched that glorious spot between her legs that made her eyelids flutter. He circled it slowly, with just the right amount of pressure to send white-hot bolts of erotic electricity through her nervous system, making her nipples tingle, her toes curl, her back arch.

Libra's breathing quickened along with his thrusts, but he waited until her pleasure crested before succumbing to his own orgasm and clung to her until they drifted back to earth.

"That was amazing," she slurred, unable to open her eyes.

"Sleepy?" he whispered, rolling onto his back and pulling her in close.

"Mm-hmm," she replied, snuggling against him and feeling more relaxed than she had in...ever.

TWENTY-THREE

THREE TIMES. THEY'D MADE LOVE three times, but it was the fun stuff they'd done in between each session that made her feel enveloped in warmth—the touching, the tickling, exploring each other:, mind, body, and soul.

Everything felt swollen and sore—her lips, her nipples, between her legs—but it was a glorious hurt. It was the kind of fiery tenderness that made her feel alive, giddy, and she wanted to shout it to the world.

Gone was the worry that he found her an offensive, savage Taiga girl. Tonight, he'd made her feel revered. He touched her with such affection, watched her with an enrapt expression, and listened to every word she spoke as if every syllable were sacrosanct.

Libra the outsider had morphed into

her knight in shining armor, her rescuer, her physical equal, her—*dare she think it?*—soul mate.

It was hard to ignore their similar upbringings despite the fact they grew up in different worlds; each had a parent die under tragic circumstances, and both were raised by emotionally absent, single parents. Both were competitive, hungry to learn, and discover new insights.

Libra brought her back from death. That had to be a sign they were fated. And the fact he was willing to help her navigate the city and find her brother elevated him to godlike status. Her own personal body-guard-escort-lover.

"We should sleep," she murmured, tracing the contour of his face with the tip of her index finger, awed by the perfection of his silhouette against the embers. "We've got to get an early start."

"You do realize it's almost dawn, right?"

"What? No," she said. "Can't be." Could it? She was too tired to roll over and check the eastern sky.

Libra caressed her arm as she slid deeper into a warm drowsy state, each stroke spreading another layer of warmth around her heart.

She tried not to think in terms of *'what's next'*, but it was hard not to imagine a future with this man, unbearable to think of one without him.

Considering she was probably homeless—she had yet to tell him *that* story—maybe she'd hang out awhile in Gomeda. Maybe he'd even ask her stay. Maybe the city wasn't as bad as she'd heard. Then again, it might be easier to convince Libra to move north and the two of them could join one of the Acadian tribes, or Prairie tribes. She fell asleep dreaming of a life together with her unexpected champion.

———

While he waited for her breathing to deepen, for her body to go completely loose and relaxed so he could make a move, he let his fingers drift up and down her flesh, amazed at how she could be so strong and so soft all at once.

After tonight, he was acutely aware of how innocent she was. Not immature, but naively mature. The bravely masked hurt in her voice as she told him about her father.

It made him hate Lewin Rush even more.

Libra knew only too well what it was like to fight for a parent's attention, but when Cleo put voice to feelings that he never realized he himself felt, it made his relationship with his own mother more real, more...damaging. He, too, tried his best to get straight A's in math and science, just like his father, but his efforts seemed to make her close up even tighter.

They were the same, but different. Where

his mother was a grieving widow, a shell of a woman who'd lost her only daughter to sickness that couldn't be cured, Cleo's father was a cold-hearted, murdering bastard.

Would it lessen Cleo's pain if she knew? Would his approval be so necessary if she realized who she'd been trying to impress?

But he couldn't tell her. Wouldn't tell her. Couldn't hurt her, even for the sake of healing her.

He felt her body slacken against his.

He should go.

A few more minutes to enjoy her post-coital warmth. Perhaps he should blame it on his incarceration with a bunch of violent testosterone-dripping dirt bags, but Libra never knew it could be this way with a woman. That the primal act of rocking and thrusting while looking into one another's eyes could be so cathartic, so liberating. They were healing each other with their bodies, patching their wounded souls, and when they finally came, together, they created a bond that was indescribably exquisite. He envied the tears that spilled down her cheeks as much as he envied her ability to release them, proof that it was as meaningful for her as it was to him.

He certainly never remembered sex ever having such a profound effect before. The third round, when she'd climbed on top of him, inhibitions set aside... for the love of all things wild, that girl blew his mind.

But just a few more minutes, to make sure she was really asleep, before he had to revert to his asshole self. What a mess, a gigantic zhanging disaster—but he'd find a way to get them out of it, find a way to make everything right for both of them. For all of them. Jaegar too. Even Achan.

He needed to go.

He didn't want to. Not yet.

Libra let his mind play, wondering what life would have been like for both of them if Cleo's father hadn't killed his, if his mother wasn't perpetually stoned. Would he and Cleo have met under different circumstances? Maybe have met at the Trading Post? Been sweethearts, lovers?

Libra cautiously slipped his arm out from underneath her, not so difficult with the air pillow cushioning them, and rearranged the blanket so she wouldn't feel the damp night air when he rolled away.

He got up and looked down at her one last time before grabbing his pack and quietly heading into the woods. In sleep, she looked so delicate and vulnerable, the antithesis of the capable, sexy woman she turned into by the light of day, with sparks in her eyes and acid in her words.

What if they hadn't met? If he'd stayed at the penal colony and refused Achan's offer like every fiber of his being warned—and that he thankfully ignored? Libra shivered, the bitter cold biting his bones, and it had nothing to do with the weather.

He couldn't imagine not knowing her, not wanting her—sexually, intellectually—always.

TWENTY-FOUR

"WELL, WELL, WELL, WHAT DO we have here?" Cleo, ripped from sleep by an unfamiliar masculine voice, rolled sideways off the air cushion before her eyes were fully open. The malice in his tone catapulted her into high-octane adrenal overload. Springing to her feet, Cleo twisted from side to side and gave her head a shake to clear any remnants of dullness.

They were outsiders, three of them, confining her in triangle formation. Libra's friends? No. Matching buzzcuts, camouflage, and monster-muscles that could only be achieved through serious conditioning and medical intervention. They could only be one thing.

Soldiers.

Gomedan Guards. Huge mother-buzzards.

Cleo swallowed and shifted her weight from foot to foot, trying but failing to keep them all in her line of sight. She and Libra were in for a fight.

Speaking of Libra... A quick flick of her eyes found no sign of him or his backpack. What the hell?

"Looks like we found ourselves a lost little savage," said the one behind her.

"And she's dressed for the occasion. Lucky us."

The eerie chuckle that followed sent a shiver of fear from the back of her neck all the way down to her heels. Why didn't she put her clothes back on during the night?

Because Libra kept her warm.

Where is he?

They moved towards her, circling, like hungry wolves.

Please don't let me die like my mother.

A cold fist of terror gripped her insides, forced the oxygen from her lungs, disabled her ability to call out or scream. She fought the suffocating feeling of impending doom, willing herself to focus, focus, focus. She wouldn't die with indignity, wouldn't leave Jag in Gomeda, wouldn't leave this earth before redeeming herself to her tribe, her father.

She would *not* die like her mother.

Anger pushed the panic from her lungs, replaced it with the instinct to survive. She took down a feral alphacat, damn it. She could take down three oaf-sized outsiders.

"Did she just growl? Fucking hell, man, did you guys hear that?"

"Zhanging *animal!*"

Cleo bent her knees slightly to lower and stabilize her center of gravity. Speed and dexterity were the only advantages she had against their bulky upper bodies and tree-trunk legs.

She needed a weapon. Her mind flitted through her options—

Libra's knife would come in handy about now. *Where the hell is he?*

Fire. Less than ten feet away, but they'd be on her before she reached the pit.

Rocks. It took only a nanosecond to see there were none around her feet big enough to do any serious damage. But if she threw it at the fire, sent sparks...

As if reading her mind, one of the Guards picked up her leathers, held them to his nose, and with a nod to the others, tossed them on top of the embers, smothering her only hope.

They crept closer still, circling to intimidate, their arms out, hands spread, caging her in. She tuned out their words, their crude comments about her body... Had to, or she'd succumb to the terror. Steeling herself, Cleo pressed her back teeth hard enough to make her jaw ache. She was ready.

Playing the helpless girl, she cowered as they drew closer, whimpered, "P-Please, don't hurt m-me."

The two within her line of sight exchanged a quick glance. One smiled. *Sick bastard.*

She inhaled sharply, taking in their scents, feeding off the charged air around her as if it were a source of pure energy. She felt the ground vibrate off her right flank. She could see him in her peripheral, edging in behind her, probably to hold her arms while the others pawed her.

Focus! Don't let the fear in.

A clear mind to anticipate their movements—it was the only way to win.

Timing was critical. Without taking her eyes off Smiley in front of her, Cleo shifted her weight and shot a leg out straight behind her. The ball of her foot smashed into a hard midsection. "Oaf!"

Smiley reacted just as she expected—by raging straight at her. She dug her heels in the soft dirt and dropped into a crouch. Smiley tried to stop himself, but his momentum propelled him forward. When he was almost on top of her, she dropped her chin and thrust upward, catching his midsection with her shoulders and propelling him up and over her.

She round-housed the third brute when he approached from the left. She spun and ducked, avoiding a punch from the one in back, who'd recovered far too quickly from her first kick. When his fist struck nothing but air, he stumbled forward, giving Cleo the perfect opening. Falling onto her palms, she swung her body sideways in a double leg sweep, knocking him flat on his ass. This time, he let out a painful grunt.

On her way back up, she grabbed a rock the size of an apple. Not much of a weapon, but it would do.

Cleo felt a rush of air behind her. Without turning, she drove her bent arms back, striking both assailants in the ribs with the hard edge of her elbows. She spun and landed a solid uppercut to the soft underside of Smiley's jaw, this time sending him stumbling backwards. He tripped over her bedding and landed on his back at the edge of the dying fire. Her arm juddered from fingers to shoulder from the impact.

A blast of pain ripped through her, radiating from her back like the tongues of a thousand blue flames. Someone had gotten in a kidney punch. Cleo bit back a cry as she sank to her knees. Her attacker stopped her descent by wrapping his ropey forearm around her neck, then pulled her into the brick wall of his chest.

Cleo had to get out of this position of vulnerability. Now. Before breathing became an issue. Before she lost it like the Banger she used the same move on.

Don't panic. Panic will kill you. Focus. Focus, focus, focus...

His other hand found her breast, pinched her nipple, hard. The sharp pain stoked her resolve. She would not die like her mother. While he groped, she thrust her head backward with all her might, catching him in the mouth with enough force to loosen a few teeth. Without a thought to the screaming pain ripping through her skull and lower back, she dodged his hold, turned, and drove her bony kneecap into his balls with every ounce of rage-filled strength she had.

He went down with a breathless squeak.

Without hesitation, Cleo spun, drew her arm back and, just as Smiley got up from his cozy spot next to the fire, drilled him in the forehead with the rock.

Damn, kicking ass felt way better than it should.

As for Libra, she was going to kick *his* ass when she found him, leaving her alone to be set upon by three rogue soldiers.

Before the trio could recover, Cleo grabbed the only garments left—Libra's thermal leggings and the shirt-to-beat-your-wife-in—and made for the river, dressing as she ran.

She had to find Libra.

The back of her head stung like devil spit

and the soles of her feet were being shredded by the rock and pine needles as she ran at top speed. She glanced over her shoulder, blinking to clear her watery vision, and sighted two of the goon squad moving amongst the trees.

"Libra!" she hissed. What if they got to him first? Killed him while she slept? What other reason could there be for his absence? What could have kept him from coming when he heard her struggling?

"Libra!" It was more than a breathy plea than the shout she'd intended.

She stumbled onto the narrow bank of the creek, trying to decide which way to run, when she spotted Libra.

He was very much alive and kneeling a few yards downstream, seemingly oblivious to the drama behind her.

"Libra? Didn't you hear me? Run! Why are you just..." Goose bumps erupted and her feet froze in midstride, her body cued to the danger her mind had time to process.

Libra's head was bowed but his pale eyes gazed up at her through his eyelashes. He didn't seem shocked to see her, nor did he speak or acknowledge her in any way. His mouth was set in a hard line and his eyes looked empty, devoid of any emotion.

"Libra?" She took a wary step toward him. "What's going on?" The muscles of his shoulders were hunched, coiled with tension, and she realized that his hands were behind his back, as if bound.

"Looking for us?" A man emerged from behind a bushy evergreen to stand next to Libra. Though dressed in sightseer clothes—hiking boots and a backpack—he shared the same bristled cut and menacing look as the men who attacked her.

And he had a gun pressed against Libra's temple.

The flat black disk he flipped between the fingers of this other hand looked familiar, like the one she'd found in Libra's stuff, except it was rimmed with a green light.

"Get away from him," she said, drawing in her strength for another fight. She had to get him away from Libra before the others caught up. She felt every bit as ferocious as a polar grizzly protecting its young. She shifted her weight onto the balls of her feet, ready to spring. "You want food? Supplies? Take what you came for and leave before I kill you."

"That's the thing," he grinned. He swung the barrel of the gun towards her, pointed it straight toward the middle of her chest. "I came for you, *Cleo Rush.*"

She didn't even hear the bang before her world went black.

TWENTY-FIVE

C LEO AWOKE TO NO LINGERING grogginess, no hazy vision, no sense of time having passed. Her eyes opened as if she'd merely blinked, her nerves still humming with adrenaline, fully aware that she was in danger.

But how much?

She was alive, all systems go, no identifiable pain anywhere in her body. The last thing she remembered was looking down the barrel of a gun. Why wasn't there any blood, or pain, other than the dull throb in the back of her head?

She was still somewhere in the Taiga, bound and alone.

Oh God, Libra... She couldn't let her thoughts go there, couldn't let her imagination run away with the possibility that he might be hurt. Or dead.

She squirmed, tugged, and twisted, but her position—hands tied behind her back and joined to her ankles—left her helpless, unable to roll anywhere but onto her tummy. Libra's thin shirt did nothing to protect her skin from the uneven, rocky ground beneath her, so any movement was hard on the ribs. Determined to escape, desperate to find Libra, she persisted until sweat stung her eyes and her heart felt as if it would bang right out of her chest.

Fear and frustration gnawed her. She needed to get the hell out of there before those men came back, but the squirming only made the knots tighter.

You're a trained warrior. Tap your skills.

Slowly inhaling, ten counts in, three counts out, Cleo decelerated her heart rate. Best she could, she blocked out the pain in her arms and legs and visualized the blood in her veins as it coursed through her, feeding her cells. She focused on the air around her, the smell, the taste, the pressure and movement. She listened. She felt. Within minutes, her body was fully relaxed, her mind opened to incoming stimuli.

It was after mid-day—the sun was already well past its apex. She counted four species of common forest birds within her immediate vicinity, but no animals—no rodents, snakes, nothing—which indicated that there had been a significant amount of human movement in the area recently. But the birds had returned, which told her it had been quiet for at least ten, fifteen minutes. Maybe longer.

She could smell water. If it was a river, it was either very big or very slow because she couldn't hear any rippling, running, or splashing. Last evening, she'd estimated that they were twelve to fifteen foot miles from the Trading Post. Now she had to figure out how far the Guards could have taken them, considering they had one, possibly *two* unconscious, bodies.

She had to know if Libra was all right.

If those goons had some kind of transportation, they could already be near the St. Mary, just miles away from the Trading Post. Or they could have gone west over the north shore of Superior. If that were the case, they could be close to the Dead Zone, which meant there was little hope of escape. There would be no forest to hide in, nothing she could use to fight back, to survive.

The wind shifted and carried snippets of conversation. The voices weren't loud, but they were certainly intense. She focused, filtered out nature's symphony to extract only that which she needed to hear.

Libra! He was alive. And he sounded angry.

"...told you I could handle it! Zhang-hell!" Cleo strained to hear what he was saying, but she only picked up the odd word or phrase. "...

coming willingly. You think she'll cooperate after this? What the hell kind of moronic—"

"No, *you* put this mission at jeopardy when you fucked her. *Not acceptable!* There are reasons we do not engage these savages—"

"She's not..." Libra's voice, unlike the other man's, was being swept into the wind. Perhaps he'd turned his back. A few seconds passed before Cleo picked up the conversation again.

"She is our prisoner and our instructions are clear." It was the other man's voice. "Now, get out of my sight and finish the job."

"I'm not... alone with you."

"But I don't *take* orders from you. You *will* go. You *will* be accompanied by Frith and Hinton. You *will* follow orders and do as you're told or I'll tell Cade you're a tribe-lover like your savage-lover of a father... *Put your goddamn fist down, son, before you...*"

Something hummed to life, drowning out the voice.

Cleo's head thunked to the ground as she tried to make sense of what she'd heard. No matter how badly she wanted to deny it, it became as obvious as a punch to the gut—Libra was with them. He was *with them.*

Drowning was an agony she wouldn't wish on her mortal enemy, but this hurt ten times worse. His betrayal cut at her insides, deep and gouging. She tried to curl her knees into her tummy but the rope pulled taut, leaving her writhing in the dirt against the physical pain.

She had trusted him. She let him into her mind. *She let him into her body.*

Cleo squeezed her thighs together, the flesh still tender, still throbbing from his invasion.

He'd befriended her, made love to her, and handed her over to the Guard, Achan's Elite. The same men that murdered her mother.

Don't trust outsiders.

Her father had drilled that into their heads. By the time she and Jaegar were teens, they'd roll their eyes and mouth the words behind him. They mocked Lewin Rush, but in the end, he was right. And Cleo was proven the fool. Again. Was there no end to her stupidity?

All the training, all the competitions, all the winning, yet nothing prepared her for Libra's kisses, for the way his hands moved over her body so reverently. The depth of emotion in his eyes when he entered her, filled her. God, she was so naïve, so stupid to think that she meant something to him, that their act of sex was lovemaking, not just...screwing.

Her tummy lurched, bringing bile to her throat.

Libra was a tool for Achan Cade, the man who destroyed her family.

For pity's sake, why did it have to hurt so much?

She lifted her head a few inches from the

ground and let it drop, then lifted it again and let it drop, over and over until the ache spread from inside her chest to her skull, a small punishment for her imprudent behaviour.

How could he, her knight in shining armor, be associated with a massive creep like Achan Cade? He wasn't army, clearly didn't have much in the way of training for survival in the wilderness. For the love of all things scaly, the man couldn't even fish! Most importantly, Libra had spent too long in the Taiga and would have been caught if he were a soldier. She wasn't sure how her people tracked soldiers who came past the Cut—something to do with their communications network, she believed, but she'd overheard Lewin and Jag discussing their c-net tracking. She regretted not paying closer attention. But Libra wasn't tracked, so he couldn't be like Trevayne. If the inter-tribal alarms had been triggered, every available warrior within a thousand square miles would have been all over them.

So no, Libra couldn't work for the Guard. But assuming as much didn't compensate for the fact that he handed her over like a trapped muskrat.

Cleo's head pounded from the hard ground, lack of water, lack of sleep, and abject humiliation. To think he was doing those *things* to her because he had to. Oh God, he must have been cringing inside, laughing at her. Did he even grow up with a single mom, or was it all an elaborate cover story so they'd have something in common? So she'd stupidly opened her heart to him. *Stupid, stupid, stupid. Naïve and stupid and stubborn and...* The shame was unbearable.

At least she could cling to the fact that those suspicions she'd had when they'd met weren't totally off. Her instincts hadn't flared up for nothing. And looking back, she ignored some pretty obvious clues. The K-Bar knife—definitely Guard issue. Not too many sightseers could afford a fine piece like that. And that damn black disc—the red flags were flapping in her face, and she had ignored them. Basic warrior training: trust your instincts.

So back to the original question, the one she should have pursued from the beginning but had been too afraid to ask because she hadn't wanted the answer. *Who is Libra?*

Cleo lost track of time as she lay on the hard ground and vacillated between anger and hurt. If she spent less time on revenge plots and more time figuring out how to get out of her current bind, she might not still be stuck like a rabbit in a snare when she heard the whirring noise.

Something or someone was coming at her through the bush. She took a deep breath, ready to scream her fool-head off if Libra appeared. Over the top of the shrubs and long grasses, the head and shoulders of a man appeared. Not Libra. It was the one who'd shot her. His movements were smooth, as if he were flying toward her.

Solar board. He sailed a few feet above the ground on a sleek black board, slowing as he approached. The low-profile wheels weren't engaged, but he hovered high enough for her to see the bottom of the rims sticking out from below.

Determined to show a brave face, she clamped her jaw and hoped he couldn't see her chest pounding against the flimsy shirt.

"Ah, Petal. You're awake!" A thousand bugs crawled over her skin at the sound of his voice. She squirmed, pulling against her restraints as he pulled up on the t-bar handle, hovering directly above her. The heat from the solar cells around the board's perimeter made the air shimmer, so when he looked down at her, lips pulled back in a twisted grimace, his face looked wavy, contorted. "Time for a cozy little chat, just the two of us."

TWENTY-SIX

Frick and Frack—Libra couldn't remember what Trevayne called them, so he made up his own names—flanked him on both sides though the corridor was far too narrow to accommodate three vehicles abreast. He twisted the throttle and gave his board as much speed as possible so they didn't have time to duck and swerve around low-hanging branches. It was very satisfying hear them curse as bows thwacked their faces. These assholes got physical with Cleo, and that sat all kinds of wrong with him.

The argument with Trevayne put him in an extra foul mood. The Colonel attempted to dump everything on Libra, but it was *he* who compromised the mission by coming past the Cut. If detected, they'd be standing before the United World Council courts for breach of security by the end of the week.

Asshole.

Libra squinted into wind. Not much farther, thankfully. He needed to turn around and get back to Cleo as soon as humanly possible.

He couldn't figure out how Trevayne found him. He hadn't activated his satcom, which was the only way the Colonel could have found his precise location...unless he accidently thumbed it when he had shoved his things in his pack, trying to hide the ampoule from Cleo. All it took for the biorhythm to register was a swipe. Zhang hell, he should have been more careful.

Cleo. His teeth ached thinking of her, unconscious and helpless. It gutted him to leave her behind, but Trevayne had him by the balls, and until he could figure out how to get Cleo out safely, he had to make nice and let Achan's Elite think he was playing along. And as long as she remained in the nerve coma, Trevayne wouldn't hurt her. Libra knew guys like the Colonel, power-hungry cretins who got off on bullying women and children, and they preferred prey that squirmed, prey that fought back, and Cleo wasn't a challenge in her current state. She couldn't feed his penultimate power—that could only be fueled by fear.

They pulled up to the Cut Road and let Libra go across alone with the shopping list.

Technically, the Guard *could* enter the Trading Post, but Trevayne didn't want anyone to know they were there, and those two buffoons were hard to miss.

The third member of their little extraction troop had been sent packing, tail between his legs, back to Gomeda after "the poncy flower let a little girl ruffle him," as Trevayne put it. Libra fist-pumped when he learned that Cleo had broken the jerk's ribs. His girl did some sweet damage. He really wanted to ask Frick about the painful-looking purple lump on his forehead but didn't want to antagonize the situation.

When Trevayne activated her implant, Libra thought he was going to pop a blood vessel. Bastard had override controls, unbeknownst to him. How stupid to not have predicted their underhandedness. How could he have been so trusting? Fresh from a deprived life in the penal colony, he'd palmed the nifty little device and thought nothing beyond *cool toy... Wonder if I get to keep it when the mission's done* instead of thinking with his brain, the one that would have told him to watch his zhang damn step around these assholes. He'd let his street-smarts slide, thinking he was playing for Team Good Guy.

Libra sighed and shifted the overstuffed duffle bag to his other shoulder. Trepidation stirred as he approached the main gates.

Mentally, he was prepared for the worst, but it annoyed the hell out of him that the Colonel didn't think it necessary to arm him with something to defend himself. He spied a broken branch, four feet long, fairly straight and a good thickness. He locked down his wheels and leaned over to grab it, stripped off the leaves, and propped it next to his console—just in case.

The Trading Post was marked by a wooden-bar gate, held open with a loop of rope, in a line of thick, dense spruce trees. He followed the wide road as it turned a bend and came into a clearing that made him grind to a stop. The Trading Post wasn't anything he'd envisioned.

Rather than a crumbled shed cluttered with a lot of junk and Bangers running around throwing axes at small children, Libra found himself in a village. He parked his board at the edge of a grassy square, grabbed his battle stick, and surveyed the encircling buildings. Sturdy structures, well-kept log buildings, flower gardens, white smoke puffing out of chimneys, and smells that made his nostrils flare and his mouth water.

Off to his left, a few old men stared at pieces on a board game under a vine-covered gazebo while two children tossed a ball to a domestic animal.

This was nothing, *nothing*, like the training videos. He wondered if Cleo lived like this.

According to the intelligence reports he'd studied, the population of Wolverine Clan was around the eight hundred souls. But nowhere did it state anything about ball playing children and quaint community gardens. Where were the rock dwellings, grimy, malnourished faces, and bloody animal corpses?

This unpolluted, quiet, charming village was the antithesis of city life. Personally, he couldn't live here for more than a few days, but it finally made sense why there was an underground of urbanites obsessed with this place, who discriminately dropped their eyes to the floor when the propaganda ads played on the holoboards. This tiny microcosm of Taiga life was hardly indicative of savagery and unhealthy living conditions.

Unless this was all for show?

A red ball came barrelling toward him, followed by the bounding domestic animal, its ears flopping and tongue hanging out the side of its mouth. Libra braced and held the stick out in front of him, across his body.

Both ball and dog came to a stop at his feet, and the latter thumped its tail and looked up expectedly.

"Throw it!" one of the kids yelled.

Libra lowered the walking stick and bent down, letting the duffel slip off his shoulder. He'd never seen a dog up close. It inched closer to him, the tail still swishing back and forth.

Watery-brown, heart-melting eyes looked at him through a fringe of fur.

"Hey dog," he said and the domestic woofed in reply, rocking a startled Libra back onto his heels. The dog barked again, dancing excitedly around the ball.

Libra reached out with his stick and rolled the ball toward the dog.

It nosed it back toward Libra.

"Not good enough, huh?"

The dog yipped as if he understood.

Libra plucked the red ball between two fingers and tossed it back in the direction of the children. The dog woofed, flipped around, and bounded after it, leaping every couple of steps.

Libra chuffed, letting a smile roll across his face. He wondered if Cleo had a domestic.

Cleo!

Shit, he had to get moving, get back to her. Get in, get out, get Cleo to safety and then return home to his freedom and his fortune. Never mind all this other stuff. These people, this village, were nothing but an illusion meant to convince the odd sightseer that they were something they're not. Civilized.

Cleo might be different, but she was the exception. She had to be. All those films the Restoration Party has shown them at youth rallies, the holoboard warnings, the travel bans. *That* was real.

With purposeful steps, he strode past the saucy orange flowers, their black centers staring at him with accusing eyes, and into the biggest of the structures that bore a rustic sign identifying it as the General Store. He scoffed at the hand-scrawled *Welcome Visitors* sign in the window.

The interior was vast and bright, filled with natural light that streamed through a high row of opened windows that invited the autumn breeze, making the place feel like an outdoor market. And there was that smell again. Libra's stomach rumbled, already resenting the Nutrishit dinner he'd have to share with Trevayne and his men.

"Help ya, sir?" A young lady, her eyes a sparkling blue, bounced up behind the counter in front of him. She wasn't much of a savage, either. She couldn't be any more than fifteen or sixteen, with apples in her cheeks and a pimple on her chin. No mud, no missing teeth, seemed to know how to articulate. Between Cleo and the people living at the post, where the hell did they find the freaks in the anti-Taiga literature?

"Your account name?" she prompted.

"I, uh... I don't have an account. First time here."

"Alrighty then, if you want to trade, we'll have to create one for you. She glanced at his forearm. "I'll need a scan."

Zhang hell. That's why Trevayne sent him. He was being set up. If Cleo's kidnapping prompted the tribers to file a report with the UWC, Libra, with his criminal history, would be back in the penal colony before sundown on Tuesday.

The data chip embedded in everyone's arm, with all identifying information, certainly made everyday life easier, but right now, it was going to screw him over. He blew out a sigh and stuck his arm out for her scanner. He'd have to think this through later, when his mind was clear, when he'd had some sleep, when he wasn't so anxious to get back to Cleo.

"Alrighty then," the girl said, entering data into the hand-held reader. "Instead of cashpoints, we work on a barter system, so you'll get credits for what you bring in to trade and you can use those to purchase from the floor, or for food from the canteen, which you passed when you came in, or for the bunk house if you care to be our guest for the night. Any unused balance gets recorded in the system and you can use it the next time you visit. Any questions?"

Libra shook his head, speechless and unable wrap his head around the fact that they were sophisticated enough to have a system of commerce. The combination of technology and snake-eating fried his circuits.

"What did you bring to trade?" she asked, eyeing the sack that weighed down his other shoulder.

Libra heaved the duffel on the counter and pushed it toward her. He had no idea what was inside but trusted Trevayne had stuffed enough in there to cover his laundry list of demands. What the hell the guy wanted with a dozen jars of blueberry jam, he couldn't imagine.

Eager hands slid the zipper across the top and dove in. The girl nodded to herself as she pulled out boxes of assorted screws, sheets of malleable plastic, various lengths of PVC piping, and a box of assorted medical supplies.

From the very bottom, she retrieved a package with the familiar DynaCade interlocking triangles logo. Retrieving a small blade from under the counter, she slit open the protective case and lifted the lid. A dozen brand-new, six-inch pocket-classroom plasma screens, lifetime batteries included, made her eyes bug out with glee.

"Oh." She popped him a quick glance. "Oh! There's going to be a fight over these! You have no idea how the schools are going to love, love, love these. "

She ran her fingers over the lid where, neatly tucked into individual slots, were the operating capsules.

"Dad!" she called.

Dad? So they didn't eat their young.

"Oh, oh, Dad, look at these titles... History of Amerada: Pre Polar War, The Rise and Fall of Zhang Bao Lin, Complete BioSciences: Basic to Advanced, Math Series one through six, and Languages of New Europa."

Her eyes peeled from the box to meet Libra's. "We get these sometimes, mostly used, but these are brand new! And the edu-chips... I've never even seen the languages one, and I don't think there's an advanced bioscience text in the entire Shield. How did you... I mean... Whoa!"

Dad peered over her shoulder and shot a squint-eyed look back to Libra. "These legitimate? We won't touch stolen goods, son."

"Family connections," Libra grunted, hoping that this stolen goods bullshit wasn't part of a sting.

The girl held digital device up to her father so he could see Libra's personal information.

"Alrighty then," Dad said, eyebrows touching his hairline. "That's mighty fine. Mighty fine indeed, Mr. Cade." The man slapped his shoulder and grinned. "Happy to do business with you."

Libra fought the urge to laugh out loud. If these folks had any idea how much he really *had* stolen in his previous life, the trader would have turned to stone. Taurus, meanwhile, hauled a cache of contraband back and forth across the Cut a dozen times a year, but he doubted whether "Alrighty" Dad ever questioned him. Taurus had that blessedly honest appeal going for him.

"This your first time up?" Dad asked.

"Yes, sir."

"I'll tally this, honeybunches," he said to his daughter. "Why don't you help the Clarks."

Honeybunches looked reluctant to go. "But Dad! How am I supposed to learn if—"

"Please," he said with a quiet voice. The girl's shoulders drooped as she shuffled towards the couple toward the end of the counter. She snuck a glance over her shoulder and zoomed in on Libra. Caught peeking, her cheeks turned bright pink. Feeling devilish, he winked and was rewarded with a wide-eyed smile.

"We usually give eighty-five creds for these, but I'll give you a hundred for each since they're new and come with the chips." Dad said, closing the box of plas-screens. "These couldn't come at a better time, considering classes are about to start."

Libra had a feeling he could have haggled the price up significantly but decided he liked these Taiga people, despite the images pounded into his head. Considering how he felt about the head of DynaCade at the moment, he was tempted to give them away for free.

"Let me just check our book, see what

these other bits will get you. It'll take me a few minutes to tally everything, so you can look around. If you need any help, just holler," Dad said.

"I've got a list."

"Alrighty, then," he said, handing over one of the wicker baskets that were stacked on the counter behind him.

There were no interior walls in the trading post, only two rows of rough wooden support columns that split the room into three distinct areas.

Libra made his way to the farthest section where wooden furniture, from bed posts to cabinets, lined the floor. With every intention to hurry his task, he couldn't stop himself from touching everything—the knots on a carved wooden chest, the smooth grain of a table—and pushed a rocking chair to see if it rocked as smoothly as he suspected.

Didn't see much wood in Gomeda, not since most of the trees in Lower Amerada had been burned for fuel during the dark times after the Polar Wars.

He moved through the center section of the building, navigated rows of shelves stocked with fresh and canned vegetables, dried meats, preserves, bundled herbs, and things he didn't know how to describe. Everything he saw, he considered. So many options, but which gave Cleo the best chance?

He found a utilitarian hammered-tin flask full of corn whisky—could come in handy—and added it to his basket. He picked up a heavy can labeled Bear Fat and felt a stirring deep in his gut. His little minx.

He moved to the tables laden with knitted clothing, leather goods, dolls, toys, but it was the child-sized feather pillow that caught his eye. He picked it up, squeezed it, and thought of Cleo saying, *"I don't need a feather pillow to get a good night sleep."* Was it only two nights ago? Seemed like a lifetime. *"They're only good for fighting,"* she had said.

He weighed the two items in his hand—the can of grease and the feather pillow, an idea tumbling around in his head and falling into place. He may have an answer for their current predicament. But would she understand? He stuffed both items in his basket, deciding it was worth the risk.

He turned to the right, toward the final third, toward the things that looked most familiar: urban wares. Solar cell kits, computer parts, an assortment of tools, medical supplies, bolts of polyweave cloth in every garish color imaginable, a few cases of Nutripacks and some genuine, factory-produced chemsoap, for that *ah, so fresh feeling*. Just what the tribers wanted after a hard day of rolling in the mud and killing animals with their bare hands.

It was embarrassing, the display of junk from Gomeda. There wasn't a thing that represented their culture, nothing of their resourcefulness.

Disgusted, he turned his back and strayed toward the huge fireplace in the center of the back wall. In front were two overstuffed couches, which, had he the time, he'd have loved to sink into and kick his feet up. The hearth was cold but there must have been a recent fire because he felt ambient heat emanating from the surround, which was constructed of the same multifaceted black stones that Cleo wore around her neck.

Libra made his way back to the service desk and waited for Dad to finish. Honey-bunches served a handful of customers, all of whom appeared to be sightseers from south of the Cut. He was sure they were from the city, but they acted differently here; they made eye contact with one another, exchanged pleasantries, didn't seem afraid to stand so close to one another. Maybe he was wrong. Maybe they were from the walled cities, further south and west.

No, that didn't make sense, either. They must be Gomedans, dressed in a weird hybrid of standard urban wear with a few Taiga pieces, like fringed leather boots and fur collars and cuffs.

That's what he needed, a replacement outfit for Cleo. It was getting cold during the nights and that thin, old undershirt wouldn't keep her very warm. He grabbed a leather outfit similar to the one she'd had and a long buckskin coat with a fur-trimmed hood.

"You've still got over three hundred points left," Dad said after subtracting his purchases from the tallied cashpoints. "You want to do more shopping, or shall I leave the balance on your account?"

"No, I've got everything I need," Libra replied. "Is it possible to transfer the remaining balance onto a friend's account?"

"Sure. Just need a name."

"Taurus—" he stopped. They wouldn't have his nickname on file. "Tate, Joseph Tate."

While Dad insisted he wrap each item in brown paper "for the journey," Libra checked out the digital board, scanning for anything interesting.

Static ads, mostly. People selling services—hunting guides, adventure trips through canyons—and looking for things like Asian cherry seeds and yard-goats.

There was a column headed MISSING. He scrolled through, disturbed by the dozens of notices: Beaver Clan sought beloved daughters *Cathryn and Olivia, last seen at the recruiter station.* Parents, tribes, siblings, all searching for news of those lost, every one *last seen in the company of recruiters* or *at the recruiter station.*

No wonder Cleo's people were wary

of Gomedans. One could argue that the youngsters went willingly, but once they drank the water, there was no hope.

"My dad's finished packing your things, Mr.—"

"Libra." It came out sharper than he'd intended, but he didn't want to hear the sound of his last name.

"Libra," the girl said with a nod. She waved her hand across the screen. "Wow, there's so much stuff up here, it's hard to read. Someone should clean this up."

Libra smiled. At that age, he doubted he would have taken the initiative either. *Someone* always meant *someone else.*

"Thanks, um...Libra." She blushed and stepped past him and plugged a code-key into the frame of the digital board.

Sweet girl, that Honey-bunches. Libra hoped her name would never show up in the MISSING column. He was just about to warn her away from the south when the board refreshed, automatically repositioning the ads to make space for updates, centering the most important and most recent in the center.

Libra felt the blood drain from his face.

It was a wanted poster...of Cleo.

TWENTY-SEVEN

THE IMAGE OF CLEO SMILING to someone off camera, as if she didn't have a concern in the world, turned a screw turned in his chest, putting unbearable pressure on his lungs. His eyes flicked to the one simple word beneath: WANTED.

"Where did you—" His voice cracked. He cleared his throat and continued. "Who's—" He didn't know how to ask the question. "Do you know her?"

"Sure. Everyone knows Cleo Rush," she said, eyeing Libra with a guarded expression. "Do you think she's pretty? It's okay if you do. The guys at potlatch get all puffy when she walks by."

"Mmm, she's okay," he shrugged.

He lied. She was stunning. And he wanted to snatch her off the wall and put her in his pocket. He drank in every detail of her face, the shy smile, the way the light reflected in her whisky-hued eyes.

Honey-bunches cocked her head. She might be young, but she was savvy. And he wasn't doing a good job hiding his interest. "Uh, what's that thing you mentioned? Potlatch?" he asked, deflecting her suspicions.

"Inter-tribal gatherings. We have them a few times of year."

"Big meetings, that sort of thing?"

"Sure, the elder councils meet. And it's a chance to exchange goods and stuff. But mostly it's a big party. Lots of food and there's dancing and we can find... so we can, y'know..." A bloom of pink crept up her face while she spoke, making her adorably blotchy. Whatever she was trying to tell him was the source of great discomfort. "For finding someone to go walking with, to make unions. Life mates from another tribe."

Life mate. Interesting. So these ignorant savages have the don't-dip-your-toes-in-the-same-genetic-pool philosophy as all the advanced civilizations. "Have you been to one?" he asked. "Found yourself a potential life mate?"

"Oh yes, I mean, no. No! I mean... Yes, I've been to lots of potlatches, but no, I haven't gone walking with anyone. Daddy says I'm too young."

"Has she," he canted his head toward Cleo's image, "made a union?" The screw at his chest torqued. Why did he ask that?

"Oh, hell no, excuse my language. Not Cleo. She's too busy winning all the trials."

"Which are?"

"Trials," she said again, as if the word alone summed it up. "For choosing the leader elect."

"So it's a competition?" Libra clarified.

"Hell yeah, excuse my language. At the call, each family puts forward one eligible member who then goes on, or is eliminated, depending on how they do in the early trials. There's lots of training and stuff, too, for like two whole years, and they do all these crazy competitions, not that I can think of any off the top of my head. They keep going until the pool of pledges gets smaller and smaller." She crossed her arms over her chest and continued without a pause. "Thank heavens I didn't have to do it because the call was made long before my significant age day—but I have done my passage," she added, as if he should know what that means. "My cousin made it to the seventh round. He was so disappointed when he lost, but we all just gave a gigantic sigh of relief that he didn't make it to the finals, if you know what I mean."

Libra pursed his lips and nodded, though he had a hard time following Honey-bunches' breathless soliloquy. "I actually don't. Why isn't it good to make the finals?"

Honey-bunches uncrossed her arms and shrugged. "You get washed. Only the leader-elect lives. The other finalists..." She ran a finger across her neck.

That explains why Cleo was on the run. "So, this...uh...person? They can't find her? Has she been gone long?" he asked, unable to keep his eyes from wandering back to the picture.

Honey-bunches shrugged. "I don't know. She was at the trials just last week, so she couldn't—"

"Are those knives?" Libra interrupted. Something caught his eye in the photo. Cleo wore a similar outfit to the one she was wearing when he met her, except leather straps criss-crossed her chest, holding what looked suspiciously like little metal handles.

"Hell yeah, excuse my language. Cleo's the best thrower in the Taiga. Bull's-eye every time."

Well that explained the alphacat, but it didn't explain why she neglected to mention her little hobby. What else had Cleo neglected to mention?

"That's quite a talent," Libra said, trying to sound nonchalant, though a million questions pushed at his teeth. "What's she wanted for?"

"Far as I know, cause she missed the swearing-in ceremony."

"Swearing in?"

"Uh-uh." Honey-bunches lifted her chin. "Cleo's going to be the new leader of Shield Tribes."

"You mean because Jaegar left, she gets the top spot?"

"How did you know about Jaegar?"

Zhang hell. Sleep deprivation interfered with this thinking. Or caused a lack-thereof. "I heard some other people talking about him," he improvised, cocking his head vaguely in the direction of the outer yard, as if he'd been chatting up the locals. "They said Jaegar was the leader-elect, but then he left. I just put two-and-two together."

"What? No, no, no. You heard all wrong." She shook her head, as if some grave insult had been uttered. "*Cleo* won those finals fair and square. Youngest person to ever do it! Those geezers out there have nothing better to do all day than to gossip about tribe politics and they're just plain wrong. I know lots of people *think* Jaegar should have been chosen, because he's older and he's a man, *obviously*," she said, cutting her eyes, "but *I* was rooting for Cleo the whole time."

"Wait a sec," he said. "You're telling me that this girl, this Cleo chick, won this competition and *she's* the leader of the Shield Tribe?"

"Hell yeah! Excuse my language. Hands-down winner. Points proved it. You look kind of pale. You okay?"

"Just tired," he said. "So why did Jaegar take off?"

"'Dunno. Probably didn't want to get washed. Simon left, too. Disappeared before the quarter-final points were even tallied. His notice has been up for over a month," she said, nodding to the board, "but nobody has seen him. Least not that they're saying. But there's always drama in the Wolverines." She lowered her voice. "I don't know if this is true or not..." She stole a glance toward Dad, who was still occupied, "but the geezers think that Cleo and Jaegar are going to fight 'til death and whoever comes back alive wins."

TWENTY-EIGHT

Colonel Leon Trevayne introduced himself as he loosened the rope that joined her wrists and ankles, propped her on the rotted trunk of a fallen tree, and offered her a green candy from a tin he kept in his pocket. She shook her head. He then proceeded to question her about the Taiga, pounding her with questions from politics to mining. His knowledge about the Taiga and their ways was unnervingly accurate in some cases and dead wrong in others, but she refused to acknowledge him either way.

Describing him as ugly would have been generous. Trevayne was short for a soldier, but solidly built. The flesh of his face looked as if it had been stretched over a bony skull, like there wasn't enough skin to allow for jowls or folds. His eyes were deep and lay in the shadow of a pronounced brow ridge. Under a pugilistic nose were lips so thin, they were almost non-existent. When he spoke, his gums showed.

He switched back and forth, from a friendly, conversational tone to one that demanded answers. Cleo marked the time by the number of candies he popped and figured they'd been at it for over an hour. Aware her actions frustrated him, she maintained silence, pressed her tender lips together, and refused to make eye contact. She was too tired, heartsick, and annoyed for this game, but what choice did she have? Sure deserved what she got for trusting an outsider. On the other hand, she couldn't afford to lose sight of her goal to get to Gomeda and find Jag.

After another hour, Trevayne began to crack. His true nature had surfaced, just as she'd suspected. Soon, he'd let his temper take over and he'd make a mistake. Then she'd make her move.

"What are you up to, Petal? Do you only talk when you have a cock inside you? Is that it?" His pupils darkened as he skimmed the length of her body, his demonic chuckle snaking up her spine. His sweet, medicinal breath filled Cleo's nostrils as he crouched in front of her. "Because that could be arranged."

She turned her cheek and drew back.

Perhaps it had been a mistake to ignore him.

The saliva in her mouth turned sour. She felt more helpless than she did facing the alphacat. The wild animals of the Taiga were justified in their instinct to kill to survive. Trevayne, conversely, was doing this for his own twisted pleasure. If he had to kill, it wouldn't be quick, with mercy. He would toy, hurt, maim. In her peripheral vision, she could see him extract a knife from his belt.

Sweat pooled in her pores as she felt the cold flat of the blade on the side of her face. He traced her scar, then down her jawline to her shoulder.

"How about I get rid of this scrap, give you some room to breathe." Trevayne slipped the tip under the thick strap of her shirt.

She let her lids drop, gathered every ounce of venom before meeting his dead black eyes with a hard stare.

"Don't. Touch. Me." Too scared to relax her jaw for fear her lips would tremble, she spoke through clenched teeth.

He leaned in closer, cocked his head to one side and squinted. "I'll do what in zhang hell I please, Miz Rush," he hissed. "My orders are to bring you back alive, not unblemished." He yanked the blade upward, slicing through the thin material. The razor sharp tip caught the side of her face, nicking her cheek.

Cleo flinched at the sharp sting of pain. She tried again to swallow, but there was no moisture in her mouth.

She could see the look of disappointment on Trevayne's face when her shirt didn't flop open to expose her. The ribbed material hugged her body closely, refusing to sag.

Inhaling deeply, she realized she'd have to buy some time before this got very ugly. "You touch me, Libra will kill you."

He laughed, a short, mean bark, and leaned in, smothering her with menthol. "Your boyfriend isn't here to protect you." He pressed his tongue to her wound and licked her blood.

Cleo swallowed the bile creeping up her throat. She couldn't tell if her fingers, numb from being bound, were shaking, but she could feel her knees begin to quake. She was not going to be this pig's toy. She would rather die fighting than let him get away with torturing her. Anger twined with the fear in her gut. She shouldn't give in. She couldn't risk letting her emotions override her common sense or she'd never get out of this alive. But no matter how hard her brain tried to out-logic her emotions, she couldn't stop herself from twisting sharply and springing back in a violent motion, catching Trevayne with her shoulder and knocking him back onto his haunches. "Get away from me, you dog."

Trevayne sprang forward, grabbed the back of her neck, and twisted her braid around his hand, forcing her to turn her face up to him. "Good enough for the pretty boy, you're good enough for me," he hissed.

He pulled her head into his crotch. She stifled a scream as the sour smell of his body infected her sinuses, as the ridge of his cock grew against her mouth.

She yelped as he yanked her head back again. With his other hand, he captured her cheeks between his fingers, pinching her face. "I know you fucked him, you ignorant little slut. Now it's my turn."

That was the last straw. The absolute last duck-loving straw!

She captured the web between his thumb and fingers and bit down until she tasted copper.

In one swift movement, he yanked his hand out of her mouth and backhanded her across the face, snapping her head sideways. "You dirty fucking animal!" he spat. He gripped the back of her neck, digging his fingers under the base of her skull so she couldn't turn away.

Cleo clamped her lips together to keep from crying out. She compacted her neck, dipped her head, and tried to turtle into her shoulders—anything to stop the pain—but his hold was unrelenting.

"Your feral brethren might get off on biting and scratching, but we civilized folk prefer our women docile." Cleo drove her bare heels into the ground against the pain but couldn't prevent her eyes from welling with tears. With a final jerk that she thought would rip the back of her scalp off, he loosened his hold but didn't release her. "Your momma should have taught you better manners."

"My mother is dead, *shithead*, so kindly keep her name off your filthy lips."

"Dead, eh?" That bark again, like it pleased him to know she suffered pain in her life. He stood abruptly, using the back of her neck as leverage to push himself up. She braced herself so she wouldn't fall off the log. The last thing she wanted was to be lying on the ground, giving him more ideas. "I thought you savages were supposed to be invincible." He spat, missing her foot by less than an inch. "What got her? Polar grizzly, rabid badger?"

"Nothing in the Taiga could have touched my mother. It was you bastards," she screamed. "Achan Cade killed my mother!"

Trevayne's eyes went wide before he began cackling like he'd heard the best joke in the world. He took a few steps back, slapping his knee as he went.

Cleo tried to control her breathing as hysteria bubbled beneath the surface. *Focus, focus, focus,* her mind chanted. She let him crack her tough veneer, damn him to hell, to the point she wanted to sink her teeth into his jugular.

His laughter stopped abruptly and he wiped the spittle from around his lips with the back of his sleeve. Black eyes glinting like a rabid fox, he turned to her. "Does Libra know?"

She squinted. "Know what?"

"About your dead momma."

Cleo's senses vibrated. Why would Trevayne ask such a question? "What does that have to do with anything?"

"That depends. What do you know about Libra?"

She clamped her lips again, unwilling to play with him, unwilling to show him how much the topic of Libra affected her. How stupid to let him rile her, stupider to let him get information about her.

Don't trust outsiders.

Okay Lewin, alright already! You were right. I'm an idiot fool.

Trevayne, clearly amused, asked again, "What lies did your lover whisper in your filthy ear while he fucked you?"

Cleo cut her eyes and remained mum.

"You know nothing," he laughed. "Nothing! I gotta give the boy credit," he said, rubbing his hands together, the smear of blood across the back of his hand forgotten. "This is almost too good to be true." He shook the tin and popped another candy.

He started to walk away but changed his mind and took a step in front of her. Trevayne reached into the flap on the front of his trousers and pulled out his cock.

Please God, no. Not like this.

If she could just lean back far enough and maintain her balance, she might be able to lift her legs and kick out, catch him in the gut. As her mind ticked through her options, Trevayne aimed a stream of urine at her toes.

Recoiling in disgust, Cleo lost her balance and fell backward off the log. She landed on her shoulder blades, her head banging onto the uneven ground, ripping the scab off her previous wound, the one she earned heading the other guy in the mouth. Her grunt was followed by more of Trevayne's sick cackling as he emptied his bladder against the log.

Cleo squirmed for a better position, but her arms were trapped beneath her, unable to give any leverage while her legs stayed suspended uselessly above. She whimpered in frustration, fighting for some kind of leverage.

Get up! Get up before the sick zhang-lover crawls on top!!

On her back, she pulled her knees into her chest and rocked. The pain in her arms and shoulders made her eyes sting, but she worked up enough momentum to roll forward into a crouch. Unfortunately, the uneven ground and inability to use her arms for balance worked against her and she tipped sideways.

"What's a matter, Petal?" he said, tucking

the short, blunt tool back in his pants. "Hurt yourself?"

Now what? She was helpless, and she hated being helpless.

She heard the crunch of his footsteps as he rounded the fallen tree. Again, she rolled onto her back, pulled her knees and rocked forward, this time landing on the balls of her feet. She was halfway to standing, struggling for balance when he got to her.

"You're an agile little creature, I'll give you that. But what happens if I do this?" He drew back his fist, but with her hands behind her back, Cleo could do nothing to evade his blow. She braced best she could, tried to turn to deflect the punch, but when his fist landed smack into her gut, Cleo buckled, lost her balance and her breath, and reeled back.

She lay stunned, her body vibrating with pain as she curled into a fetal position. Her head rang with his laughter...and something else. Somebody called her name.

"Cleo!" Libra crashed through the brush on a solar board. She never imagined she'd be so grateful to hear the sound of anyone's voice, let alone the bastard who got her here.

"What the hell do you think you're doing?" he yelled, presumably at Trevayne, and leapt over the log into her sight lines. He dropped down and scooped her into his arms.

"You okay, darlin'?" he asked, pressing

his lips into her hair. She groaned as he jostled her into position and lifted her back onto the log. His hands were everywhere at once—palming the side of her throbbing face, picking leaves out of her hair, running his fingers up and down her bare arms. "Did he hurt you? Why is your face bleeding? What happened to your shirt?"

Without waiting for her to answer any one of his questions, he turned to Trevayne, a knife magically appearing in his hand.

Cleo recognized it immediately. Short handled, double edged, perfectly weighted: it was a Taiga throwing knife.

"Talk fast, Trevayne, unless you want this between your eyes."

"Settle down, Petal, your whore is unblemished." Trevayne said and took two paces forward. He didn't even have the decency to look contrite in the face of Libra's blade. On the contrary, mischief danced around his eyes. "We were just having a chat, the missus and me," he said and winked at Cleo. "Getting better acquainted. Weren't we?"

Cleo shivered. She regretted sleeping with Libra, regretted trusting him, but at the moment, he was the closest thing she had to an ally and he didn't intend to harm her or let her be harmed. While allied with the enemy, it was clear he didn't understand how dangerous or unpredictable Trevayne could be.

"Libra," she whispered, hoping he'd interpret her warning.

Trevayne misunderstood. "Aw, how precious. She thinks you've come to save her, rescue her like some kind of hero." He glanced back and forth between them, looking sickly gleeful.

Cleo had a bad feeling. A very bad feeling. Whatever was coming next, she wasn't sure she wanted any part of it. In fact, she wished, more than anything, she was back in the river, about to go over the falls. She wanted a do-over, even if it meant staying dead.

"You two seem to be awful close considering you've not been formally introduced." His voice dripped with venom, drawing out each word, emphasizing each syllable. "Miz Cleo Rush, allow me to introduce Mister Libra Cade, Achan's one and only beloved grandson."

TWENTY-NINE

C LEO HADN'T UTTERED A WORD to anyone since Trevayne opened his lipless gob. Libra desperately needed to get her attention, but she wouldn't even look at him, going out of her way to turn her head, staring past him into the trees, looking anywhere but at *him*. If he could only explain, make her understand his predicament, and assure her that despite how bad it all looked, he never meant to hurt her.

But he couldn't pacify Cleo, here, in front of the league of extraordinary moronic gentlemen.

The evening sun began its descent, leaving them in the long, extended fingers of shade. He offered Cleo his windbreaker, but she ignored him. Fine, he deserved to be ignored, but she didn't deserve to be cold, so he draped it around her shoulders. She shrugged it off. She probably would have taken it if she had any idea that her nipples were practically poking holes through her undershirt. He sat next to her, hoping some of his body warmth would comfort her. She sat stoically on the crumbling tree trunk while Frack, tasked to watching over her, mouth-breathed behind them. He seemed to be having a problem with his nose, which, Libra suspected, had something to do with Cleo.

Though Libra was just as determined to get Cleo in front of Achan, collect his inheritance, and be gone, he was equally as determined to see that his Taiga lover remain safe, unharmed, and returned home.

Everyone remained silent. They tracked Frick as he prepared an evening meal as if it were a fascinating new spectator sport.

"What do you want for dinner, Colonel? We have Nutristew or Nutrichik-in-gravy with veg."

"I'm not eating any of that shit." Trevayne turned to Libra. "Where's my jam?"

"In the duffel, right on top."

Trevayne dragged the bag from where Libra had dropped it and slid the zipper open. He removed the top package, laid it on the ground, and with the care of a mother unswaddling a newborn, opened the brown tissue paper. His thin lips peeled back in what Libra suspected was an attempt at a smile. "Where's the rest?" he asked, squinting.

"That's it." Libra said.

"One jar?" Trevayne's eyes bugged out. "Not acceptable." He held it in his fist and shook it at Libra. "You had enough to trade for a hundred zhanging jars of jam, and you brought one?"

Libra shrugged. "That's all they had."

"You'd better have had more luck with the rest," Trevayne sneered, pulling the rest of the stash out.

"What's this?" he asked, pulling out the leather outfit he'd picked out for Cleo.

"You didn't let me bring anything from our camp this morning, including her clothes."

"She got clothes on."

"No, she's got *my* clothes on, and I want them back," Libra said, contrarily. "Wouldn't you agree it's rather necessary to present her to Achan wearing clothes?"

"And this?" he pulled the buckskin coat, his eyes squinting with disbelief at the extravagant beadwork on the cuffs and lapels. "How was this necessary?"

"Don't want her to freeze on the boat."

"I'd have kept her warm," Trevayne scowled, eyeing Cleo with lewdness that made Libra grind his teeth.

"You won't touch her." Libra's voice dripped with threat.

Next out came the little feather pillow. He didn't wait for Trevayne to speak, just jumped up and snatched it out of his hand. "For her head. She doesn't sleep well without one." Without looking at her, he tossed it onto her lap, hoping she'd understand.

Trevayne, worked into a frenzy, tore the rest of the packages apart with unbridled fury.

"Crackers, cheese, rose-hip tea, and what zhang hell is this? A knitted cap?"

"It's a... tea cozy. Keeps the pot warm."

"Not acceptable!" The veins on the side of Trevayne's neck throbbed as he waved the blue-and-orange warmer in his fist. "Where's the other stuff? The mineral oils, the nickel pellets, copper wire? How the hell am I supposed to sell this bloody junk?"

"You're not. It's for my *beloved* grandfather. He enjoys a nice cup of tea with his cheese and crackers. And since he obviously supplied the goods..." Libra shrugged.

Trevayne uncovered the can of bear fat, eyebrows knotted as he tossed it aside, and reached for the last and heaviest item, a lumpy, ten-pound sack. "At least you had the good sense to get the... What in zhang hell?" He pulled out the burlap sack and dug his fingers into it. Apoplectic with rage, he growled, "This isn't grain!"

"Potatoes," Libra corrected. "Had a hankering for a little delicacy called French fries. Ever had 'em? You cook 'em up in that there bear grease. Delicious."

Trevayne ignored him, his white knuckles twisting the empty duffel. "What did you do with the rest of the trade credits? Those Educhips alone should have got you thousands."

"Supply and demand, my friend. Seems they recently had a big deposit of plasma screen devices, so they weren't paying very much. I haggled best I could, but barely got forty creds per."

Trevayne looked ready to flay him alive, but it was totally worth risking his skin for the sight Libra caught in his peripheral vision: the smirk on Cleo's lips.

Treveyne left with one of his goons to prepare the boat while the other, the one Cleo had cracked in the head with a stone—obviously not hard enough—stayed behind.

He told Libra to unbind her feet in preparation for the walk to the boat, but Trevayne made it clear her hands were to remain tied. Libra argued on her behalf, that they be at least tied in front—so long as she promised not to use her teeth on the knots, to which she solemnly acquiesced—so she could at least scratch her nose or break her fall if she stumbled. Golly gee, it was almost enough to make a girl swoon.

Libra could have used a knife to cut the cord, but instead, he knelt at her feet and made a project out of fiddling with the knots. He was trying to make nice. Why?

He peeked up under her lashes, but she pretended not to see him and kept her eyes averted. She wasn't prepared to show him an ounce of mercy, if that's what he was looking for.

"You need to put those clothes on," he said.

She lifted her chin to the sky.

"Cleo, listen," he whispered in a gruff voice that still somehow, against all logic, resonated straight through her and into her heart. "You can't wear a torn—practically see-through—Cleo, these guys are pigs. Every time Trevayne looks at you—" his sighed, his implications obvious. "You don't have to think of it as a gift, or a favor," he continued. "You don't owe me anything. I'm just replacing what was taken from you."

Cleo shook her head. He didn't understand.

She would wear his flimsy beat-your-wife shirt and leggings as a reminder to herself, and to him, of his two-faced betrayal.

"Fine," he said. She expected him to walk away in a huff, but he stayed to massage her ankles. Her feet were so cold and numb, she hadn't felt the cord slip away, but now that the blood was rushing in, they hurt. The heat from his hands sent pain shooting clear to her heart. He washed them with water from his canteen, gently brushing away the grime, pebbles, and stink of Trevayne. Before she realized what he was doing, he slipped a moccasin onto her foot.

"I bought these, too," he said, his voice taking on a sterner edge. "You'll wear them, and the coat. I won't have you freeze to death when we get out on water."

She could argue, but she wasn't stupid. She'd need shoes and the coat if she were to get away.

"How did you get here?"

His fingers stilled on her ankles. "What do you mean?"

"It's a simple question. How did you come to the Taiga in the first place? And don't bullshit me. What do you want with me? Were you following me? Is that how you were able to pull me out of the falls?"

He rose, his sudden movement almost upending her. Libra tore the knife from the sheath around his waist, leaned over her shoulder and cut the ties around her wrists. The intimate press of his body against her filled her nostrils with his smell, eliminating any lingering remnants of Trevayne. Had she been thinking straight, had she had a moment to collect herself, she would have decked him and ran as fast and far as her aching legs carried her.

He grabbed her arm and jerked her up, knocking the pillow to the ground. He shoved her cramped arms into the sleeves of the buckskin greatcoat and sat her back down. Angry, hurt, confused, and crazy-tired, she was just forming the words to protest as he retrieved the undamaged length of polycord and applied it to her wrists. A string of invectives danced down her tongue but as she opened her mouth, she realized that he'd barely put any tension into the rope. The bindings were loose enough that with any amount of surreptitious manoeuvring, she could slip free.

"No," he said tersely, but Cleo didn't know which of her questions he was addressing. "No, I didn't come by boat and no, I wasn't following you. That was a fluke, serendipity."

"Serendipity," she spat. "Fancy words won't make me believe you."

Libra bowed his head and held her hands in his palms. She was inclined to tug them away, but the uneven rhythm of his chest as it rose and fell made Cleo curious enough to remain still. A range of emotions flicked across his face as he opened his mouth to speak, then closed it into a tight line and squeezed his eyes shut. When his chin jutted up and his eyes opened to meet hers, they were cold, masked of any emotion. He squeezed her hands, then pulled away, leaving hers to fall into the emptiness between them.

"You just happened to be in my jump zone."

"What does that mean, jump zone?" A woozy feeling overcame her, a tingling sensation that started at her toes—like her limbs were falling asleep in a wave that worked its way up her spine. "W-what does that mean?" Her voice sounded thin and distant, as if she were speaking through a long pipe.

"It means I jumped out of an orbital glider." His eyes flicked up to hers. "An airplane."

THIRTY

"Fainted, huh?" Trevayne peered over Libra's shoulder. "She didn't strike me as the delicate type."

It happened so fast, Libra barely had time to react. The blood drained from her face, her eyes rolled upward, and she crumpled. If he hadn't been standing a foot in front of her, she would have hit the ground.

"She hasn't eaten since yesterday and hasn't had a sip of water all day."

"I offered," said Trevayne. "She refused. Couldn't force her, could I?"

Ignoring him, Libra railed, "She fought off three men who outweigh her by at least a hundred pounds *each*, was stunned unconscious, manhandled, and kidnapped. I don't think *delicate* applies."

Libra looked down and found his actions

at odds with his temper, his trembling hand on her forehead gently pushing back stray strands of hair that had come loose from her braid.

"Not my fault she refused dinner, either," Trevayne said. He unhooked a small flask from his belt and dropped it. Libra caught it, one handed, before it hit Cleo on the chest. Trevayne kicked dirt over the smouldering piro-brick fire. "Just make sure she can walk to the boat, 'cause I am *not* carrying her. We scram in ten minutes." He turned his attention to Frick. "You're with me." And then to Frack. "Stay behind these two."

Trevayne picked up the last of their gear and stopped in front of Libra. He looked down at them, skewering Libra with his black stare. "Ten minutes, Mister Cade. And no funny stuff. Your grand-pappy might have told me not to kill her, but he didn't seem to care whether *you* made it back alive or not."

Libra fingered the handle of the knife strapped to his waist as Trevayne strutted from the clearing. He'd never taken a life, never been tempted to, but he didn't believe that Trevayne's demise would cause him any long-term psychological trauma.

Cleo moved. He unscrewed the cap of the flask and poured a bit of water into the cap. He held it to Cleo's lips as she moaned softly, as if she was awakening from a disorienting dream.

"Here you go, darlin'. Drink up." He tilted the cap slowly, letting a thin trickle pass her lips.

Her tongue darted out, swept across her lower lip. He quickly refilled the cap and poured more water into her. He slid his arm under her shoulders and pressed the flask to her lips, letting her take a few gulps. She raised her hands, still joined at the wrists, and tilted the flask higher. Her eyes flitted open and she stared at him with a poisonous expression while she drained the water.

A hard knot coiled deep in his gut.

Cleo hated him.

Libra helped her into a sitting position, then dug in the pocket of his cargo pants. "It's kind of squished," he said, holding out a bun wrapped in waxed paper.

Cleo turned her face away.

His shoulders sagged. "Take it. Your next meal won't be until we reach Gomeda."

She didn't budge.

"Come on! You've got to eat, Cleo. It's from the Trading Post. I found that woman you told me about, Valentina."

"You tried to make me believe there was no aer-o-plane." Her voice was tight with anger, with hurt. "You questioned my sanity, my education, and you insulted me."

He thrust the bun in her hands. "There's bacon inside."

"I don't want it." She didn't throw it back at him, like he expected, but let it roll from her fingers with eerie calm. He watched it drop off the curve of her thigh and onto the ground. "I don't want anything from you."

———

Her stomach growled. Loudly. But there wasn't a chance in hell Cleo was going to pick up the food. "On second thought, I do want something from you," she said, changing the subject to get her mind off the hole in her stomach. She glanced over her shoulder at their watchdog, busy wiping out evidence of their campsite. "I want answers. What do you want with me? Why are you even with them?"

"I'm not one of them, if that's what you mean." Libra dragged his fingers through his hair and shook his head. "It's complicated."

She snorted. *Complicated.* "Did you come north to get me specifically?" She reached forward and grabbed the bun, her stomach ruling her actions. "Or were you looking for any sucker stupid enough to go with you?"

"You. I was sent for *you.*"

"How long have you been tracking me?" *And why didn't I notice?* Tracking was her forte! How could she have been outfoxed?

"I told you, it wasn't planned like that." His eyes looked like a stormy grey sea, a trick of the twilight. "I just happened to be there."

"There. Where's there? Did you see me turtle the kayak? Did you watch me, leave me to drown before pulling me out and playing hero?"

"No Cleo. I wasn't following you. It happened just like I said. I was just there, at the bottom of the cliff. The clearing where I made our camp was supposed to be my drop zone, but I missed the mark and landed on the other side of the river. I was barely out of my parachute harness when I saw you go over the falls. And I didn't know it was you when I jumped into the water."

"When? When did you know?"

"I don't know," he said with a shrug. "Not at first. You were similar to the description, so I had my suspicions, but I wasn't sure until you started thrashing around and talking in your sleep."

Cleo scrutinized his face. He sounded earnest, but she couldn't trust herself anymore.

"But why *me*? Why *now*? Does this have something to do with Jag going to Gomeda? Is he in danger? Because so help me God, if anyone has touched my brother, I will destroy you, Libra *Cade*." She spit his last name like it was acid on her tongue.

He held his palms aloft, to calm her, hold her back, she wasn't sure which. "When he recruited me, Achan—"

"Your *grandfather*."

He huffed. "Yes, but it's not what you think. I don't have anything to do...haven't had a relationship with the man in a very long time."

"Yet you work for him."

Libra dropped his chin. "It's complicated."

"So you said." She watched his lips disappear into a tight line. He was losing his patience. Good. She liked him unhinged.

He glanced around, making sure Frack wasn't paying attention.

"Come on," he said, rising. "We've got to get to the boat before Trevayne comes back."

Cleo's stomach did another rumbling growl.

"You really need to eat that, darlin'," he said, looping his arm through hers as he guided her down the path that would take them to the river.

"Don't call me that," she hissed and pulled from his grip. "Just keep talking. I want to know everything."

"My original mission was to get your brother. I probably wouldn't have taken the assignment if I knew..."

"If you knew what? That I was a savage girl?"

"If I knew you'd steal my heart before I could steal you."

Whoa! That was not the answer Cleo was expecting.

He took advantage of the silence and continued. "They provided me with a cover story, a list of scenarios to play out to get your brother alone. It was supposed to be a simple drug and drag operation. Day before the flight, before we left to come here, they changed the mission."

"Why?"

"I don't know," he said, too quickly. "Why did you lie to me about Jag?"

Cleo stumbled, her foot caught on a...She looked down. Nothing. She tripped on nothing. Libra linked an arm through hers. "I didn't."

"Really? Because the gal at the Trading Post was very chatty."

"What gal?"

"The teenage daughter of the guy who runs the store."

"She's a child. She can't possibly know or even understand—"

"She told me *you* won, Cleo. That *you* were the leader-elect, that *you* beat Jaegar." Accusation dripped from his words, like her victory was a hanging offense. "Is it true?"

"Kind of. It was tie, so they made us do this extra trial—"

"The bear grease thing?"

"No," she said, surprised he'd remembered the story, seeing how he was just pretending to listen, pretending to be interested in what she had to say.

"What then?" he asked, his tone way pricklier than it should have been, considering it was she who was wronged.

"Have you ever heard of thanatosis?"

"Bad breath?"

"Not halitosis, *thanatosis*. Never mind. Suffice to say, I won."

"Well then, you answered your own question, Cleo. My dear old grandfather wants the leader. Not Jag, the favorite to win. *You*. And I gotta tell you lady, the entire Shield has their collective breeches in a twist over you ditching the swearing in ceremony—"

"How do you know—"

"And there's a rumor going around that Jag left to avoid being *washed*." Libra's voice grew louder, his words spilled together. "And what about Simon's disappearance? Did you go off a waterfall looking for him, too? There are a group of old men who are calling it an unfair competition, and saying you and Jaegar went off to fight until the death. Or maybe you're both going to hunt down or take down this Simon fellow. I really can't figure out what the fuck is going on in your zhang-damn tribe, Cleo, so how about you take a moment and fill me in on the games you and your brother are playing, cause this whole mess is making me feel like a dirty monkey in the middle."

"None of that is true," Cleo said. "It was a clean win. It wasn't my problem that Jag couldn't possum. Technically, I *am* the leader-elect. But I'm not going to kill anyone. I'm going to bring him home."

"So he can be *washed*. And why do I feel that's a code word for kill?"

"That's ridiculous! You're confusing everything!" Cleo shook her head. How could she possibly explain the rules to an outsider? "I don't know where Simon is but he has nothing to do with this. And yes, I did win. But Jag should have won. Not because of the stupid competition, but because he is a better leader. Those people need him. They adore him, they look to him for guidance, they trust him. Me?" she shrugged. She'd never put voice to her feelings, but it felt right to confront them here and now with the one person who wouldn't care to judge her. "I'm just about winning. Nobody wants to follow me. I don't fit with people, never have. Besides, I could survive the wash. Jag couldn't."

Libra's face went blank.

"It's complicated! You can't possibly understand how it all works—not without spending time with the tribes. All you need to know is that I did something to disqualify myself, but Jag doesn't know that yet. That's why I have to find him. He's the leader-elect by default."

"Then they must know. Achan, the Energy Collective—somehow, they know you won. They know he doesn't have the authority, hence the change in orders."

"Authority for what?"

"Something to do with signing papers. All this," he said, spreading his arms, "is about a signature on a line. Mining rights or something. So sign the damn paper and go home."

"Why wouldn't they just go to my father?"

"They did, Cleo. They were unsuccessful."

"No they didn't. I would know if any kind of negotiating was going on. I would have heard the talk—"

"It was twenty-one years ago!" he said through gritted teeth.

"How is that relevant? I was barely born—"

Lightning struck. A big, horrifying bolt of enlightenment. "That's why the Guards came? To negotiate?" Finally, after all the years of evasive answers from her father, the truth about her birthday came from the mouth of her sworn enemy. "So then what?" she challenged. "My father wouldn't sign, so they murdered my mother?"

"No," he said, yanking her arm forward to hurry her. "The soldiers went to support the negotiator, a scientist, Doctor Bronson Cade."

"Doc Bee," she muttered. "Yes, I know about him."

"That was my father. He went to negotiate but ended up being held captive, for months. *By your clan.*"

Libra's words fell like a trickle of ice water

down her back.

"No, no. That's not right," she muttered. "You have it all twisted." Cleo's feet dug into the pebbled stones of the shoreline, just steps from the thick metal plank that would take them aboard the boat. She spun through memories, snippets of conversations, whispered stories, and unanswered questions, until the connections began to form. Doc Bee, Doctor Bronson. Gomedan Guards. Libra's father, murdered on the same day as her mother, on the same day she was born in the stone cottage in the woods.

Frack pushed past them, jarring her from the past.

"You're wrong," she said, her voice barely a whisper. "You're all wrong."

"No, I'm not. I'm sorry about your mother, truly I am. But your tribe murdered my father, a peaceful, unarmed scientist, acting as negotiator. She was probably caught in the fray."

The pressure in Cleo's chest grew until she thought her heart and lungs would crush from it. She bit the inside of her cheek but couldn't hold back the tears.

No, no, no! He was wrong. She shook her head and glared at him. His jaw was locked and his nostrils flared with each breath. His ignorance, his refusal to listen, to understand, snapped her. Her head buzzed as if swarmed by angry bees. "Listen to me, *urbanite*! I don't know what exactly happened to your father, but I do know *my* father wouldn't speak of Doc Bee with such respect and affection if he'd had anything to do with a murder. Doc Bee wasn't a captive. He had, *has*, his own cottage, which my father still visits every damn day, like it's some kind of shrine! He won't let anyone occupy it. Lewin might be a first-class warrior, but he would never, ever *murder* anyone."

She was done with Libra Cade. She would go with these people to Gomeda, sign whatever they wanted her to, find Jaegar and leave. She pivoted with the intention of getting on that damn boat and away from the *outsider*.

His grip locked on her upper arm and he spun her back around.

"Well he *did*, Cleo, so get used to it. I don't know what lies you were told—"

"Shut up, *shut up!*" If only her hands were free to cover her ears. Instead, she gripped the warm stone that hung against her chest while her heart pounding angrily beneath against her breastbone. "You don't know what happened! You weren't there!"

"I know exactly what happened! The story is family lore. And worse, I saw the pain on my mother's face when my grandfather broke the news. She crumpled to the floor like a heap of rags. I see the scene replayed in my head every time I look at her. And she's still a crumpled heap of rags!" His breath was coming as fast and hard as hers, but his tone became eerily quiet. "I was only four, Cleo, but I remember wishing I had magic powers so I could lift her back up and fix everything. But I couldn't." His voice cracked. "My father was gone and I had to take care of her and Libby, but I didn't know how."

Without easing the grip on her arm, he leaned in close. "And how can you even *defend* that bastard after the way he's treated you? How can you say he's not a murderer when he won't even look in your eyes?"

"I know what my father is, I've no illusions. But *he* didn't kill you father. The soldiers did."

Libra's eyes squinted. "Do you know what you're saying? Those soldiers work for my grandfather. Do you understand what you're implying?" He tightened his hold on her bicep.

"The guards *raped* her! Raped her and beat her because she tried to defend Doc Bee while my gram went to get help, to find my father, because he wasn't even there." Cleo tried to rub her face into her shoulder to dry the wet tracks down her cheeks. "She was pregnant with me at the time. Do you understand, you ignorant son of a bitch?" She swung her head to the side and thrust her jaw out so he'd get a good look at the evidence. "And when he got there, he had to cut me out of her stomach because *she was dead.*"

The damn holding back her rage crumbled as tears coursed down her cheek.

Libra dropped his hand and took a step back, his face devoid of any emotion.

"Don't you believe me?" Her voice hitched. "Don't you?"

He flicked his eyes toward the boat, to Trevayne, who stood on the deck holding up a dark shape, with a green light glowing inside.

"Look at me, damn you!" She got his attention by pounding her fists against his chest. "You have to believe it because that is how it happened. That's the truth."

His face remained passive and unflinching. He glanced at her, then back at Trevayne.

"Damn you!" she screeched, pummelling him. "Look at me, urbanite. *Tell me you believe me!*"

He nodded at Trevayne and her world went black.

THIRTY-ONE

THE BOAT WAS A LONG, narrow metal tube resembling a half-sunk submarine. Solar inductors rimmed the perimeter, giving the vessel stability and power. By day, they were too hot to stand near, but at night, they acted as a deck. The hold was divided into three sections—Trevayne would be in the wheel house up front and no doubt the goon squad would land in the day quarters, which took up the largest section in the middle, so Libra took unconscious Cleo to the engine room at the back. He made a nest from a pile of tarps and ropes and laid her unconscious form in the middle. He placed the slightly soiled feather pillow, into which he'd slipped the throwing knife, under her head.

With mechanical indifference, he undressed her, numbing his mind to what she felt like, what she looked like in the dim light. After re-bandaging the wound on her leg and treating the cut on her cheek with first-aid ointment he found onboard, he dressed her in the new outfit.

He felt shitty about signaling Trevayne to activate the implant again, especially having to witness the satisfied glint in the asshole's eye as he pressed the button, but it was the only way Libra was going to get Cleo onto the boat. And the only way he could get through this.

If only she hadn't become hysterical. But he couldn't risk her wrist bindings coming off while she pummelled him with her fists. Trevayne would have retied them himself, and she'd have no hope of wiggling free, or having blood circulate into her fingers.

Nor could he bear her accusations or the hatred in her eyes.

Her story was wrong. Had to be. And her impressions of his grandfather were way off. Achan could be a hardass, a manipulative bugger with single-minded purpose, but he wasn't a monster. He would never sanction the heinous act of violence she described. The old man would buy his way out of a situation before he got his hands dirty. That wasn't his style at all.

But it bothered him that *she* believed the Taiga fairy-tale they made up to appease the little girl who'd lost her mother, conveniently casting Achan Cade as the big bad wolf.

Libra tried to dredge up some animosity towards her, some contempt. He reminded himself she lied about her status, her purpose, anything to cause him enough annoyance to replace the ache of losing her trust. Nothing came. He still saw a beautiful, smart, vulnerable girl whom he'd wronged.

Libra scrubbed his hands over his face. He felt ripped in two, poisoned, and possessed.

He leaned over her to tuck a note into the pocket of her buckskin coat but couldn't resist touching her, just once more. He pushed back the silken strand of hair that had fallen over the side of her face, surprised by the jolt he felt when he came in contact with the warmth of her cheek. He let his hand linger, smoothing her scarred cheekbone with his thumb, wishing he could erase the mark she loathed. Not the visible scar—that was part of her, part of her unique beauty—but the emotional damage beneath.

Zhang-damn, he ached for her. He ached for the baby whose passage into life was marred by tragedy and for the self-conscious little girl who craved the love of her father. He ached for the woman whose conscience drove her to please the men in her life—men that were indisputably unworthy of her. Himself most of all.

Libra drew in a ragged breath as he tried to memorize her face, burn her image into his brain so he'd never forget. Not that he ever would.

It pained him to leave her here, in Trevayne's hands, but he had no choice. Their fight and her subsequent nerve-coma meant he had to alter his plans at the last minute. And Libra had no intention of breaking his promise to find her brother and get both of them out of the city. He just wouldn't be directly involved, but he knew just the man for the job. From this point on, he'd oversee but not be seen. It would be unbearable, for both of them.

Libra boosted himself out of the hold and made his way to the deck. The boat slid through the water at an amazing speed. His knees wobbled, and he couldn't seem to get his bearings in the dark. Which way was shore? Which way was home? He'd never before felt so...directionless.

Chilly spray from a wave hit the side of his face, stinging his skin with its toxic content, but that didn't stop him from leaning over the thin rail. The motion of the boat as it skimmed through the Dead Lake made his head spin and his stomach burn. Or maybe he got an ulcer from eating snake. He gagged, wishing he could throw up, get the whole sick mess out of his system.

There are some felonious talents you pick up as a rebellious teen that serve you well into adult life. Lifting Trevayne's satcom had risks, but Libra had a knack for picking pockets and breaking lock codes, and a singular determination to play by his own rules. Frick and Frack's, respectively, were even easier to steal since they clipped them to their belts. He didn't know if their coms could override the implant controls on his own device, the way Trevayne's could, but he couldn't chance it.

The first stage of his plan was to make sure Cleo stayed unconscious for the journey. It was better for everyone that she not awaken. As long as she remained quiet, Trevayne would leave her be. After programming her implant, he slipped two of the stolen coms over the starboard rail, holding on to his own and Trevayne's. He had calls to make.

The first was to his team. Those guys knew how to deal with a call to action and didn't waste time asking a lot of stupid questions. Libra issued them a brief directive and they were ready to go.

The second communication proved more difficult, but it had to be done.

"It's me," Libra said.

"This is quite a surprise. I didn't expect to hear from—" Achan paused a moment before resuming in a cool tone. "What happened?

Did she get away?"

"No. She's here."

"Good. How long until you get her to me?"

"Tomorrow, if the weather holds."

"Don't bring her here until after curfew."

Of course. Achan wouldn't want a triber to be seen walking into the head office of DynaCade. Libra stifled an urge to scream. "I just wanted to make sure you haven't forgotten your part of the bargain."

"You're a free man. The records are purged."

"No, that's not what I mean. I was referring to—"

"The money? Libra, my boy, you surprise me," Achan chuckled. "You always pretended you didn't like my wealth."

Libra gritted his teeth. "Don't."

"You'll find that I'm a man of my word. I'm transferring the money into your account as we speak." Libra linked to his bank and felt the slightest release of tension upon seeing the balance rise. He coded in a password to initiate a sequence of transactions that would move all his money into a dozen fake accounts that would take Achan's accountants a decade to trace, just in case they had any notion of fouling the deal.

"I see it. Thanks. But that's not what I'm talking about," Libra said. "You told me this was a simple business deal."

"That's what I said."

"Mining rights. That's all you want? She signs them over and you let her go?"

"Flowery details, son. No need to concern yourself."

"But I do. What did you find up there that you suddenly need access to?"

"I don't have time for this now. Come and see me when you get back. We'll talk."

"Now. Or I don't bring her to you."

"Have you forgotten why you were sent to the colony? What motivated you to do what you did?"

"People needed those medical supplies to survive."

"And you care about those retched beings over in New Chicago?"

"Of course I do. They deserve to live, to have basic human rights."

"So you justified stealing from one to aid a few." By 'one', he meant himself. It was a Dynacade warehouse they'd sacked.

"I justified it because you greedy bastards put a price on basic human rights. You charge exorbitant prices for basic medicines and drug therapies; things that would help them survive! But you deny them access and—"

"You and I are no different, boy," Achan said, cutting off his rant. "You think it's okay to steal from those who have and give it to those who don't. Well, the Taiga has the resources to give us the power we need to help those very same people. No more rolling blackouts, no more shutting down factories. More supplies, lower costs, we could not only provide more jobs, but give them the ability to pay for the things you've been stealing for them."

Libra blew out his breath. Achan's twisted logic offended his honor code. Right now he needed some distance, needed to think, to either justify or rectify everything he'd been a part of. "Listen, I need you to promise me you won't lay a hand on her or I don't bring her in."

Abrupt silence made Libra think the old man had hung up.

"So it's true then," he replied. "Trevayne intimated that you had a little thing for the girl, but I didn't believe him. Honestly, Libra, how could you sully yourself with such a creature?"

Libra felt his blood heat but refused to play into Achan's mind games. All through his early childhood, his grandfather considered it a sport to press his hot buttons and watch him implode. Said it would help him handle adversity. Then he'd throw some comment to his mother about not raising him right. Asshole.

"Just give me your word, Achan. Give me your word that you won't harm her, that you'll let her go once she's signed."

"This is a simple business transaction, my boy. She will sign and leave. I shall be the perfect host, as always."

Libra disconnected, barely able to stop himself from crushing the satcom in his hand. He'd need it later. He reached deep into his pocket and extracted the tin flask. Right now, he had some friends to make. Then would come the performance of his lifetime.

THIRTY-TWO

Much like she had in the clearing by the river, Cleo awoke fully alert, but with a crick in her neck and a pain in her side from slouching against a hard, vibrating surface.

As she straightened up, three things became immediately apparent: She wasn't in the Taiga, she was wearing a different set of clothes, and Libra wasn't with them. She sensed his absence like she sensed a gathering storm. She wasn't sure which one of the three caused a bubble of panic to rise in her chest, maybe all three, but the inability to fill her air with lungs was the only thing that stopped her from screaming.

Frick chose that moment to turn around in the seat in front of her. He took one look at her and his forehead creased. "Hey," he shouted. She felt her eyes bug as she struggled to breathe, tried to move her hands to her throat, but they remained numb in her lap. He reached across the seat, grabbed her upper arms, and rammed her into the back of her seat, jolting her from respiratory paralysis.

Oxygen rushed into her lungs and she coughed until her throat hurt.

"You'll be okay," Trevayne said, his tone passive. "Just a side effect."

Side effect of what?

Her head dropped sideways against a dusty windowpane as her breathing returned to normal. How the hell did they keep dropping her like that? Her tongue was thick and dry from thirst, but she didn't dare ask Trevayne for a sip from his canteen. She'd die before she put her lips where his had been.

Where's Libra?

Tinted windows, coupled with the thick cloud cover, made it impossible for her to tell the time of day. They knocked her out just before full darkness, but when? Last night? The day before? Days ago? Without the sun or the forest sounds, she was completely disoriented.

The utilitarian transport vehicle travelled along an arid, barren corridor, bumping over ruts and jostling the occupants. An unfamiliar-scented breeze trickled into the cabin via the air vents in the low ceiling, and helped to dispel the musky scent of her three companions.

The vehicle's interior was a wide, rectangular box, with plastiform seats—two per side of a narrow aisle, four rows in total. Trevayne was directly across from her in the back row, with a Frack two rows in front of him. The other buzzcut sat directly in front of her, and next to him was the only visible exit. The operator was concealed behind a dark partition that blocked her view of whatever lay directly in front of them. Presumably Gomeda. Escape, as far as she could see, was impossible.

This isn't how she wanted it to be. She wanted to enter Gomeda on her own terms, not trussed up and presented on Trevayne's arm like a prize doe.

Low buildings cropped up on the horizon, along with the odd wall and heap of rubbish, and she could see distant fields of the wind turbines that Libra had mentioned, though none appeared to be turning.

Hover board traffic increased and impatient operators zipped around them, weaving on and off the corridor. One rider, in particular, caught her eye. With his shoulder-length dreadlocks and shearling vest, he bore resemblance to a character from the Wild Boys comic books. Taiga kids considered the graphic novels, about a band of troublemakers ever questing for the elusive Ghost Warrior, mandatory literature.

Wondering if the others noticed him, she feigned a stretch and glanced around. Trevayne was looking out the opposite window, Frack was playing with his bootlace, and Frick was snoring.

She pressed her forehead to the glass for a better look. The Wild Boy coasted at the same speed as their vehicle, as if wanting to be noticed. He canted his head in her direction before shooting forward, but she saw what she needed to. A few of his dreads were encased in silver-pointed charms, just like the leader of the Wild Boys! A seed of hope germinated in her belly.

Jaegar! It could only be her brother's doing. He was sending her a sign to let her know everything would be okay. He must have found out she was captured and sent someone only she would recognize, to assure her that everything would be alright.

Whomever the hover rider was, his presence changed the game, gave her hope, renewed her spirit. She just had to wait patiently for a signal, some cue, a call to action that only she would understand.

Another sight kept her transfixed on the world outside her dusty window. She watched as the faint glow on the horizon grew in intensity. Finally, as the sky darkened behind it, the brilliantly lit skyline of Gomeda came into focus. And it was beautiful. Radiant, beckoning, it unleashed a sense of excitement. No wonder her people came here and never returned. She wrapped her fingers around her stone pendant and craned her neck for a better view.

She felt a slight vibration in her cheek a yoctosecond before shutters clanged down, completely obliterating her view. Foggy interior lights flickered on, bathing everyone in sickly yellow.

"What's happening?"

"Security. Can't go through the New Chicago with the windows exposed."

"For how long?" she asked, feeling the space close in around her. Thankfully, the ceiling vents remained opened.

"Until we open them," he sneered. "Are you impatient to see Mr. Cade?"

Screw you, she wanted to shout.

Jaegar was going to kick this jerk's ass.

"Speaking of the Cades," he said. "You haven't asked about your boyfriend? How come?"

"I don't give a badger's ass about the Cades. Any of them."

"Good. It won't bother you then."

There was something in Trevayne's manner that compelled her ask. Not that she cared. "What won't bother me?"

"That he's dead."

Cleo stared at Trevayne, the lipless gash of a mouth curling up in the corners.

No. Libra isn't dead. He is not dead. Trevayne was goading her. He wouldn't be so cavalier if it were true. Would he? Libra probably took off, mission accomplished. Probably didn't even get on the boat.

"You're lying."

One of the buzzcuts chuckled in a knowing, smug way that made her want to drive her foot into the back of his head.

"Your lover boy got himself dead drunk and fell overboard back in the Dead Lakes," Trevayne said. "We didn't stick around to watch the flesh melt off him."

Libra. Dead.

A slash of pain, quick and deep, like a blade under her ribs, snuck up on her before her brain snapped to the obvious conclusion—the bear grease, of course! He planned it, that zhang-loving bastard. She'd given him the method, he took the opportunity.

Coward.

Just wait until she got out of this mess, she'd hunt him down and flay him.

Not dead...

She hated that she felt relieved. It would be easier if he had died. She'd never see him again, never be tracked by his silver-blue stare. Her cheeks grew hot at the thought of him dressing her in the new outfit. He had stripped her of his clothes like he stripped himself right out of her life. He had removed his very existence, and she had nothing of him left but memories that were too unbearable to recall.

But the disgusting, self-injuring truth was that she didn't want to forget Libra, and she was scared that if she pushed those moments too far away, his image would disappear forever.

Cleo shivered and sunk deeper into the fur-trimmed coat. She tried to swallow but couldn't manage to dislodge the lump in her throat. She felt as helpless and desperate as she did when the river took her, shook her, and dragged her to her death. What kind of fall would she face at the end of this journey?

He was dead, in a sense. Dead to her. He'd served his purpose, got her to Gomeda. She could do the rest alone.

She bit the corner of her lip and blinked to erase the sting in her eyes. Crying didn't stop pain; this she knew first-hand. Crying just made you look weak and vulnerable and this warrior, third-class, was neither weak nor vulnerable.

Just...*alone.*

Libra crouched next to the towering needle that protruded from the roof of the Energy

Collective Headquarters. Even without the satellite control spire, the ECH was the tallest building in Gomeda, a carefully considered optic when they designed the city. It was also no accident it grew adjacent to the DynaCade compound. The two buildings were conveniently joined by a sky tunnel so that the president of one could traverse the sky tunnel and become the CEO of the other without getting the soles of his shoes dirty.

The Restoration Party Headquarters were some miles away, straddling the inner and outer ring so that the thousands of government employees didn't clog the gates into the sanctum at the beginning and end of each workday.

But here, at the core of energy-hungry Gomeda, this is where the real power was. And his grandfather controlled it all.

From his loft above the city, he was able to track the army transport vehicle from the moment it passed into the inner prefecture. Libra's palm grew warm from holding the flat black disk he'd reclaimed from Trevayne, watching the green indicator light move toward him and wondering if the colonel even realized it was gone. He held it tightly, a tenuous link to Cleo.

Libra touched the auto-focus on his binocs and tracked Trevayne's group as they escorted Cleo across the rooftop concourse of

DynaCade and to the drop plates that would lead them to Achan's personal suites.

She looked good and didn't appear drowsy or drugged. The last twenty hours had practically killed him, not knowing.

She was in Achan's hands now. Safe. The old man would coax her with his politician's charm, she'd sign the papers, have a nice dinner, and be escorted out in the morning. Knowing his opportunistic grandfather, there'd be a photo op with handshakes and a smiling representative from the UWC to ratify the deal.

He rubbed his face into the crook of his arm. He'd need another hot shower or three to wash the stink off him before he liberated Jaegar from the dorms of the Ministry of Opportunity. That would be easy. He knew a girl who knew a girl. One or two calls, a promise of contraband... It could wait a few more hours.

It shouldn't be this hard to walk away. Cleo was nothing more than an assignment. Mission complete. He had his freedom, he had his cashpoints and he should be feeling like the king of the zhang-damn world.

But he didn't. He felt as greasy and rank as the bear grease still oozing from his pores. He rubbed his sternum to ease the pressure deep in his chest and looked out over the city, so different from the peaceful vista atop

Raccoon Ridge. The night was still and quiet, everything but Gomeda's inner rings bathed in a consuming darkness. The curfew patrols would soon be out, ensuring the safety of the inner prefecture and not giving a damn about the rest of it. Status quo.

He strode to the edge of the rooftop and leapt over the side onto the deck below. Over the buildings, one by one, he jumped, rolled, crawled, and ran, moving as fast as his unpractised limbs allowed. But he couldn't leap fast enough or far enough to escape Cleo's tinkling laugher, her stunning beauty, or her singular uniqueness. He couldn't outrun the poison of their last exchange.

But God, he tried. He ran until his sweat and grease mingled to sting his eyes. He limped the rest of the way to his old home, to Glory Cade, hoping to find her sober. Only his mother could clear up some nagging thoughts he'd had regarding his father's work in the Taiga, and maybe give him the perspective he needed to get over Cleo Rush and the mess she's made of his heart.

ACKNOWLEDGMENTS

SPECIAL THANKS TO MY DEAR friend Elba, who encouraged me to leap and then held my hand during the entire adventure. I'm eternally grateful.

My heartfelt appreciation to my beta readers—Rebecca O'Sullivan, Shana Baptista, Sherry Patterson, and, with minimal coercion, James Watkinson (who saw the heavily redacted 'PG13' version)—for their feedback and direction.

I'm blessed with an amazing and supportive network of writers that include Katy Evans, Cynthia Sax, Olivia Loch, Christine D'Abo, J.K. Coi, Amy Ruttan, and Maureen McGowan, who inspire, push, challenge and enlighten me. They make me laugh, listen to me whine, let me cry, and know just when to snark-slap me back to reality.

ABOUT WYLIE SNOW

MOST AUTHORS WILL TELL YOU **that they wanted to be writers** from a very young age. Not me. I wanted to be a detective like Nancy Drew, or a wildlife expert like Jim Fowler, or an archaeologist like Indiana Jones. I even wanted to own my own island resort and make fantasies come true!

I didn't do too badly... I married a detective, worked in a zoo, explored ancient shipwrecks, and spent 18 glorious years living on a sunny island.

As for those fantasies... That's another book ;)

I love to hear from readers. You can write to me at wylie@wyliesnow.com

Visit my website for information on upcoming books: www.wyliesnow.com

Like my FACEBOOK page if you'd like to hear about upcoming contests or 'coming soon' excerpts: www.facebook.com/pages/ Wylie-Snow-Author/496092523761066
Follow me on Twitter: twitter.com/WylieSnow

OTHER BOOKS BY WYLIE SNOW

GAME ON

Secrets, lies, lust ... whatever it takes to win.

CLARA BEAN, EUROPE'S MOST RESPECTED restaurant critic, lands on American soil to do a promotional tour with a sports icon. But how will she keep her career-ending secret from her deliciously handsome new partner? She quickly learns that all games have rules, even falling in love.

LUC BISQUET CAN'T SEEM TO score any points with sassy, sexy Clara despite the palatable chemistry between them. But he's willing to endure as many penalties as it takes to crack her icy reserve, because winning is everything. *Game on!*

Now available on Amazon Kindle, Kobo, iBooks, Smashwords.

Here's a sneak peek at the next book in
the Jump Zone trilogy...

JUMP ZONE

LIBRA RISING

PROLOGUE

City of Gomeda

I'd always presumed that being in love would feel fuzzy and warm.

It's not. Love is painful. And cold.

Love is lonely.

Five days ago I died. Then he *showed up to revive me, only to kill me again, slowly, from the inside out.*

Every part of me hurts, even more than when the frigid river tugged me under, even more than when the crushing pressure burned my lungs and I was tossed like an arbitrary scrap of flotsam over an eighty-foot waterfall.

If I even think *his name, I get piercing sting in the middle of my chest that makes me want to howl like a dying wolf. The pain radiates through my limbs and I have to fight to keep from curling up in a ball.*

There are moments I loathe Libra Cade with blackness darker than a moonless night in the Taiga, and a yoctosecond later, I yearn to gaze into his pale blue eyes, feel his breath against my hair, see the half-smile that makes my knees turn gooey.

Then I remember that it was his fault that I died the first time, his fault that I smashed my kayak because his mythical aer-o-plane distracted me. I hate him.

Then suddenly I feel his phantom touch, his thumb grazing over the scar on my cheek with aching tenderness, or his lips softly kissing the notch on the curve of my ear. He made me believe I was beautiful, even if for just one night.

Trevayne and his human hounds told me that Libra died on the trip south to Gomeda. They said he fell off the boat in the middle of the night and the acidic water of the Dead Lakes melted the flesh from his bone.

But I know differently. I know he used my technique of slathering on bear grease, just so he could escape being around when I awoke from the most recent blackout.

I press my palm against the cool glass of my prison and marvel at the city aglow in lights. It's awesomely beautiful and I though I want to go home even more than I want to breathe, a piece of me is excited by the odd angles and curves of the tall buildings, the strange glittering colors of the skyline.

Libra is out there. He's lost himself amongst the eleven million people of Gomeda and I'm betting he'll never set foot in my Taiga forest again.

He'd better not.

I'll kill him if he does.

COMING DECEMBER 2013

www.ingramcontent.com/pod-product-compliance
Lightning Source LLC
Chambersburg PA
CBHW020240200626
46816CB00001BA/60